THE STARLET LETTER

A CANARY HOUSE MYSTERY

THE STARLET LETTER

A CANARY HOUSE MYSTERY

Julie Mathison

Starr Creek Press

First published in the United States by Starr Creek Press.

ISBN: 978-1-7350037-9-5 (paperback)

ISBN: 978-1-959067-90-0 (hardcover)

ISBN: 978-1-959067-91-7 (ebook)

Library of Congress Control Number: 2022901306

Cover design by Robin Vuchnich.

Starr Creek Press, LLC
922 NW Circle Blvd. Suite 160
P.O. Box 212
Corvallis, OR, 97330

www.starrcreekpress.com

ALSO BY JULIE MATHISON

OLD RUS TALES:

Vasilisa
Elena the Brave

STAND ALONE:

Believe

TABLE OF CONTENTS

CAST OF CHARACTERS

The Family:

Vivian Belle Van der Beeck: Twin, heroine of our story, bankrupt heiress, amateur sleuth.

Viola Blythe Van der Beeck: Same.

James "Jimmy" Wilbur Van der Beeck: Vivian and Viola's father, erstwhile playboy, charming drunk.

Giselle Adilene Van der Beeck (née de Bourbon): Jimmy's wife, society iconoclast, twins' mother, in that order.

Lavinia Matilda Van der Beeck: Twins' great aunt, self-styled nemesis of THE Mrs. Astor, devout gossip.

Cornelius Phileas Van der Beeck: Twins' eccentric grandfather, last seen in the foothills of the Himalayas.

Theodore "Teddy" Silas Van der Beeck: Twins' uncle, deceased.

Titus Sylvester Van der Beeck: Same.

Joost Van der Beeck: Sixteenth-century progenitor of the Van der Beeck dynasty, infiltrator, charming drunk.

Johann Van der Beeck: Joost's son, New World émigré, prominent citizen of New Amsterdam, thief.

The Household:

Mary Lurch: Housekeeper, former Canadian Mountie, Jacqueline of all trades.

Alma "Cookie" O'Sullivan: Beloved family cook, technophobe, scone aficionado.

Augustine "Mistress" Dubois: Twins' governess, widow, guillotine enthusiast.

Dixie Abel and Dolly Bates: Part-time maids, cousins.
Horace Rummage: Gardener, hoarder, Civil War veteran.

The Tenants

Barbara "Babs" Le Roy (née Appleby): Washed-up Follies star, occupant of the mysterious turret room.
Victor Sparrow: Pianist, heartthrob, aspiring composer.
Alastair "Al" Feeney: Bootlegger, good fella, nice guy.
Agrafena "Madame" Koslova: Philanthropist, mountebank, Russian émigré, devout spiritualist.
Fatima Sphinx: Poet, devout Sufi, thorn in Madame Koslova's side.
Dr, Wilhelm Weber: Eminent psychiatrist, Freudian scholar, confirmed bachelor.
Ambrose Sharma: Retired diplomat, hypochondriac, genius.

The Detective Bureau:

Detective Samuel T. Flanagan: Detective in charge of investigating undisclosed mystery, softie, grump.
Sergeant Adam "Adi" Kowalski: Flanagan's right-hand man, youngest cadet ever appointed to the Bureau.
Detective Johnny Broderick: Foil, braggart, comic relief.
Jane Hart: Foil, dark-haired Bureau secretary, unwitting romantic rival.

Famous Folks:

Florenz Ziegfeld, Jr: Legendary Broadway showman known for his lavish revues, spendthrift, lady's man.
Caroline Schermerhorn Astor: New York society maven of the Gilded Age, known for exclusivity.

"But this had been a sin of passion,
not of principle, nor even purpose."

~ Nathanial Hawthorne, *The Scarlet Letter*

THE STARLET LETTER

CHAPTER ONE
Enter the Seven

The Van der Beecks had always been considered slightly disreputable in New York Society. Oh, sure, they were of solid Knickerbocker stock, going back to the days when the city had been called New Amsterdam and Wall Street was just a wall. Johann Van der Beeck, the twins' great-great-great-great-*great*-grandfather, had arrived in 1642 to set up a windmill and had later been named a Great Burgher, and after that, various Van der Beecks had made and lost fortunes in beaver pelts, banking, and the odd misadventure into real estate. That's what people did, after all, and by *people*, one meant the Old Guard. And yet it was the family's fate to be always like that child quietly forgotten when introductions were made.

For they were unmistakably different.

Take the ancestral home at 63 Central Park West. All the right people lived on the Upper East Side where you never stayed out past dark and the talk at dinner parties was of horses and yachts and what had happened at Newport. And if you ever had an interesting thought in your head, you mustn't let it show, for Fifth Avenue was *comme il faut*, how things were done. Now, the Upper *West* Side—well, there were theaters and concert halls and other vulgar entertainments that went on well past midnight, and you might even see a revolutionary stumbling home late, singing ballads about the world to come.

Grampy Cornelius had built Canary House, as it was called, back before the Great Crash and even before the Great War, back when Central Park was just a muddy field and there was nothing to look out on but pig farmers, chicken wire, and a small house or two. The design had come to him in a dream—half château, half Kremlin—with plenty of gables, turrets, pinnacles and peaks, and a few domes thrown in for good measure. Father and his brothers had been born there, and it was not until 1909 that Grampy took up with a traveling mystic and left for India, never to be seen again.

The Van der Beecks had a talent for disappearing.

It was all there in *the diary*, a centuries-old volume cataloging the unusual, unwholesome, and untimely deaths, the ill-fated expeditions and ill-advised marriages, and a general habit of absconding with entirely the wrong sort.

"It must be to do with the curse," Viola said as she nestled beside her sister in the bay window, leafing through the journal's tattered pages.

"Oh, not that old rot," Vivian said. "People make their own rotten luck. You know, Lala, you really ought to stop reading those horrid Gothic novels."

"That's not all I read!" she cried. And it was quite true that Viola had memorized nearly half the books in the family library, if you can call it memorization when something just sticks in your head.

Vivian and Viola had been born over seventeen years before on the very same day, at almost the same time, as most twins are. They were identical, only they were opposites too. Vivian was possessed of a preternatural gift for persuasion. She enjoyed pulling the wool over the eyes of mere mortals, and she prided herself on living in the real world, whereas Viola liked rummaging around inside of books and only came out because she couldn't bear to be without her twin. They had the same fine blond hair pulled back from a high forehead and heart-shaped face, the same striking gray eyes smudged mauve somehow about the lid in a way that was strangely becoming. They were long-limbed and wispy with knees that bowed slightly back, and the only difference in their appearance was that Viola sometimes wore glasses.

Strangers always looked at them twice.

Truth be told, they had their mother's looks, who was French by birth and educated in Egypt and whom everyone in Society envied and no one liked. Gisele cared not a whit. "Let them eat cake," she would sometimes joke, and while Vivian would applaud and Viola would search her mother's eyes for hidden sorrows, to all the world it appeared that Gisele was a world unto herself. Father was a trickier specimen. Viola was certain he had suffered badly in the war, for even Mrs. Lurch said he'd come back changed, but James Van der Beeck—Jimmie to his friends—was cheerful to a fault and reckless too, and it seemed that with him each day was made to be squandered.

Other than that, there was only Great Auntie Lavinia.

For the sad truth of the Van der Beeck lineage was that by the year 1931, with the Depression on and the world reeling from a decade of excess followed by a very Black Tuesday, there were only five twigs left on the family tree. The day the stock market crashed, two Van der Beeck uncles followed suit, plunging to their deaths from the rooftop of an eighteen-story building—the most lamentable suicides ever to be cataloged into the diary. The stocks and bonds were worthless, the estate in the Hamptons sold for creditors, and all that remained was Canary House with no means to support it.

"If we're under a curse," Vivian continued, "then why all our good luck?" And she didn't need to explain herself because she and Viola shared one brain, a *meta-brain* Vivian had coined it (after hearing a lecture on quantum physics), invisible yet somehow connecting their synapses so that everything one twin said the other understood at once.

"I suppose you're right," Viola agreed. "Think of it! We never would have met Mr. Sparrow!"

"Nor heard his tortured ruminations at the piano late into the night," Vivian said, sounding much more like her sister than herself. She only waxed poetic for Mr. Sparrow.

"And think of Miss Sphinx!"

"And Mr. Sharma!"

And before they knew it, they'd reminisced their way through all the tenants who would never have come into their lives had the Van der Beecks not been forced to make ends meet.

"Canary House must be the most interesting boarding house in the history of the world," Viola sighed, and for once, her sister did not correct her excesses. All toted up together, the house boasted six tenants: a pianist, a poet, an erstwhile diplomat, a psychiatrist, a bootlegger, and a philanthropist who was always short on cash. There was a vacant room in one of the turrets, but whosoever took up lodgings there did not stay long.

And they say that seven is a *lucky* number.

But luck and calamity are often mixed, and seven had secrets to tell. When Grampy Cornelius wandered into China after seven years spent levitating with a Hindu fakir, he'd learned those secrets the hard way. For in the Book of Changes, seven is a *yang* number, an active number, its pronunciation much like that of the word meaning *gone*, and it is used to release dead souls from purgatory.

Words are power, and power is fate, and the twins' ecstatic declaration had not gone unheard by the powers that be. For although it seemed the Canary House could not be even one iota more interesting than it already was, someone was already walking up the winding path to the door under the glow of a streetlight, stumbling and straightening as she broke her heel.

Babs Le Roy rang the bell.

CHAPTER TWO
Tragic Airs

Mrs. Lurch cast a stern eye upon the young woman who stood in the front hall, starting with the bottle-blond hair set in a marcel wave, roving past the beaded scarlet dress that showed beneath her coat well above the knee, and on down stockinged legs to the broken high-heeled shoe.

"I was given to understand you got a room," the woman said in a high, nasally voice, as if she had a handkerchief stuffed up her nose.

There was a pause while Mrs. Lurch audibly sniffed.

"Why do you suppose she puts them through it," Viola whispered from the corner around which she and her twin peered, one head over the other like a mythological beast.

"Test of character?" Vivian guessed. "Or maybe she's just having a lark."

The young woman shifted her weight to the bung shoe, stumbled slightly and recovered.

"Did you see that?" Vivian hissed.

"Jazz!" Viola whispered excitedly. The two-headed monster had spied upon many a party and recognized a nimble step. "She looks like she might break into the Charleston any minute now."

But the young woman only opened her mouth a few times, like a fish out of water.

"Guppying," Vivian said.

Fitch and Brewster cheeped and twittered from their gilded cage on the landing, starting up a chorus from their feathered friends in adjoining rooms.

"Right, come along then, missy. Can't bear a lollygagger." Mrs. Lurch snatched up the woman's suitcase and headed across the wide hall, her sensible shoes silent on the Persian carpet.

"But . . . but . . ." the young woman see-sawed along behind in her mismatched heels. "Don' cha want references? Don' cha even want to know my name?"

"I know who you are, Miss Le Roy." The housekeeper stepped smartly up the stairs, as if the suitcase were full of nothing but eiderdown. "I didn't fall off a turnip truck yesterday, and I don't plan to do so anytime soon."

"But . . . what about the owners? Ain't they got a say about it? I cain't believe they ain't got anything to say about it, this being their house and all . . ."

And then the pair of them turned the bend on the landing and continued upwards, their voices dwindling to the usual Canary House whisper and creak.

Vivian whistled. "Babs Le Roy. What a break!"

The monster disengaged its heads, and two bodies followed from around the corner, resolving into a pair of identical girls, still otherworldly in aspect, like the reflection of a nymph in a sylvan pond.

"Where do you suppose she's been all this time?" Viola said as they turned to follow the housekeeper and their new tenant up the stairs, trailing slender hands upon the banister. Viola was always asking Vivian what she supposed about this or that, having somehow formed the notion that it was her twin who knew everything.

"It's a mystery." Vivian shrugged as she walked ahead. "Why, she hasn't been seen on Broadway in over a year. Liv and

Betty said she must have taken up with a mobster and come to a lamentable end at the bottom of the East River, but I told them there wasn't a shred of evidence for such nonsense."

"Maybe they've been reading too many Gothic novels," Viola said with a wry smile.

Her sister cast a wide-eyed look behind. "Lala, I do believe you've made a joke."

They paused on the second-floor landing, gazing up the darkened stairs to the upper floors, where the tenants lived. Right about now, the starlet would be surveying the turret room under Mrs. Lurch's watchful eye.

Viola sighed. "The stories she could tell."

"*Will* tell," Vivian said, for as the saying went, she could squeeze blood from a turnip, even one that had fallen off the turnip truck. "Come on," she said, turning toward their adjoining rooms in the east wing. "I'll show you the latest lovesick claptrap from Tommy Parker."

On entering the twins' quarters, one might have thought the Van der Beeck fortune still intact. The two chambers were connected by French doors, dressed in the same chintz that graced the row of tall, narrow windows, looking down upon the avenue and beyond that to Central Park. The bed sets were Louis XVI with vanities to match, and the carpet had been shipped by Grampy straight from Kashan and was respectably threadbare. The beaded lampshades cast patterns upon the silk wallpaper and toile bedspreads.

Mother had been firm with the creditors, who were uniformly male.

Viola flopped belly down onto Vivian's bed. "I won't sleep a wink tonight, I won't, not with Babs Le Roy up there in her turret, the single lamp casting her silhouette upon the wall as she opens her lonely suitcase. Oh Viv, did you see her tragic airs?"

"Did you hear her tragic grammar?" Vivian replied, feeling some correction was in order. "Really, Lala, you say the strangest things." She sat on the edge of her bed, taking a silver-handled brush to her hair in long strokes. "*I* want to hear about all the good stuff, about Hollywood and what it's like to be in the talkies, and whether Marlene Dietrich really draws on her eyebrows."

"Oh, speaking of eyebrows, you were going to tell me about Tommy!" Viola said, hitching up onto her elbows.

Vivian was used to her sister's flights of association, and it was true that Tommy's fine eyebrows were his one strength. "Poor sop," Vivian said, rising with a sigh to retrieve the letter from her trinket box. "I'm not encouraging him, am I, Lala? Tell me I'm not."

"You're not," Viola said, even though Vivian most certainly was. Viv had to be protected from her weaknesses, of which vanity was one, but it wouldn't do to let on about it, because she detested being coddled. "Come on, what does he say?"

Vivian dutifully read the letter, taking pains not to laugh, which even she owned would be bad form. It was a trial though, for the letter was full of things that could not possibly be true, like—well, Vivian was likely the most beautiful girl Tommy had ever met, Lala excepting, and it was true that Viv's sparkling wit was the talk of the Fifth Avenue set, though it was usually cast as a fault, but even Tommy could not possibly be losing whole nights of sleep in pondering her limpid brow.

"Could he?" Vivian asked, dropping her hands into her lap.

"It really is a lovely phrase. *Limpid brow,*" Viola said, trying it out. "Oh, Viv, he isn't half so bad as you make him out."

This led to a debate on the qualifications of the ideal suitor as the girls prepared for bed, slathering their alabaster cheeks with cold cream, jostling at the sink in their shared bathroom. The tube of Dr. West's toothpaste erupted in a blob of goo, but neither girl would own up.

"You really ought to clean that before someone steps in it," Vivian said archly, skirting the mess.

"I don't see why," Viola grumbled, even as she swiped it up with a sheet of tissue.

Off went each to their respective beds, though Viola made her feelings clear by cinching the French doors closed.

Moments passed as clocks ticked in the hall and one of the downstairs canaries cheeped. Vivian flipped over on her silk sheets and punched her pillow twice. At last, she could stand it no longer.

"Move over, will you, Lala?" she said, tucking into bed beside her twin. "I'm dead beat, and there's a horrid draft from that busted window in my room."

Viola took off her glasses and snapped shut her dog-eared copy of *Persuasion* to set on the bedside table. She knew all of Jane Austen's works by heart, but there was no substitute for turning pages. "I forgive you too, Viv," she said softly and then turned off the light.

CHAPTER THREE
Breakfast and Banter

"Now, Auntie, you really must eat," Viola pleaded, settling the tray over Lavinia's skinny lap. "Cookie hates it when you send your oatmeal back, and you know what a tyrant she is."

The old woman pouted as she sat in bed, propped against a cloudburst of overstuffed pillows, then shot her favorite grandniece a sly look.

"That'll teach her to leave the raisins out."

Vivian perched herself on the brocade bedspread and started on a pile of mail with an ivory-handled letter opener. "Perfect nonsense. Yesterday you told her you would send her packing back to Ireland if she so much as looked at the raisin jar." She paused, then added without looking up, "And don't pretend for a moment that you don't remember."

Great Auntie Lavinia's gaze lost its vacuous look as she scowled at her *least* favorite grandniece, who was rather too much a pea beside her in the pod. It was no use playing the dotard with *that* one. "If there's anything in that pile from that old dough-faced, addle-brained battle-ax, I don't want to know."

"Auntie!" Viola protested, "Mrs. Astor was always very kind to—"

"Oh, you mean like this?" Vivian shot her twin a sharp look as she flicked up a lavender envelope, then read on the front, "'From Her Magnificence *The* Mrs. Astor to the Aging Dowager Mrs. What's-her-face.' Goodness, Auntie, does she mean you?"

"That lily-livered, liver-spotted crouton!" Lavinia snatched the letter from Vivian's hand and tore it open. "'It pains me to say,'" she read aloud, "'that so old and venerable a family as yours must be excluded from fashionable society and lumped in with the other upstart arrivistes'—why that pimple-pocked, scissor-hearted old coot!" she cried, then fell to raving, her skinny arms punching at air in their floppy linen sleeves.

Lumped in? Viola mouthed, but her twin just shrugged. It didn't much matter what words Vivian used in her souped-up forgeries just so long as she stoked the feud with the late and great Mrs. Astor, who cast a long shadow, even in death. Auntie must have known it was all nonsense, but everyone needed something to live for, and what with her brother Cornelius gallivanting off to the Himalayas, there was nothing else for it. Viola only hoped the excitement wasn't bad for her heart.

They left the old lady with her half-eaten bowl, and a pen and paper to craft her reply, then hurried on to their own breakfast.

"What do you suppose Miss Le Roy looks like in the morning," Viola said as they glided down the stairs. "All made-up or au naturale?"

"She wouldn't go anywhere without her lipstick on," Vivian said, but when they turned the corner into the dining room, the starlet's chair was empty.

"Mes belles enfants," Mother said from the head of the table, waving her folded newspaper to usher them into their seats. "Hurry, my darlings, or you-know-who will deny to us our scones."

The girls slid into the two empty chairs between Madame Koslova and Mr. Sharma.

"Where is Mr. Sparrow?" Viola asked with a tad too much disappointment in her voice. Vivian stepped on her toe. "Ow! I mean, is he well?"

Father sat at the end of the table. He glanced to the empty chairs on either side where the two newest tenants should have sat, then waggled his eyebrows.

"Perhaps they're getting better acquainted," he said, which led to an uproar of protest or merriment depending on the person. The twins were appalled at the thought for purely selfish reasons.

"Sorry I'm late." Mr. Sparrow rushed in just as the girls began to despair.

"Fear not, Vic." Father snapped his napkin out to tuck it into his collar with an upward thrust of his chin. "Cookie hasn't rolled out the cart yet, so we won't suffer for your sins."

"The gentleman prefers Veector, is that not true Meester Sparrow," Mother said, affecting more of an accent than usual. Mr. Sparrow turned red and was unable to muster a reply.

"Ah yes, *Victor.*" Dr. Weber, the eminent psychiatrist, peered at the pianist over his glasses. "Derived from ze Latin for *conqueror* I believe. A heavy burden for any namesake." The young man blushed deeper.

"I'd go with Vic, myself," Al said, a fork and knife already clenched in opposite hands. "Take me fer instance. My parents named me Alastair. What kind of a name is that fer a man of, ahem, business?" He harrumphed a laugh. "Some sense of humor some folks got."

The twins exchanged a knowing glance. Bootlegging was *big* business these days.

"Ah, but what is true victory?" Miss Sphinx asked, smoothing a ringed hand over her ebony hair. "Is it not found within? 'Once you conquer your selfish self, all your darkness will change to light,'" she quoted with a raised finger. "The great poet Rumi has much to say on this subject."

Madame Koslova heaved her ample girth onto one hip, placing a bangled wrist upon the table. "Fatima, Fatima," she tutted, shaking her head, "If only you would study the works of Madame Blavatsky, Spirit guard her soul!" she said, referring to the late Russian spiritualist. Madame Koslova claimed to have donated a large sum to the Theosophical Society back in the 1890s—of someone *else's* money, of course. "Matter appears to have conquered Spirit, though it be but illusion."

The twins were awaiting the next profundity when Babs bustled in.

"I ain't late, am I?" she said, settling into her chair. "I'm famished, Lord help me if I ain't."

This ushered in a lengthy discourse on the subject of God and whether His almighty job description included meddling in gastronomical affairs. Miss Sphinx, being Moroccan by birth and a Sufi by faith, was warm to the idea with Madame Koslova taking, as usual, the opposite view. Everyone had their say except for Mr. Sharma, who seldom spoke on account of his nervous condition.

"You all's an interesting bunch," Miss Le Roy said appreciatively as the breakfast trolley arrived.

Cookie was puffing away behind it, red-cheeked, tucking strands of wild, graying hair back under her bonnet. She pined for the old days when her kind presided over seven-course meals, though such scions were invariably French. But that was Canary House for you, where everything was topsy-turvy with an Irish cook, a Canadian housekeeper, and two part-time maids from Georgia. No one knew where the groundskeeper, old Horace, hailed from because most of his teeth were gone. Even the governess, Mistress Dubois, though certainly French, did not quite fit the role.

"Tell to me, Miss Le Roy, are you a countrywoman?" Mother asked, passing around the scones, followed by scrambled eggs. Cookie kept chickens in the conservatory.

The starlet froze. "Oh, no, no, I ain't from the country," she said, wide-eyed and pale.

"But are you *French*, ma chère," Mother said, buttering her scone casually, as if Babs were not floundering like a beached halibut.

"Me? French? Oh, I get it!" Babs laughed, high and staccato. "Oh no, Missus Van der Beeck, Le Roy is what they call a stage name."

"Ah, the stage," Father said, easing back from his meal with hands clasped behind his head. "Where you and I first met, Gisele darling. Or was it at the opera house?"

There was a slight, awkward pause. Jimmy Van der Beeck had acquired a vague quality somewhere between the Battle of Cantigny and the attack at Meuse-Argonne, though Gisele filled in the details so seamlessly, one hardly knew.

"Saratoga, my love," she said, gently. "You bet most extravagantly on that beautiful thoroughbred—*aie!* What was his name?" She chewed her lip charmingly, though the twins weren't fooled. Viola blinked back tears, and Vivian reached over to clasp hands in her sister's lap.

"Old Rosebud," Father said, his eyes softening so that for a moment he was *there*, and the twins took a shaky breath as one.

There was more talk on horses and gambling, but the twins had stopped listening because Miss Le Roy was acting strangely. Vivian noticed now that her lipstick was askew, as if applied by a child, and Viola thought she glimpsed tortured ruminations in those wide-set blue eyes.

All of a sudden, Mrs. Lurch was at their side with Dixie and Dolly in tow, helping to clear the plates.

"Girls, I'll need you to assist Miss Le Roy in getting settled before your lessons begin," she said with a wink for the twins.

"Oh, gee, Missus Lurch," the starlet mumbled, "thanks, but I don't rightly need—"

"Chop chop," Mrs. Lurch said, having magically popped over to Babs's side to whisk away her half-finished meal. "Many hands make light work."

Good old Mrs. Lurch! She was all-seeing and all-knowing, just like God, only more reliable. Having spied the twins' distress, she'd known just the fix, a rollicking good tale. And what better one than the story of the mysterious Ziegfeld star!

CHAPTER FOUR
Rattled

The turret room at the very top of the house was small and paneled in beadboard, like the cabin of a ship. It appeared octagonal at first glance, but like everything in Canary House, appearances deceived. The peculiar magic of seven had already stolen Grampy's fancy well before he suffered its treachery, and he had instructed his architect to encode seven and its multiples into many of the mansion's features, from roof pitches to room heights to the number of tiles in the bathroom floors. The seven walls of the turret room were each set with a stained-glass window, transforming the city beyond into a gallery of fantastical landscapes.

"Some room." Babs turned to face the girls and wrung hands that were surprisingly large and capable looking. "You know, I really ain't got anything for you girls to do," she began, but Vivian shut the door with a decisive click. She could already feel her twin weakening. Lala was far too considerate of people's feelings, and it was clear Miss Le Roy did not want them here.

But *why?*

"Oh, that's Mrs. Lurch for you," Vivian said brightly as her twin stood beside her, awestruck by the starlet's tragic airs. "She was probably just trying to get us out from underfoot. We're an awful nuisance, don't you know."

The starlet's penciled eyebrows shot up, and she giggled through her nose. "No kidding." She sank into an armchair, already strewn with silk stockings. "Don't that beat all. I wouldn't have known it to look at the two of you, being so . . . so . . ." she made circles with her hands, as if to oxygenate her brain, "so high-class, and all. Now, take me. I know I look like a prize when I'm all dolled up, but I used to be quite the tomboy, climbing trees, chasing my brothers all up and down the—"

She stopped mid-sentence and guppied for a moment or two.

"Farm. You romped up and down the farm, isn't that right, Miss Le Roy?" And the way Vivian said it, it was not only perfectly natural, but noteworthy, a point of pride. "I read in an article that you rose to fame from humble origins."

"Humble origins." Babs tried it out. "Humble origins, yeah, sure, that's it." She sat up straighter yet seemed reluctant to say more. Viola came out of her swoon to shoot her twin a canny look. Babs's rise from obscurity was part of her glamour, so why try to hide it? "How kin you tell I grew up on a farm?" the starlet asked, eyes widening. "You got psychic abilities?"

Viola started to laugh, but Vivian crushed her foot, for the second time that day.

"I dabble." Vivian shrugged, modestly. "In fact, I'm a member of the Theosophical Society. Shall we test my abilities?"

Viola knew exactly where this was headed. She noted now what her sister had observed upon entering—that Babs's hands were used to rough work, and that she'd already hung up a Norman Rockwell print of a housewife feeding farm hands at a long table. It was likely the first thing she'd done when Mrs. Lurch had closed the door, leaving her alone in a strange room. Babs spoke like a mobster's gal, but beneath her city airs, there lurked an unmistakable country twang. Viv's deduction was no psychic feat, and soon she'd have Babs spilling her guts all over the place, just so she could sort through them for the shiny bits.

"Gee, I don't know," Babs said now. "Will it hurt?"

"Not a bit." Vivian strode briskly to the other stuffed chair, leaving her twin to stand behind, frowning. "Here's how it works." She pulled up to the starlet so that their knees were touching. "I take one of your hands in my own, focusing my astral senses on your aura—which is where your past resides, sort of like a shadow. I'll tell you what I see, and you can tell me if I'm right or not."

The starlet looked torn. Famous people were notoriously self-centered, but this one was shut up tight as a clam. And yet it seemed to Viola that Babs's burdened soul cried out for solace, and to Vivian that a crude curiosity animated the starlet's otherwise vapid mind.

"Shoot, why not," she said suddenly, thrusting one large hand into both of Vivian's delicate ones. "Have at it."

Vivian closed her eyes and was silent for a time, then gave a small moan which, as a measure of her powers, managed to be charming. Her lids fluttered open on a glassy gaze.

"I see a house," she said dully, as if someone had slipped her a mickey.

"Oh, sure!" Babs chirped. "That would be Ma and Pa's place. Is there a big elm in the front yard?"

"Yes, an elm," Vivian droned, "with a . . . swing?" Her gaze groped briefly across the starlet's face. "Or perhaps it is the imprint of a young child's wishes."

For a moment, Vivian feared she'd gone right over Babs's head, but then the starlet brightened.

"Oh, I get it, sure! I always did want a swing . . . er, didn't I?"

Vivian let the question hang. "But who is this on the front porch?" she said. "A woman . . . and a man."

The young woman's eyes misted over. "Tell me, Ma's crying, ain't she. Oh, tell me she ain't crying."

Vivian paused, then said, "She isn't crying."

"Are the . . . little ones around?" Babs's voice caught.

"My, yes, quite a . . . hmm . . . quite a horde."

"*Horde* means a whole bunch, don't it," Babs said fondly. "Ma always did have a gift for breeding."

While Vivian was having her lark, Viola, and her attention, drifted about the room. She'd just started a marvelous book by Nathanial Hawthorne called *The Scarlet Letter,* which reminded her of Babs and her plight—whatever that might be. Hester Prynne, the book's main character, maintained terribly tragic airs and had secrets galore piled up in her metaphorical closet, plus a mysterious suitor.

"But . . . there is *another* man," Viv said now, perhaps hopping on board Lala's train of thought, via their meta-brain. "Is he . . . young . . . or is that an . . . er . . . shadow across his face?"

This was a safe bet, because a young man could always be pawned off as a brother, and an older one as an uncle. But Vivian must have hit some kind of jackpot because the starlet gasped and withdrew her hand, wiping it on her dress. "Ain't you somethin'. Well, I do believe your powers is tuned up just fine, but I got to get my toilet done before rehearsal this afternoon." Vivian flinched at the word *toilet,* stripped of its French intonations to sound less like powdering one's cheeks, and more like something that flushed. If only she could coach the starlet, her airs might not be so tragic. But at least Vivian had learned a little something.

"Isn't this darling!" Viola burst out from across the room, bending over the bedside table. Manners prevented her from lifting the tiny silver baby rattle as she yearned to do, but she bent close to inspect it, sweeping her flaxen hair over her shoulder with a graceful hand.

"Do come again, girls." Babs flustered out of her chair, hustling the girls toward the door like chickens to be herded. "Any time, just not today or this week or next." Her cheeks were pale beneath their rouge. "I'll tell you what. I'll get you both tickets to my opening night at the show. Now, wouldn't that be grand? Off you go now." And she shut the door right in their astonished faces.

Vivian turned to Viola and raised one elegant brow. She did not need to voice her question, which concerned the writing traditionally etched into silver keepsakes.

"*That which binds us,*" Lala said. "And there were some initials too: *F & B forever,*" she recited, as they turned to head back down the spiral staircase.

"A mystery man, a baby rattle, and the initial *F*," Vivian said, her angelic features by turns lit and shadowed as the girls circled down past gaslit sconces.

"It doesn't necessarily mean anything," Viola hedged, though her highly associative mind was already weaving connections, a madman's quilt hiding the thread of genius.

"Not necessarily," Viv said, "but even so, I'm not letting that woman out of my sight."

CHAPTER FIVE
A Star is Torn

As it happened, Miss Le Roy remained out of Vivian's sight for several hours. There were chores to be done, for even two Georgian maids and a Canadian housekeeper could not stay abreast of all the dusting, mopping, washing, and waxing that a large house required. The tenants had the run of the main floor—both parlors, the library, living room, and conservatory (arranged charmingly with wicker chairs amongst the coops)—and truly they were just like children, always leaving ancient texts or recently declassified documents lying around amongst the silk scarves, gum wrappings, and other detritus of their cluttered lives. Al had once mislaid a loaded pistol in the conservatory, but Mrs. Lurch had set him straight so that he never forgot it, and neither did the chickens.

The girls worked on the sly, for Mother, though democratic in the abstract, did not hold with housework.

"How long until the rat arrives?" Vivian asked as the girls nipped into their suite after dusting the second parlor.

"You really shouldn't call her that," Viola said with a small disapproving frown, a rebuke, one might expect, of her twin's unkindness. But, alas, in this instance, she had fallen under Vivian's sway. "Mistress Dubois is much more of a vole," Lala mused, "or maybe a mole, or some other small rodent that blinks a lot and likes burying things."

For all their sleuthing, the twins had not yet learned to look beyond appearances.

"I suppose," Vivian shrugged. "Oh, look at that," she cried, picking up the crystal clock beside her bed. "It's almost ten o'clock! Old pincer-grips will be here any minute."

"If you're going to take that tack, old mussel-mouth would be just the thing because of her pursed lips," Viola said. "Or how about scuttle-hustler, you know, because she's always shooting sideways like a crab, or—oh, Viv, what *are* you doing?"

Vivian was elbow deep in a box she had pulled from the armoire, spilling bits of newsprint as she rummaged.

"Shh. No time. Ah, here it is—" and she plucked out a snipped page from one of those gossip rags that folks were always reading down at the candy counter in Schrafft's.

They laid flat on their stomachs, side by side on Vivian's bed.

"Stars don't always fall from the sky, and so it was with Mr. Ziegfeld's shining orb, Babs Le Roy, a femme vivant who clawed her way up from the mud and slime," Vivian read. "That is catchy," she exclaimed.

"Really, Viv," Viola said, wrinkling her nose. "And you say *I'm* impressionable."

On they read. The high-stepping Miss Le Roy learned to hoof at Zelda Delaney's Dancing School in New Jersey, living as a boarder in a house for aspiring starlets while she hustled any gig she could land.

"Hoof!" Viola said, with a derisive snort. "Gig!"

"Life isn't all violins, Lala. If Miss Le Roy can get down in the dirt, so can we. Just pretend you're an anthropologist."

Babs danced her way all through the next paragraph—tap, musical comedy, acrobatics, polka, ragtime, you name it, she did it. Meanwhile, Ziegfeld was busy just over the harbor, upending Vaudeville with his new revue, full of glitz and glamour and girls galore. Police raided the stage—then joined in the finale cancan, all part of the act.

"I wish I could have been there," Vivian said, biting the corner of her lip in a way that had once caused Tommy Parker to spill his cherry fizz in the lap of a visiting marquis.

"You would have gotten into mischief, you know you would," Viola replied.

Babs's big break came on tour when Mr. Ziegfeld discovered her, high kicking the back of her own head. He paid her ten dollars a week to join the Follies chorus, but in no time, she was promoted to specialty dancer, bobbing her hair and donning the short, loose beaded dress that would become her signature look. In 1925 the rising starlet was declared winner of First Beauty Honors in eight states.

"They do go on about her legs and flanks and things, just like a horse," Vivian complained. "Next thing you know, they'll be examining her gums" But they soldiered on, because the next bit was golden.

Hollywood!

Lights! Camera! Action! It was a stroke of luck for Babs that the silent era was still at its zenith. Her tragic grammar was heard only by water boys and makeup artists, and if she forgot what scene they were running, she could always roll her black-lined eyes and rend her hair. Her star had cleared the mud and slime, and on it rose, carrying her back to New York to headline Mr. Ziegfeld's latest show, where she arrived at the New Amsterdam Theatre, chased by hordes of men wielding diamond bracelets, Persian lamb coats, and gallons of perfume. But Babs was deaf to their pleas. Was her heart already spoken for? But by whom, if not . . . Mr. Ziegfeld Jr. himself.

"Mr. Ziegfeld?" Viola cried.

"*Florenz* Ziegfeld," Vivian said, with a significant sideways glance.

"The initial," Viola breathed, for she had just been thinking about *The Scarlet Letter*, in which Hester Prynne was forced to wear an A on her dress, on account of being branded an adulteress. "But don't you think the *F* might stand for more than just a name?"

"Why on earth should it?" Vivian demanded, pushing up to sit and swiveling her legs out in front of her.

Viola couldn't answer this, for it was really more of a feeling, and that would get her nowhere with Viv.

There were only two sentences left by this time, all that was needed for Babs Le Roy to vanish from the limelight quite suddenly, before the season was even through.

"This must be her big comeback. Did you hear that she'll be joining the Follies of 1931?" she began, but then Viola gave a cry of dismay.

"Oh, look at the time!" The crystal clock now read ten fifteen. "Mistress Dubois will already be pacing."

"She'll have our feet in the fryer," Vivian agreed, hurrying off the bed and out the door.

Viola gave a shudder as she followed after. Viv did come up with the most barbaric original sayings.

"Life is barbaric, Lala," Vivian noted, as if her twin had spoken aloud. They paused before the nursery door to smooth their dresses and straighten each other's scarves, then plunged in.

"Bah, mes enfants! Look at the time!" Mistress Dubois was short and squat, with a wart on her nose the size of an island nation. She scurried sideways to snatch up a clock and ogle it, as if it had much to answer for. "How am I to do my work in these conditions?"

"Now, now, ma bonne maitresse," Vivian cooed. "Did you hear that the stock market fell another fifty points today?"

Suggestibility was Mistress Dubois's one saving grace.

"Quel dommage!" she cried, dropping the clock and clapping paw-like hands to her cheeks. "How can this be? Was the market of stocks not already in the twa-let, as they say?"

Mistress Dubois pronounced *toilet* in the French way, getting it wrong, like Babs, but in the opposite direction.

"May I suggest we start our lessons with a discussion on the perils of overindulgence?" Vivian suggested, guiding the black-clad governess toward the door. "Perhaps we can sit in the front hall. It's so nice to have the canaries around."

"Fifty points!" the woman moaned, still manhandling her cheeks as they headed out the door. "But how much more can it fall? Is this American twa-let so very large?"

Just why Mother had hired the aging Mistress Dubois was beyond the twins. She had none of the required attributes of a governess. She was not pretty, nor petite, had no dark secrets and was in little danger of attracting the attentions of the household patriarch. The choice could be marked down to one of two things: Giselle's vanity or her benign indifference.

And yet . . .

There was something endearing about the hapless dear. She was a bit like the last puppy left in the box. The girls exchanged a glance as they ushered her down the stairs.

"Let's sit here," Vivian said, pulling several chairs around in view of the stairs, just in case Babs took it into her head to leave. Just why she was so curious about the starlet was a matter of some confusion, even to Vivian herself. Perhaps she was bored, her mind thwarted at every turn by the dogged tutelage of Mistress Dubois. Had Vivian been sent to Miss Chapin's or one of the other posh schools attended by the Upper East Side girls, surely she would have ruled the roost, for despite her taint, such was her charisma. And even in exile, she maintained a kind of scandalous mystique, sparking whispers beneath the eaves of those Beaux-Arts mansions, half-spiteful, half-admiring. Who knew what Viv Van der Beeck might do next?

But perhaps it was more than boredom that drove Vivian to ghost her mysterious subject. She had a nose for trouble, and when it came to Babs Le Roy, something stank.

Sure enough, they'd only just settled into their seats when the starlet bustled down the stairs, a brown-paper parcel tucked beneath her arm, her eyes puffy and red. She walked out the door with nary a hello.

Distracted! said the twins' shared glance.

"Mistress Dubois, I feel suddenly unwell," Vivian said, placing the back of one hand to her forehead. She rose to fetch her smart, woolen coat with the velvet collar from the hall tree. "I think a bit of fresh air would do me good. What do you say we all take a turn about the neighborhood?"

CHAPTER SIX
Morning Constitutional

Hardly a minute had passed since Babs's red leather pump, recently repaired with a dollop of glue, disappeared out the front door. There they were, assembled on the threshold, the twins in their coats and low-heeled boots, and Mistress Dubois, hastily bundled into her familiar plaid monstrosity. As Vivian tugged a blue turban down over the woman's brow, Mistress Dubois looked vaguely seasick from all the commotion.

"You feel unwell, you say? And is it catching, this leetle bug of yours?" The twins whirled her around toward the porch. "Zut alors! Why is the lamp of streets upside down?"

"The streetlight is perfectly upright, Mistress Dubois," Vivian said, reassuringly. "Come along. Nothing like a brisk walk to clear the mind."

Off they all went at a Herculean pace. Babs could still be seen, halfway down the block amid the crowd, her taffeta hat at an angle as it bobbed in and out of view. She was headed down West 66th Street toward Broadway.

"But why do we not walk in the beautiful park?" Mistress Dubois moaned, as if certain now that she had caught Vivian's mysterious ague. "The trees, the lake, they will make me feel better, no?"

Viola and Vivian hoisted the governess between them to urge her along.

"Oh no," Vivian said. "Fresh *urban* air is what you need, Mistress Dubois. Why, I'm feeling better already."

The worthy lady took to gazing about like a baby as she was trundled along, head lolling back to take in the brownstones that had sprung up in the years before the market crashed down. On they raced, past the polo rings of the New York Riding Club, through the traffic light at Columbus Avenue, then past the small triangle of Empire Park where beggars slept under sheets of yesterday's news.

Viola stumbled and pretended to wrench her ankle, limping over next to one of the newspaper-covered heaps. It was smaller than the others, with one bare foot sticking out, and one ragtag shoe.

"Here," Viola hissed as she ducked a peek under the paper tent to slip the poor urchin a nickel. "I'm sorry it isn't more."

The wide eyes gazed back at her, dark in the shadows.

"Lala!" Came Vivian's voice from behind. "Where on earth did you—oh, *there* you are."

Viola straightened and hurried back into the street, still limping, but Vivian merely shook her head.

"Really, Lala, where are your priorities?" She flung a hand up and gazed into the crowded maze. "She could be anywhere by now."

Viola's priorities were her own, thank you very much, but there was no use going on about it.

"There!" she pointed. "Isn't that her hat?"

This ploy did the trick. The twins broke into a run, as best they could with the governess hoisted between them.

"Ouf! Why do we run? Are we being chased by les criminels?"

"Just relax, Mistress Dubois," Vivian huffed. "All part of the cure."

Beyond Broadway, they paused again, looking in all directions. To the south stretched the jazz clubs and bordellos of San Juan Hill; to the north, the luxury apartments of Riverside Drive; to the west, the Hudson River; eastward—nothing but home.

"Oh, look!" Viola cried. "She's behind us, after all!"

"Mais non! *She* is behind?" Mistress Dubois parroted in her confusion. "Is it that les criminels are the ladies?"

"Never you mind, dear," Vivian said with a pat on the arm as they steered her around. "It's just a little game we're playing."

As luck would have it, Babs had paused to look into a storefront window and was back on the move, northward up Columbus Avenue. Mistress Dubois had taken to dragging her feet, testing the twins' strength.

"I think she turned in up there," Viola managed between breaths as they slogged along.

"Of course, the parcel!" Vivian said, who was slightly more athletic than her twin. "What terrible dopes we are, Lala."

The neighborhood post office was hardly a grand affair, nothing like the one near Penn Station with its palisade of marble pillars. This one sported only two pillars and several gargoyles clustered about the eaves.

"I'm just going to pop in and mail a letter," Vivian said. "Lala, why don't you two find a bench. Mistress Dubois looks peaked."

Viola returned her sister's pointed stare with a scowl that could not help but be dainty. She hated to be left on governess-sitting detail, but there was nothing else for it.

"Come along, dear." Viola patted the woman's arm. "So, tell me, what do you think about the Dust Bowl?" she began, throwing her twin a final, long-suffering look. "Those poor Okies are just parched for rain, don't you think?"

Vivian hurried up the wide stair to the double glass doors. Good old Lala. The question of this mysterious Dust Bowl would occupy the governess for at least ten minutes, what with wondering what size it was and why a bowl would be set down in the middle of a prairie and whether the poor drought-inflicted farmers would ever be able to climb out.

Once inside, Vivian stepped aside, shielded from general view by a potted plant. The velvet-roped aisle zigzagged across the floor toward the wall of teller windows, but there was no line at this time of day. Babs stood waiting for the lone postmaster on duty to finish up with a gentleman in spats.

"Next," the postal agent droned as the gentleman hustled off in New York style.

Babs wasted no time, either. The parcel was placed on the ledge with shaking hands, soon to be weighed, stamped, and tossed into a rolling canvas cart, ready for transit.

But to *where?*

Shrinking into the shadows as Babs turned from the counter to click-clack out the door, Vivian drifted up to the teller window.

"Pardon me." She drummed her nails on the ledge and leaned in close. "I do hate to trouble you, but is there a package for Evelyn Wier?" She graced the postal agent with a self-deprecating laugh. "I'm just a mess waiting for it, and it should have arrived weeks ago."

The young man gazed at her as if stricken, then seemed to recover himself. Touching his visor, he hurried off behind the screen in search of the missive, perhaps lost in transit from Heaven itself. Vivian hoisted herself onto the ledge to peer down into the canvas cart, knocked askew in the man's haste. She could barely spy the address written on the uppermost parcel.

Appleby Farm, Box Holder, Rte. 145, Preston Hollow, NY.

As the agent rounded the screen, the bell tinkled, signaling that his angel had taken flight. He touched his visor again, gazing out the glass doors and into the crowded street. Perhaps she was just a vision, after all.

"*Finally,*" Vivian groused when she spied Lala and her aged charge, tromping back up Columbus Ave. "Where on earth did you get to?"

"We tailed her, Viv," Viola said, breathless with excitement at having nabbed some of the action. "She got onto the Sixth Avenue El, not two minutes ago, and that's not the only thing."

"Well? What is it?"

"A *man,*" Viola whispered. Mistress Dubois squinched her eyes shut and clamped hands over her ears.

"Aaand?"

"I'm just certain she knew him, Viv, even though they didn't stand together, and well, I suppose they didn't really look at each other either what with being on opposite sides of the car, but I'm certain of it, she was meeting him, Viv." She looked deeply into her sister's eyes. "It was a *rendezvous.*"

Vivian took up her post on the far side of Mistress Dubois and steered her around, shooting her twin an approving glance.

"Excellent work," she said, and when her sister beamed, the last bit of peevishness left her heart. If only *she* were as generous as her Lala . . . but then, that's why nature made twins. As for the mystery man, time would tell. Lala's flights of fancy often veered off the map, but one thing was certain: Lala never forgot a face.

CHAPTER SEVEN
Al Dishes the Dirt

That the twins were blessed with unique gifts was not surprising when one considered the ancestral line. Indeed, Joost Van der Beeck, progenitor of the modern dynasty, was himself a savant, though his gifts were . . . controversial.

Joost had a peculiar genius for opportunity.

It all began in 1590 in a town called Breda, situated in the low country of the fledgling Dutch Republic. After the town was conquered by the Spanish in a surprise attack, the Calvinists, led by Maurits of Nassau, devised a counterattack, infiltrating the besieged city in a Trojan Horse operation that was only slightly tawdry by comparison. Sixty-eight Dutch soldiers were smuggled across the moat in the leaky, pungent hold of a peat boat, recapturing the city with a minimum of bloodshed. The boatman was later deeded a house in gratitude for his daring feat, named harbormaster, and lauded down the years to generations of Dutch school children. Less known is that the plan was hatched in a pub (where Prince Maurits found himself waylaid between campaigns) and was the brainchild of a certain Joost Van der Beeck, who had consumed one too many pints of good Dutch beer.

Joost was deeded a house as well, quietly, on the promise that the plan's beer-soaked origins would remain obscure. And so began the legacy of fortune and ignominy that would mark the Van der Beeck line down to the present day. Joost's grandson, Johann Van der Beeck, would cross the ocean a half century later, charged with the construction of a windmill, only to abandon his commission on the shores of the New World for the promise of beaver pelts, wampum, and the hand in marriage of a French girl named Martine. Success would follow, but so too would that taint, like an odor that could neither be quite identified nor shaken.

Around the time that Johann was building a house in the muddy streets of New Amsterdam, the fictitious Hester Prynne, heroine of Viola's much-loved tome, would have been suffering her own ignominious fate a few hundred miles to the north. As it happened, Viola was thinking about Hester Prynne—and Babs *and* Johann—while she sat in the conservatory with her sister, playing chess. It was their favorite spot, what with the chickens clucking about in the damp, tepid air, and the smell of oranges, and rain pattering on the glass roof. It was good for thinking, and it struck Viola now that Johann, Hester, and poor Babs had a lot in common—except for Hester's fictitious nature, of course, and the fact that Johann was a man, and, well, that he had lived several centuries ago and had never seen a Ziegfeld Follies show much less worn a candelabra on his head. But still, there was some *thread*, wasn't there? And as the self-appointed family historian, Viola was intrigued by the thread that bound them, that disreputable air, and a darkness that seemed to threaten all around them, pressing in like night.

"Viv, how do you suppose the curse began?" she said out of the blue, moving her rook one square to the right.

"Really, Lala, I thought we'd agreed that the curse was nonsense."

Viola toyed with her rook, arranging several captured pawns just off the chess board, as if they were loitering around the castle.

She could have pointed out that *Viv* had decided it was nonsense, but that Viola was free to think what she liked, thank you very much. But at the moment, she was distracted by the notion that the ousted pawns were plotting rebellion.

As for Vivian, she was bent on victory.

She pictured the game of chess as a maze in four dimensions. For every step one took, corridors branched off exponentially so that one had to project the intersecting probabilities of the two mazes, one represented by one's own moves, and the other by one's opponent's, applying a rudimentary knowledge of human psychology and social dynamics.

Lala played by instinct. She often won.

But Vivian was sure she had her this time. "Queen to king's knight seven!" she crowed. "Check!"

"Oh, that is good," Viola said admiringly. "I could take your queen with my own but there's your noble bishop, protecting his imperiled regent, though it must spell his doom. Well played, m'lady!"

This sort of flowery nonsense was the price of a chess game with Lala. Her pieces invariably acted out subplots only vaguely connected to strategy. But the taste of victory made Vivian magnanimous.

"Really, Lala, anyone could have fallen into that trap. I only came up with it because I know how much you like to keep your pawns close to home."

"*Peasants*, Viv, peasants. And how can they be expected to toil in the fields and stock the manor lord's coffers day in and day out and still have time to go to war, let alone hoist the maypole come springtime. It's too much to ask." She tilted her head. "Besides, I haven't left them all at home. I decided *this* one's a page. You were so busy with all that court intrigue that you forgot all about Frederick over here, the lonely page who longs to marry the princess, and—oh, look at that! If my Queen takes your Queen and then your Bishop takes my Queen, and I take your Bishop with my horsie, you can't take my horsie with your King because of good old Freddie, my trusty page!"

It was precisely at this moment that Al strolled in from whatever speakeasy or gin mill he'd been frequenting in the name of, *ahem*, business. And not a moment too soon.

"If it ain't my two favorite dames," he said, jingling change in his pockets as he swaggered up, then bowed. "And what is you fine ladies doin' on this inclement afternoon?"

Vivian glanced up archly. Losing put her in a *mood*.

"Oh, we're just knocking off, aren't we Lala. We simply aren't getting anywhere with this silly game. I do believe Lala has written a dozen novels in her head, just while we're sitting here."

"Don't say," Al said, cocking his head politely toward Viola. "And speakin' of which, Miss Lala, ain't you promised to confabulate me a little somethin' for when my boys is, er, waitin' to be otherwise occupied."

Al had hatched the idea that he could better his associates with literature, if only it were lurid enough. Consequently, he had engaged Viola to write his boys a real page-turner.

"I'm almost done with it, Al," Lala said fondly. "I made the liquor agents real pills, just like you said, always fretting the establishment with their sneaky little ruses."

"Lala!" Vivian said. "And here you are, always saying *I* read trash!"

Viola blushed. She had rather enjoyed her detour into the darkened alleys of organized crime.

"But those poor racketeers, Viv!" she protested. "They have to start somewhere." She leaned out to pull over a third chair, then patted the cushion. "Sit and chat with us a while, Al," she said to change the subject. "How's business?"

Al doffed his hat as he sank into the chair, slinging one leg over the other. His wiry body was never still, and the dangling foot kept time with the clucking of the chickens. He twirled his fedora in his hands, then popped it back onto his head.

"To tell you ladies the truth, it's been better."

This was saying a lot because, according to Al, the underworld was littered with uncomfortable things like turning state's evidence and being taken for a ride from which one never returned.

"I got this new place, see, and I's callin' it The Night's Tale, on account of that book you read to me, Miss Lala, only it's a joke, see, 'cause it's *night* with a—"

"*N* not a *K*," Viola said excitedly. "Oh, that is clever. It's a pun on *The Knight's Tale!* I just knew you'd love Chaucer, Al, especially if I got the voices right." Granted, she'd adapted it, somewhat. Al wasn't quite ready for Middle English.

The bootlegger shrugged but looked shyly pleased by the compliment. "I wanted to get a more, er, sophisticated kind of Joe in there, see, and I figured those high-class chums might get the joke. But, that ain't my problem. I got Owney sending his guys over lookin' for a job, see, and I ain't keen to have a Madden man takin' hats and dishing up grub in my establishment, nothing against Owney, mind," he said hurriedly with a furtive look over his shoulder. "I mean we all got Owney to thank for cleanin' things up, what with his bein' so gentlemanly, unlike that Legs Diamond—why, that mug'd string you up soon as he'd talk to you, and for nothin' more than chattin' up the wrong dame . . ."

Viola could tell Al had wandered from his subject and would soon be lost in the deep grass, sniffing daffodils, and staring at the sky. He was like her in that way, a poet at heart, but with the mind of a plumber, always taking things apart to marvel at how a few pipes and elbows could carry away a whole load of raw sewage.

"Now, this *Owney*," she began, helpfully, "isn't he the one that's such a favorite of Warden Lawes?" But Vivian had other ideas.

"Forget him," she said, leaning in with a gleam in her eye that belied their soft creases. "Tell us about Diamond. Does he run a club too?"

That did it. The following talk ranged from Hell's Kitchen to the rogue's gallery of Sing Sing, from The Drool Inn to The

Cassanova and every club in between until Al stumbled unexpectedly on a familiar face.

"It was at The Fair Lady that I first saw Babs dance," he said, and the twins guppied as one.

"Babs!" Vivian cried.

"Sure. She danced in Luigi's place for a few months, didn't she, right up until Ziegfeld snatched her up for his big show."

"But the newspaper said—"

"Aw, don't credit them rags," Al said, waving her off. "Unless it's one of Winchell's plugs, it ain't worth readin'. I always wondered if that was why Ziggy and Luigi got off on the wrong foot, seein' how Luigi was sweet on Babs, as much as a mug like him can be, and Ziggy bein' so slick about the whole thing. But Babs has always got fellas hangin' around." He leaned in. "Why there's one up there right now, ain't there, come callin' not twenty minutes ago."

This ushered in a second round of guppying before Vivian took the situation in hand.

"Oh, Lala, look at the time," she breathed, glancing at her bare wrist. "We ought to freshen up before Mistress Dubois arrives, oughtn't we?"

Lala didn't like the look in her sister's eye. They would barge in on the mysterious visitor using any old excuse they could get their grubby hands on, then start ransacking poor Babs's heart for loot. But alas, Viola was bound by the Twins' Code—*two minds, two hearts, one will*. This was something Viv had come up with to keep Lala in line, but they both knew whose will they were talking about.

"Right," she sighed and rose. "Bye Al. Do stay out of trouble."

"Youse too," he said with a crooked smile, as if that were a grand joke, what with the twins being much too fine for monkey business.

If only he knew.

CHAPTER EIGHT
A Private Grief

The spiral staircase to the tower room flickered in the gaslights. No one had ever bothered to wire Canary House for electricity before the Great Crash, and it was unlikely to happen now. Viola liked the ambience, the stone walls shimmering like something out of a tale by Poe, and rain streaming down the gray-clad window-panes as the girls circled by, ever upward. There might be anything lurking behind that great oaken door at stairway's end, its black hinges hand-forged and shaped like fleurs-de-lis, stout enough to hold firm against whatever heaved and strove against the straining planks . . .

"It's bound to be a suitor," Viv whispered conversationally, breaking the spell. "I read in *The Scribbler* that she gets at least a dozen proposals a week, or at least she did so before she vanished. A mobster, Lala! What if Betty and Liv were right? How on earth will I bear it?"

She fell silent as they neared, creeping up to place an ear upon the door. Viola wavered, twisting her hands like a wet towel, then followed suit when she could stand it no more.

"Oof shudduff hant fome!" came Babs's muffled cry.

"Hay fadooseeyoom!" was the deep-toned reply.

The girls pressed their ears closer, though this yielded diminishing returns. Vivian was just on the point of mastering the application of optimal pressure without muffling the ear drum when the door was flung wide, and the twins tumbled in.

"Girls!" Babs cried.

"Oh, look at that," Vivian laughed, as if falling into someone's room was the most natural thing in the world. "We were just leaning in to knock! What were the chances?"

Babs was clad in a red silk kimono and her hair was piled on top of her head willy-nilly. She wore not a smudge of makeup, and both girls were taken aback by how pretty she looked with the faint sprinkling of freckles across her nose, her eyes red from crying. Younger somehow, fresher.

"Well, I . . . that is . . . what is it I kin do for you young ladies?"

Behind Babs, a man stood, shoulders hunched as he gazed at the hat in his hands. Suddenly, decisively, he jammed it on his head, grabbed his sodden overcoat from the armchair, and brushed past them out the door—but not before both twins glimpsed his face.

Babs's eyes widened as she watched the man depart, then hardened into resignation.

Vivian cleared her throat. Even she could feel the horror of their intrusion, for never had she expected to find Babs so self-possessed, so dignified by some private grief, and this almost compelled her to guilt. Almost, but not quite.

Why was Babs crying? And *who* was the young man?

"Oh, dear, we've done it this time, haven't we?" she breathed, her hand alighting on Babs's wrist. "We've just come to return this." She pulled a tangle of stockings from her pocket. "Can you believe, it must have stuck to my skirt when we left in such a hurry the other evening."

Viola *couldn't* believe, and it was only years of conditioning under the Twins' Code that saved her from a telltale eye roll. But the Code's power was such that she felt the mingling of shame at her complicity and admiration for her sister's forethought, for Viv had surely snatched the stockings just to afford the pretense of returning them.

That girl never missed a beat.

Babs took the stockings from Vivian, staring blankly at them in her hands as if unable to place an acquaintance.

"You're not yourself, dear," Vivian said, taking Babs's arm and guiding her to the armchair so surely she might have been the elder. Babs sank back and turned her cheek against the cushions, stopping her mouth with the back of a trembling hand.

"I'm sorry, girls. You've caught me at a bad time, see, why I . . . it's just you kin see I got lots of things on my mind."

Viola rather hoped that Viv would tread gently. No doubt being a brilliant tactician was a trial, but Viv did so tend to look down on others, and she could be a terrible snob on occasion.

But Vivian only handed Babs one of her own clean hand-kerchiefs. "We're the ones who are sorry," she said, leaning down to smooth a tangle of bleached blond hair back from the woman's forehead. "You rest up, now. We've got to be going anyway, haven't we, Lala."

Viola shot her twin a startled glance. What, no third degree? And with Babs ripe to spill every bean she had ever hoarded?

"Come on, Lala." Vivian ushered her twin toward the door, sweeping an arm down to scoop up the newspaper that lay folded on the side table. Vivian had a way of moving that was so mesmerizing, one hardly noted what she did.

"Goodbye," Viola cast hoarsely over her shoulder, just before the door closed. She couldn't even enjoy the pathos of the scene, not when Babs was in such a state. "Oh, Viv! It's just like that moment when Hester Prynne comes out the prison door to find her life bereft of solace!" she cried as they circled downward. "At least she had a babe in arms to comfort her."

"Really, Lala. What *are* you talking about?" Vivian was already perusing the newspaper she had nabbed.

"I can't help it," Viola said, her lovely face miserable in the half-light as they left the bottom stair and passed across the third floor gallery. "There's just something about her that reminds me of Hester, even though Hester has to wear that awful plain dress, well, except for the *A*, while Babs is just the opposite, what with all that powder and rouge and—oh, Viv, did you see how lovely she was au naturel? And with those darling little freckles all over her nose. Why, if she only went around like that all the time, I'll bet—*Viv*! How can you read the news at a time like this?"

Vivian had stopped midway across the carpet, frowning as she scanned the columns of newsprint, like a fair-faced harpy that had spied its prey.

"What an awful, dreary day," she grumbled, squinting in the muted light. "It's a terribly sad article, Lala, all about this poor man who got hit by a car not three blocks from here just a few days ago, on September 26. Listen—he had just crossed Central Park West when a black sedan sped up onto the curb and just knocked him down. He's quite dead."

She had thought to distract her sister from the vicissitudes of Babs's fate by way of a substitute tragedy. Just why she had snatched up the paper she didn't know, except that it was lying around looking like evidence. Having returned the stockings, she didn't want to leave empty-handed.

Viola came to a startled halt. "Do you suppose *that's* why Babs was crying?"

Vivian laughed. "Oh, Lala! Well, of course not! Not everyone is as soft-hearted as you!" This might have been taken as a slight if Vivian hadn't been gazing so fondly at her better half. "It had to be the young man who drove her to tears. It's only logical."

Viola felt that logic was overrated. But why belabor the point when Vivian would only use logic to support her position, thereby reinforcing the initial fallacy?

The irony of her own logic made her cranky.

"Oh, bother, Viv! Have it your way then," she cried with such uncharacteristic rancor that Vivian softened and took her arm.

"No, Lala, we'll have it *your* way. Why, Einstein himself said that logic will get you from A to B, but imagination will get you everywhere, or something like that."

Viola placed a hand over her twin's where it lay on her arm. It took very little to soothe her nature, and a kind word from Viv was more than up to the job.

"You're just saying that to make me feel better," she said with a small smile that Vivian couldn't help but return. "You don't believe a word of it, even if Einstein is a genius."

As the twins basked in their sameness, Vivian was struck by an even happier thought.

"Come, Lala." She grabbed her sister's hand to drag her down the hall. "Babs's opening night is only a week away, you know. Let's pick out our dresses, and then there's just time for me to do up your hair before old huff-and-puff arrives."

And they raced down the stairs to the second floor, laughing and jostling to see who would get there first.

CHAPTER NINE
The Curtain Calls

The Ziegfeld Theater was a sight to behold, with its Parisian Art Deco facade, lit by floodlights from below in the early dusk of an October evening. The grand limestone front bowed slightly out onto the sidewalk, decorated above the marquee by a zigzag of plaster relief like piping on a wedding cake.

"It *does* look yummy," Viola said, finishing her twin's thought.

"Oh, I don't know." Vivian tilted her head to one side, her flaxen hair coiffed in a side chignon. "It's no New Amsterdam." *That* legendary theater had housed Ziegfeld's Follies all through the last decade, until he'd gotten it into his head to build his own.

Viola sighed. "If only we'd been old enough, Viv. Or think of the Moulin Rouge! Why, we weren't even born then."

"Then you can't have missed a thing," Mrs. Lurch observed with her typical prairie wisdom. Having grown up on a ranch in Alberta, she saw no reason to gild a cow patty.

The girls were silent for a moment, gazing on the smattering of theatergoers, milling about the entrance. It wasn't so much the architecture that disappointed as the times themselves that had grown a little dingy.

Kind of like Babs Le Roy.

"She doesn't even have top billing," Viola complained as they ventured closer to the windows flanking the theater doors.

"Come now, Lala. The show's been running since July. She can't possibly expect to have simply waltzed back into the limelight." Vivian peered closer at the playbill mounted behind the glass. "Is that Helen Morgan? I can't quite tell."

Mrs. Lurch sniffed from behind, where she looked on over their shoulders. "'Glorifying the American girl,' indeed. Someone ought to lend that girl a coat."

The poster pictured Miss Morgan, former nightclub torch singer, draped in nothing but a fur stole, one hand placed strategically over her, *ahem*, chest. Vivian frowned. She didn't know why it should bother her, but lately she'd begun to wonder if being a glamour girl was everything it was cracked up to be, what with all the oohing and ogling and poking and prodding.

"I'm sure *that* old fuddy duddy would agree with you." She cast her eye on a tall man dressed in black, perched on a crate at the edge of the crowd. His ravings were lost in the general murmur, until a few strident words rang out.

"And so, it is written," he cried, wagging a finger: "Upon the wicked he shall rain snares, fire and brimstone, and a horrible tempest! This shall be the portion of their cup!"

Mrs. Lurch snorted, a rare departure from the usual sniff. "Can't abide Bible-thumpers, never could." She turned to usher the girls toward the theater doors. But Viola wouldn't budge.

"That man," she murmured, wandering a few steps closer to where he railed on—but just then, a long sedan pulled up to the curb and they all turned to look. Flashbulbs popped as the handful of newsmen who had turned out for the evening rushed the car.

"And are we not told all we need know in Romans 8:13?" The preacher's voice trembled in a way that brought Viola's gaze back around, striking pity in her heart. Such lonely people, fanatics, what with only their terrible missions for company. "For if you live according to the flesh you will die, but if by the Spirit you put to death the misdeeds of the body—"

He broke off as the sedan door opened wide. Out stepped Babs Le Roy, even though there was no red carpet to receive her, only the sad gaggle of theatergoers.

Vivian snagged her sister by the elbow as a barrel-chested man thundered by wearing long tails and a collapsible top hat that were decidedly démodé.

"Honestly, you're going to get trampled like a wounded wildebeest"

But Viola's gaze was still fixed on the preacher, perched atop his makeshift pulpit, silent now as he watched Babs hurry toward the theater doors. "He loathed his miserable self," she breathed, thinking of a line from *The Scarlet Letter*, but the quote was lost on Vivian.

"Not you too, Lala," she chided, absently. "What *are* you talking about?" But her gaze was also distracted—by Babs's agitated state as she hurried up the aisle, as though she were fleeing death itself. Could she really be that nervous? Maybe her absence from the limelight had shaken her confidence. Vivian turned her attention back to her twin. "Next thing you'll be raving away just like that ridiculous man."

Viola ignored her twin's rebuke. "He's just exactly like Dimmesdale, Viv, the preacher from my book. Oh, it all fits so perfectly. You see, when Hester Prynne passes Reverend Dimmesdale—her secret lover—in the public square, she always casts her tortured eye down to avoid—"

Her musings were cut short by the arrival of Mrs. Lurch, striding over to collect them like two calves who had strayed onto the back forty.

"In we go," she ordered crisply, elbowing her way through the crowd with her charges in tow up to the plate-glass doors. "Give way, give way," she scolded so roundly that even an ample man in a pin-striped suit stepped aside, eyeing her with chagrin.

Inside, beyond the oak-paneled foyer, the lobby was a haven of velvet, carpet, and gilded paint. A staircase swept up to either side, papered with scenes of harts cavorting through a stylized leafy wonderland. They paused to shoulder out of their coats, then drifted up to the mezzanine, the girls dressed in sleek, backless evening wear, cut on the bias in the nouveau style, Mrs. Lurch in her black frock and sensible shoes. The woodland fantasia extended into the egg-shaped auditorium that was the theater's hallmark, covering the walls up to the domed ceiling with floating castles and other displays of whimsy so ornate that Mrs. Lurch snorted for the second time that day.

"Rather like a Gustav Klimt painting, don't you think?" Viola ventured, and Vivian had to agree.

"You have to hand it to Ziegfeld. He has style."

"I do wonder how long he can hold out, though," Viola said, "with the talkies being all the rage. I tell you, Viv, it's positively the end of an age."

The girls traded predictions about the future of entertainment as seats slowly filled in the balconies, scalloped to either side of the proscenium, and down by the orchestra pit, where violins were already being tuned. Something about the hush of voices, punctuated here and there by the toot of a French horn or the trill of a flute, worked its way into their joint imagination, magnified in the half-light of the great chandelier like a child's fears, finding monsters in nursery shadows. Only this was magical and delicious, and as they poured over the program, leafing past advertisements plugging women's hose, Coty perfume, and the Sanforized-Shrunk men's shirt, they chatted in the comfort of Mrs. Lurch's silence. By the time the curtain rose, they were on the edge of their seats.

After the overture, Faith Bacon got the show off to a brilliant start with a rousing number called "Bring on the Follies Girls."

"There she is!" whispered Viola, pointing discretely with a gloved hand. And indeed, Babs was among the plumed figures drifting down the broad, curved staircase to the stage. The Ziegfeld girls were clad in silk and chiffon, pausing to pose like mannequins before venturing on, as if the stage were a department store window come to life. Some of the headdresses were downright unwieldy, sprouting candelabras and the like, and again, Vivian felt the troubling brush of a new sensation, a kind of claustrophobia that made her want to rush out onto Sixth Avenue for a breath of air. They *did* all look so very like one another, but for the variety of household objects balanced on their heads, on display, like their long limbs when they paused to strike a pose. What was the point of it all? More to the point, what was wrong with her?

Thankfully, this train of thought was derailed by a disturbance, just a few rows ahead of where they sat. The silhouette of a man stood abruptly, unsettling his neighbors as he gathered up his overcoat and lumbered over crossed legs on his way to the center aisle. The grumbling settled back into silence as he stepped free and turned up the aisle, where his frowning face was briefly lit by a ghost light pooling on the carpet. The twins drew a joint breath.

"That's him!" Viola hissed. And there was no need to explain, for Vivian didn't need her twin's photographic memory to recall the young man who had rushed out of Babs's room.

After that, it was hard to pay attention, no matter how Ziegfeld's spectacle sparkled and spun. Gladys Glad was presented as the Follies Girl of 1931, and Harry Richman crooned a song about helping yourself to happiness (and perhaps a helping of Gladys herself). Then followed a tableau from the Grand Hotel peppered with comedy bits, impressions, and dance numbers, including several scenes in a loosely plotted parable about Prohibition, complete with gangsters and their molls. The girls would have enjoyed it all terribly if it hadn't been for the conundrum of Babs's mysterious visitor.

"Oh, look, Viv, Babs is in the next number, finally," Viola whispered, pointing at the program, which listed Babs in the role of a mobster's gal.

The curtain opened on the Club Piccadilly with Ethel Borden in the role of that legendary, wisecracking queen of the speakeasies, Texas Guinan. Ruth Etting made the rounds as a cigarette girl, looking smart in a skater's skirt and pillbox hat, while hard-talking mobsters sparred with fast-talking con men.

"Where is she," Viola whispered, as the show within the show took to the stage upon the stage. "Do you suppose she's taken ill?"

"Good question, Lala," Vivian said grimly. By the time the curtain fell, both girls were half out of their seats with the intrigue of it all. But before they could utter a word, Mrs. Lurch took the matter in hand.

"Look sharp, girls," she said, rising with a wink as the lights rose on the hustle and bustle of intermission. "Let's have a look in on Miss Le Roy. Won't do not to congratulate her on her opening night."

CHAPTER TEN
Ziegfeld's Folly

The Ladies' Lounge was packed to the walls with dolls, dames, and debutantes, looking as sleek as sardines in a rolltop tin.

"Drat that cherry fizz," Viola lamented as she elbowed her way out of a stall and over to the bank of vanities, inlaid with porcelain sinks. She did her best to wash up, assaulted on one side by a gold lamé puff sleeve and on the other by a fox's head dangling grotesquely from a stole. Poor creature. It was perfectly detestable, wearing dead animals, just as lah-de-dah as you please. By the time she got out to the retiring room, she felt she was somewhat in need of a rest.

"It's about time," Vivian said, rising from a divan in the corner that beckoned in the dappled light of a beaded lampshade.

"No rest for the wicked, I suppose," Viola said with a sigh, but already she felt her spirits quicken. The sight of Viv, taut as a drawn arrow, reminded her of Babs's plight—if plight it was.

"Funny you should mention wickedness, Lala." Vivian linked arms with her twin as they exited the anteroom and re-joined Mrs. Lurch. "Do you suppose it's come to that? I mean, it is rather in the air."

Perhaps it was the reappearance—and sudden departure—of Babs's afternoon visitor that suggested the possibility of foul play to Vivian's restless mind. Or perhaps her fancy had merely been piqued by the atmosphere of the darkened theater. After all, most likely Babs had just fallen prey to a spot of nerves. And yet, Vivian's gut, always voluble, told her something was amiss. The starlet's emotional behavior, her air of secrecy, and now, her failure to appear on the most important night of her comeback—it all felt wrong.

It took some doing to find the basement stairs, but finally they spied a door marked STAFF ONLY through which they proceeded with Mrs. Lurch leading the way, just exactly as if they were late for an appointment. Down they trod, emerging into a warren of narrow passages, all lined with doors that were constantly opening and closing as half-clad showgirls and frantic stagehands came and went. A robed gentleman with slicked-back hair sauntered by, chased by a makeup artist, desperately waving a rouge brush.

"It's terribly exciting, down here," Viola breathed, forgetting for a moment the mystery of the missing Babs in the general melee. They turned down several halls, dodging all manner of props and scenery, then came abruptly to a halt.

"This will do, if I'm not mistaken," said Mrs. Lurch with the unerring instinct that had oft served her when flushing out rabbits on the prairies of her youth. Without deigning to knock, they barged right through the door marked only with a fading star.

Inside, a circle of faces looked up in surprise.

"For crying out loud, what now?" said a short, broad-shouldered man in a gabardine coat. He sat on a stool, half-swiveled in their direction, his elbow thrust behind him on the makeup table.

"Hmph," Mrs. Lurch said, ignoring the man. She stepped aside to wait just inside the open door, arms folded over her chest like a bouncer in one of Texas Guinan's joints.

It was all just exactly as Vivian had suspected. She did not miss a beat, stepping to the fore with, "Excuse me, sir. We're here concerning the disappearance."

"Here concerning the . . . but how on earth did you . . . *look here*, young lady . . ." The man rose from his stool, parting his trench coat to place a hand on each hip, but Viola knew he didn't stand a chance. With a gracious smile, Vivian strode to meet him, as though he'd offered his hand, which he most certainly had not.

"Oh, that is decent of you, but you needn't get up, sir. Really, we came as soon as we knew. Perhaps it's just a case of nerves—we saw her looking quite frightful on her way in tonight. But then, I suppose it's always possible that—oh, goodness, is that a ransom note?"

A tall, youngish man stepped out of the glare cast by the naked bulbs framing the vanity mirror. As he leaned down to snatch up the piece of crumpled paper, Vivian couldn't help but notice how white his shirt looked against the tan of his neck. He folded the note, then tucked it into the breast pocket of his suit.

"Look, little lady," said the man in the coat (who could only be a detective, what with those wide lapels and that bunched up fedora on the makeup table), "I really must insist that—"

"Thank you, but no," Vivian said, gesturing toward the gently spinning stool as if declining to sit. "I'm quite fine standing, but you *are* a gentleman. Tell me, is the mob involved? Far be it from me to offer theories at this tender stage, but I understand Babs was once in the employ of a certain—"

"Mob! Why, that's preposterous."

This exclamation brought all their heads around to stare at the third member of the party upon which they had intruded. They'd hardly taken note of him before, but now Vivian recognized with something of a shock the shrewd, wide-set eyes of Florenz Ziegfeld Jr.

"Mr. Ziegfeld! Oh, pardon us. This *is* an honor and a delight," Vivian said with perfect self-possession. "May I express our sympathies regarding this dreadful turn of events. I know you and Miss Le Roy have a long and, well, intimate history, if that's not straying too far. You did discover her, after all. How distressing for you, finding her simply *gone*. Why, she'd hardly time to take off her candelabra, had she? Before—poof! And then, this note! How beastly. I assume the miscreants are demanding money for the return of your once shining star. Truly, it's absolutely *beastly* . . ."

On she prattled as she scanned the room, taking in the lay of her disheveled surroundings. Babs was a slob, there was no other word, her robes and stockings and scarves strewn all about like tickertape after a New Year's Eve bash. She noted the detective's scowling face as contrasted with Mr. Ziegfeld's markedly pale one, dangerously pale, now that it came to it—but then her eyes locked momentarily with those of the young man, who must be the detective's sergeant, and she felt her cheeks grow hot.

She'd best watch out for that one. He didn't miss much.

"As I was saying," she began, trying to recover, but the moment was lost, and she knew it.

"As *I* was saying," the detective said, taking her by the elbow a tad roughly and turning her toward the door—only to come face to face with Mrs. Lurch. No one handled *her* girls that way, lawman or no. He seemed to take this in at a glance, coughing a few unintelligible words as he let go of Vivian's arm, then smoothed his lapels with such discomfiture that Viola thought him rather dear, just an old softie under that hard-boiled exterior. "Now," he said with forced courtesy, "we have business to conduct, so if you ladies would be so kind as to excuse us?" He extended his arm toward the still open door.

"Of course," Vivian said, though *her* forced courtesy smacked of such genuine hubris that the detective's brow un-grizzled before their very eyes. "Goodness, you've a crime to solve, we quite understand. May I thank you for you service, sir," she said with a nod that only partially concealed a final glance at the young sergeant. There was the unmistakable glint of laughter in his thick-lashed brown eyes. Honestly! The conceit of some people.

Vivian turned to Mrs. Lurch, who hadn't budged and was still staring the inspector down like a bull getting ready to charge. "We'd best get back for the second act, hadn't we, Mrs. Lurch," Vivian said breezily, leading the way out into the corridor. Viola followed just behind with a friendly backward wave at the detective, whose arched brow betrayed his utter bewilderment. Mrs. Lurch came last, her eyes lingering until the very last moment with what Viola knew must be chilling intensity. When one had taken on the Royal Canadian Mounties in pitched battle and lived to tell—well, let's just say that for all her prim manners, the worthy Mrs. Lurch was no buttercup.

"What a perfect waste of an opportunity," Vivian fumed, but Viola only took her arm and snuggled in close as they wended their way up the corridor.

"Come now, Viv, the *pity* is that Babs is missing, don't you think?" she chided, gently. "Besides, it wasn't an utter waste. It's such a terribly intriguing message. Why, we might ponder it for ages and still not get anywhere. All that business about 'paying the piper,' and 'trinkets and treasures,' which is quite poetic when you think—"

Vivian stopped cold in the crowded hall causing a commotion behind as a stagehand collided with Mrs. Lurch's back.

"Lala, are you telling me—"

"That I read the scribblings on that ghastly note?" Viola looked sidelong at her sister with a mischievous smile. "It was a tad trying with it being upside down in the mirror and all, but *oh*, the message was so intriguing, Viv, just as I said. Though not nearly as intriguing as what that poor preacher was saying from atop his pitiful little box. Now, Viv, I know you'll say he was only raving, but I tell you, as soon as I recognized him, I just *knew*—"

"*Recognized*—Lala!" Vivian began in exasperation, but Viola only giggled and took her by the arm again, pulling her back into stride.

"Didn't I tell you?" she said, and now the mischief in her voice was unmistakable. "Why Viv, I recognized that preacher outside the theater at first sight. You know I never forget a face. It was the man from the Sixth Avenue El—the man from Babs's rendezvous!"

CHAPTER ELEVEN
Bumps in the Night

Mrs. Lurch had only just let the girls in through the front door after a long cab ride home when they all heard the ruckus coming from the kitchen down below. The front hall canaries Peisinoe, Aglaope and Thelxiepeia (named for the sirens of yore who called sailors to their deaths) were twittering their familiar welcome from the hanging cage by the staircase when a crash came, followed by a hearty round of Irish cursing.

"If you'll excuse me, girls." Mrs. Lurch removed her coat and hung it in the hall closet before clip-clopping across the carpet and out of sight. Vivian and Viola exchanged a haunted glance. Father was such a happy drunk, one should think it harmless, really. Yet the sight of him sometimes, bent over his knees with laughter because of some joke no one could fathom, or throwing his arm around a stranger's shoulders to whisper sloppy nothings in his ear, or simply nodding off as he sat, slumped in a chair and fighting slumber—invariably, such prospects contrived to tie a knot in the twins' collective insides, binding each to the other.

The only thing worse than seeing Father in such a state was *hearing* him.

"I suppose we ought to look in," Vivian said, reaching for her sister's hand. Viola gave a sober nod, and off they went, hand in hand, across the wide hall, through the dining room and butler's pantry, then down a flight of stairs at the rear of the house. As they neared the kitchen, a shriek met their ears.

"James Wilbur Van der Beeck, what am I going to do with ye? You do be a right handful!"

The girls pushed in to find Cookie, frazzled hair peeking out from beneath a head rag as she held Father by the ear like a naughty boy caught at mischief. He was bent double, sobbing with laughter as one hand slapped the butcher's block beside him. The floor was littered with shards of china, the remains, no doubt, of his failed attempt at a bedtime snack. There was Mrs. Lurch, turned away at the rear counter as she poured a cup of coffee from the silver carafe. Moments later, she brought it hither, corralling Father by the chin to administer the black elixir directly into his mouth. He sputtered, still chuckling, then stood upright and wiped an arm across his mouth. But soon, he was giggling again, face thrust into the crook of his elbow to stifle his snorts.

Just then, Mother breezed into the kitchen from behind the twins, coming to stand beside them. Father looked up and fell silent at once, arm dropping from his face as he groped behind him for the counter. A chastened look entered his eye, as if he were frightfully sorry, though for what he could not quite recall.

The air trembled between them.

"But *look* at you, mon cher." Mother breathed in her husky voice, breaking the spell. She glided across the flagstones, avoiding the shards without looking, and took Father gingerly by the arm while she tutted and cooed. "It is a sickness with you, but I tell you, it will not do, no mon cher, you who are l'amour of Giselle's, you must not treat yourself so."

"I'm sorry, darling, I . . . I . . . we stormed the field, don't you know, the whole battalion." He stroked his temple with one finger as Mother led him away. "I . . . I got the call you see, so I sent them over the top, my beautiful boys, all over the top, down to a one, and all the while that *beastly* rattling of guns was going on and on and *on* . . ." he murmured, just exactly as if he were explaining a bother that had happened down at the club and not one of the worst battles of the war.

The door swung shut behind them, followed by a second pause. The four of them looked at each other as Father's voice drifted into silence.

"Well, that's that, then," Mrs. Lurch said briskly.

Cookie was still swaying on her stubby legs, furiously brushing hair from her eyes with the back of one pudgy hand.

"A right shame, 'tis," she said, looking up blearily into Mrs. Lurch's eyes. "Remember him as a lad, Mary? My word, what a scamp! Ne'er were there a rascal like our Jimmy, always scrappin' 'round the kitchen with his hoop and stick or coming in with some wild tale about . . . about . . . and *now*—"

She mashed the back of her hand to her mouth as Mrs. Lurch patted her shoulder. It wasn't just Father that Cookie was remembering. The twins knew full well that she was also picturing in her mind's eye two other scamps who had scrapped about her kitchen in the years before their double suicide on Black Tuesday—Father's young brothers, Uncle Teddy and Uncle Titus.

But the family never talked about them.

Mrs. Lurch fixed the girls with a canny look.

"There, there, Alma, nothing to be done about it," she soothed. Cookie was the only person in the household with whom Mrs. Lurch was on a first name basis. "And you two," she said, flinging a finger toward the door, "off to bed. Won't do to lollygag." The words were stern, but there was something in Mrs. Lurch's eyes that eased that knot in the twins' insides. *I've seen worse,* her eyes seemed to say. *We'll get through this too.*

They retreated upstairs through the silent house and were almost to their bedroom door when the sound of a low cough turned both their heads. There was Mr. Sharma's long face, peeking around the corner of the second-story hall, his black hair slicked back from a neat middle part.

"Why, Mr. Sharma, what are you doing up at this hour?" said Vivian, venturing closer as Viola trailed behind.

He stepped fully out into the hall, clasping his slender, dark hands before him. Vivian never got over how tiny he was. Born in India, raised in England, and now marooned in New York, a world away from the Oxford halls of his youth, Mr. Sharma seemed perpetually unsure of his reception. Vivian pitied him, but really, just now she was in no mood for his bumbling inquiries.

"I say . . . ahem . . . I was rather hoping . . . er . . ." He cleared his throat again, looking everywhere but at their eyes. "I've been t-t-tasked with a bit of research by the Society," he said, referring no doubt to his volunteer work with the New York Historical Society, "and, well, your family has c-come up, you see, and . . . well . . . there's something I-I-I—"

"Mr. Sharma, we've had rather a trying night," Vivian said around the lump in her throat. It came out more curtly than intended.

Finally, his eyes snapped to hers as understanding dawned. "But of c-course. This is not the time." He started to turn away, then swiveled back and said, all in a rush, "It's not his fault, you know."

The lump in Vivian's throat grew.

"*Whose* fault?" she asked, obstinately.

"Now, Viv," Viola chided, ghosting past her sister to take Mr. Sharma by the arm and lead him closer, "you know perfectly well he's talking about Father."

It was what Vivian should have said, but gently, as only Viola could say it. Vivian's cheeks flamed.

"Where were you stationed, dear?" Viola asked, turning to Mr. Sharma as she let go of his arm.

Stationed? But of course, Mr. Sharma had been in the war too. A historian by training, a professor by occupation, he had ended up in the British Foreign Office through a succession of circumstances no one quite understood. And in an age of shifting allegiances, Mr. Sharma had been quietly instrumental in securing the alliance between Russia, France, and Britain—the Triple Entente—that would ultimately prevail in a war that left over eight million dead, overturned three monarchies and four empires, and spelled the end of European colonialism. Vivian could recall in detail the profile she'd read in the *Daily News*.

But as usual, it was Lala who understood.

Vivian sighed, and the lump in her throat eased. If Lala could be kind, the least she could do was to be courteous.

"Come, Mr. Sharma, let's all have a chat, shall we?" She opened the door to their adjoining chambers. "The sitting area by the windows looks terribly cozy." Already, her mind had turned to the marvelous feats of diplomacy their humble tenant had improbably achieved, chatting up grizzled world leaders over a spot of tea. Had he always been so tongue-tied? "I've been wondering, Mr. Sharma, how *did* you manage to convince those Brazilian fellows to enter the war?" she inquired with genuine curiosity as she gestured to a chair.

Half an hour after Mr. Sharma had returned to his small, monkish chamber on the third floor, Vivian finally nestled in beside Viola, where she was reading the diary in bed.

"I simply won't have it, Lala," Vivian said. "You'll have to give up this curse nonsense. Those Gothic novels have quite addled your good judgment."

Viola was forced to own that the notion of a curse had been growing on her in recent days. Perhaps Viv was right—it was a bit gruesome for a seventeen-year-old girl to dwell so on doom and gloom.

"But look, right here, Viv," she persisted, placing a finger on the entry that read *Florence Constance Van der Beeck, died, age 28, by means of a falling piano.* "And here." She moved her finger down the page a couple of lines to where two names were scribbled, Lawrence and Leopold, conjoined twins who had enjoyed a spectacular debut in Barnum's American Museum, only to perish the following day when Leopold choked on a plum pit. Lawrence followed soon after.

"They were perfectly happy for a while," Vivian said, though her voice was doubtful. "You should know that better than anyone, Lala. They always had someone to talk to."

"But a plum pit, Viv. How *tragic.*" Viola closed the ancient volume and set it gently on the bedside table, snuggling down under the covers. She hadn't brought up the deaths of poor Uncles Teddy and Titus, though she knew it was fresh in both their minds. Perhaps that's why Vivian was so dead set against the subject of family tragedy, which in other respects did not bother her at all. "Do you suppose we're paying off some kind of ancestral karmic debt?"

Vivian turned onto her hip to face her sister, head propped in one hand. "You're only saying that because of Grampy Cornelius. Honestly, Lala, you didn't even know the man! Why, he was gone years before we were born, traipsing off into the ether, and all because of some mumbo jumbo about mysteries encoded in the universe. Auntie said it was utter nonsense."

She finished on a firm note, but already, the corner of her mouth was twitching, and one look into her sister's eyes sent the two of them into a fit of giggling.

"And she should know," Viola managed in a garbled voice, tears squeezing out of the corners of her eyes. "Being an expert, and all."

Vivian's eyes grew wide in mock astonishment at her sister's temerity. But it was true—Great Auntie Lavinia was truly a nonsense aficionado. She believed just about anything she read in the penny press.

"Well, you may be right about one thing," Vivian said when they were able to talk normally again. "We seem to have had more than our share of accidents in this family, though I'm betting some of that is plain bad judgment. You know I love Father like my own—well, I suppose he is my own flesh, isn't he. But he does make some terrible decisions." This observation, a departure from Viv's typical offhand manner, sobered them both and was perhaps a bit too earnest for her taste. She added archly, "But to say that it's a mystery, well, I simply won't have it, and that's all there is to it. Now, Babs's disappearance—there's a mystery."

Viola let the warmth from their laughing fit settle on her insides like a soothing balm. She continued gazing at her sister and tried to imagine life without her. "Maybe you're right, Viv," she said fondly, with just a trace of sadness for the rest of the twin-less world. "Leopold and Lawrence were truly blessed, just like us, even if I am rather glad we don't share organs. And poor Babs, she seems so woefully alone. Viv, do you suppose—"

But Vivian never had a chance to suppose one way or the other, for at that moment, the distant ring of the doorbell reached their ears, announcing the arrival of someone on the front stairs.

Vivian was out of bed in a flash.

"Come on, Lala, you know who it is, don't you?" She hurried into her best kimono and ran a brush through her hair. "Who else would be calling at this hour? It's the serg—the detective, silly. They've come to talk to us about the case!"

CHAPTER TWELVE
The Parlor of Babel

Samuel T. Flanagan, detective first grade, had only recently joined the Major Case Squad of the Detective Bureau, having served for many years in the Gangster Squad under the leadership of one Johnny Broderick, whose crime-busting exploits were a favorite subject of the penny press. The two detectives had lived strangely parallel lives. Both had been born in the Gashouse District along the East River, amid the hulking, cylindrical tanks for which the district was named. Both had been admitted to the force in 1923 and had worked the Broadway beat, where Detective Broderick earned a reputation for violence and rose quickly through the ranks, making detective first grade in a mere three years, while Detective Flanagan had achieved that distinction only after leaving the Gangster Squad last year.

He was not a favorite of Tammany Hall.

Flanagan's young associate never mentioned the detective's rival in his boss's presence. Sergeant Adam Kowalski, Adi to his mother, was the youngest cadet ever to be appointed to the Detective Bureau and at 20 years of age possessed the acumen of officers many years his senior. A third-generation Polish American, his grandparents were dissidents who had fled after the insurrection of

1863, seeking the sanctuary of a Brooklyn farmstead, crowded on either side by warehouses, ropeyards, and breweries of lager beer. As the son of a doctor, Adi had been the object of all his mother's hopes and dreams, but from a young age had wanted only one thing: to solve crimes.

"Is that, ahem, everyone, then?" Detective Flanagan said as the last of the Canary House tenants crowded into the parlor where the family had already gathered.

"What are you waiting for? A royal invitation?" Auntie Lavinia groused from her nest of pillows on the divan.

"Quelle nuisance!" Mother said with a flick of one hand. "Tell to me, Inspector, do you always make the calls at such an hour?"

"Where is that blasted drink?" said Father, rolling his head back against the sofa to look behind, as if the waiter had wandered away. Alas, he found only Mrs. Lurch, stationed behind the sofa in her nightcap and flannels.

"It's Detective, ma'am, not Inspector," Flanagan said, choosing to address himself only to the incomparable Giselle. His blush was faintly evident in the gaslit incandescence. He cleared his throat again, shifting in his chair. "Sorry to disturb you all but I'm afraid in a kidnapping case such as this, time is of the essence. Now," he crossed his legs and licked his pencil tip, balancing a notepad on his knee, "when did Miss Le Roy first take up residence here?"

The parlor erupted in conversation. Madame Koslova and Miss Sphinx, who were sitting close enough to ignore each other, struck up spirited discussions with Mr. Sharma and Mr. Sparrow, respectively. The worthy madame, whose room happened to be situated at the base of the turret stairs, told of comings and goings in the dark of night while Miss Sphinx shared a poem she had recently penned, inspired by the downtrodden star. Mother was speaking in rapid French, Father in rapid drunk, while Auntie began recounting (to no one in particular) an anecdote she had recently read in the New York Sun about one Detective Johnny Broderick, who had knocked out gangster Francis "Two Gun" Crowley with a single punch. Mrs. Lurch and Cookie were discussing the state of Miss Le Roy's chambers while the eminent Dr. Weber's dissertation on dissociation and the female mind was lost in the din, (fortunately, as Mrs. Lurch did not abide such nonsense). Only Al lurked silently in the shadows, having conceived a professional distrust of detectives.

Vivian caught her sister's eye. High time she took things in hand.

"Detective *Flanagan*, was it?" she said politely from where she stood nearby. "Miss Le Roy joined us on the evening of September 17, at approximately 8:40 p.m. and I believe you'll find she took up lodgings here soon after her return from upstate New York where she had been living with her family of origin, that being a fact she took pains to hide upon her arrival."

The effect was immediate. Vivian had established herself as the lone voice of sanity among the babbling fools. Both detective and sergeant turned to her at once. Flanagan's florid face showed relief so profound the effect was comic. Still standing beside his boss, Sergeant Kowalski's face betrayed only polite, professional interest, though his not unappealing brown eyes, when they met hers, did seem a tad impressed. Not that she cared one whit, of course.

"You know about the child, I assume," she went on with perfect nonchalance, noting with satisfaction that the detective most certainly did not. "By my calculations, Miss Le Roy's baby must be at least six months old by now and is likely being reared by Miss Babs's mother as a small addition to the impressive family brood. I can supply their postal address if that would be useful."

The detective guppied for a beat or two. A small smile lodged at the corner of Sergeant Kowalski's mouth as he eyed her, then looked away.

"You've done a fair bit of sleuthing yourself, haven't you," he said, and Vivian was taken aback at the sound of his voice, which was somehow both strong and soft around the edges. Not that there was anything strange about the act of speaking itself. It was just that the sound seemed to render the sergeant real in a way he hadn't been before, as if a picture had become flesh and blood. The room *did* seem warm, didn't it? What with the whole household crammed in, cheek by jowl, still jabbering about this, that, and the other thing. They'd long abandoned Babs for other topics ranging from medieval haberdashery to the importance of iodine in maintaining dietary health.

"Why isn't Detective Johnny Broderick investigating this case?" Auntie Lavinia suddenly shouted from her divan, where she had lain too long neglected. "Who ever heard of Detective Finnegan anyway?"

A vein throbbed on the side of the good detective's neck. He reached a finger into his collar to tug it wide.

"It's *Flanagan*, ma'am," he growled. "Now," he turned to Vivian with a look of defiant determination in his eye, "you were saying, miss?"

Vivian proceeded to tell him almost everything she knew. She had to keep some bits for herself, of course, or there would be no fun to be had for a good, long time. Having tasted real intrigue, she was loath to go back to Mistress Dubois's anemic offerings, which were bland as a baby's pap, even when they did make sense.

"There was that *fellow*," Viola began once, so softly that only Vivian heard, just in time to bring her slippered foot down firmly on her twin's. Babs's mysterious visitor was one of the bits Vivian was *keeping*, and with Al as the only other witness, they weren't likely to be scooped. He was too busy flitting from one shadow to the next, twirling his fedora like a majorette in the Easter parade.

Vivian had just finished giving Detective Flanagan a thorough accounting of Luigi Luciana's fling with Babs during her time at

The Fair Lady when she felt the touch of someone's gaze and looked up to find the sergeant studying her with an infuriating steadiness that did give one a tingle about the knees.

"You're sure there's nothing else?" he said.

Drat that sergeant and his superior ways. And if there *was* more, what business was it of his? If Vivian's logical mind noted the fallacy introduced into this statement by the fact of the sergeant's occupation, she gave no sign.

Ignoring the warmth in her cheeks, she graced him with a brittle smile.

"Quite sure, Sergeant, but you'll certainly be the first to know if we discover anything at all."

The detective rose to his feet. "Well, I must say, you've been quite helpful, miss," he said with such frank gratitude that Vivian felt the brush of chagrin. He really wasn't half bad, even if the gabardine coat was un peu trop.

"Humph, Detective Floridian, eh?" Lavinia shouted, struggling upright from the drift of her pillows. "Sounds like some kind of newfangled toothpaste, if you ask me."

Detective Flanagan opened his mouth, then thought better of it. He tucked his small notepad into his breast pocket and swept his coat open to place both hands on his hips, turning to his sergeant.

"Kowalski? We've got a few more stops to make tonight so we best get going."

The sergeant nodded. "Thank you, ladies," he said with a small smile for Viola and Vivian, each in her turn. Viola thought him a fine officer, a bit of a "fuzz," Al would say, which was professional slang for a diligent copper, not a palooka or a sap like so many of the gumshoes out there. Oh, Al *would* be pleased with her progress. But more to the point, Viola could see there would be no living with Vivian for quite some time. The last time she'd seen her sister like this was when . . . when . . . well, truth be told, Lala had never seen her twin like this. For all the love letters Viv kept stowed in her trinket box, Viola firmly believed she'd never cared a whit for any of her suitors. It was really something of a fault. And now, there was Viv, looking anywhere but at the two men as they gathered their things.

"Come, dear, we'll show you out," Viola said, stepping up to take Detective Flanagan's arm. His befuddlement seemed tinged with gratitude. Poor dear. How ghastly to always be going about interrogating people who might otherwise be perfectly friendly. A thankless job it was, and nearly as lonely as the desperate pursuits of Al's underworld associates, who had scraped around as best they could since birth and couldn't be held accountable. If only people could get along.

"You first," Sergeant Kowalski said, extending his arm as Vivian studiously avoided his eye.

CHAPTER THIRTEEN
Ruminations

The whole household slept in the next day. It was Sunday, after all, and the family had not made the pilgrimage to the Trinity Episcopal Church since Auntie had so spectacularly fallen out with *The* Mrs. Astor over the Van der Beeck's exclusion from "The 400" (an ingenious ploy devised by the dowager to hand-pick the *Who's Who* of New York Society). Whether Auntie was riled at being left out, fed up with "the old harpy's" snobbery, or merely peeved at not having thought of such a ploy herself was anyone's guess.

This left Sundays free for lounging about the conservatory after a leisurely breakfast of Cookie's scones and (if they were lucky) a piano concert in Mr. Sparrow's room.

Breakfast was not ready until eleven, and the tenants wandered up to Mr. Sparrow's third floor suite with scones in hand (in contravention of Mrs. Lurch's standing orders that no crumb should encroach upon the commonweal). But the drama of the preceding day had clearly made her soft, and she turned a blind eye as the tenants, one by one, skulked out of the breakfast room, plates clutched in one hand and steaming cups of coffee in the other.

Vivian and Viola were already settled on the low divan under the casement windows when the others arrived. Mr. Sparrow was allotted two rooms for his tenancy, one for his bed and desk, his piles of books, and whatever instruments he happened to be playing, and the other for his piano. Officially, the occasional Sunday concert was granted in payment for the extra room, but Viola was sure he would have played for free. He loved nothing so much as cracking his marvelous long-fingered hands over the ivories, hovering for one instant in the silence of anticipation, then laying into Ravel's *Gaspard de la Nuit*, or one of Chopin's smart Études, or (increasingly of late) some rag by Fats Waller that would send the keys jumping, like the ghostly gyrations of a player piano.

Today, it was all jazz.

"Oh, he *is* in rare form today, don't you think?" Viola whispered, nestling against her twin's shoulder. She still thrilled to see his unruly, sandy blond hair falling over his eyes as he pummeled the keys, as if punishing them to new glories of expression. It was terribly romantic, even if his ruminations were, in truth, less tortured than rapt. And was it her imagination, or had he been coming home late these days, drifting up the stairs with a creaking tread that only the twins had learned to recognize?

"What? Oh, yes, hmm," was all Vivian said.

Viola scooted away to look at her sister's profile. Oh dear. "I do believe he's taken up with someone," she tried. "Probably at one of those 'rent parties' in Harlem they're always going on about in *The Scribbler.*"

Sure enough, Vivian cast a brief glance at her sister before resuming the consumption of her lower lip. "I say, Lala, don't believe everything you read."

It was true then. Not even the prospect of Mr. Sparrow's defection into the arms of another woman was sufficient to break the trance. But was it the young sergeant or Babs's case that had commandeered Viv's single-minded train of thought?

Viola hoped it was the latter.

Mr. Sparrow put the finishing flourishes on "Birmingham Blues," an old favorite, and the tenants erupted in applause. Father and Mother were nowhere to be seen, which pricked Viola's peace of mind a bit, but then Father was likely sleeping it off, and Mother did so like to keep an eye on him. Mrs. Lurch was busy with Cookie in the kitchen, and the maids and Horace had the day off. With just the tenants here, away from their keepers, it was a golden opportunity for gossip. Viola wouldn't have noticed had she not been forced to think of it on Vivian's behalf, but that's what twins were for. Besides, it felt a little lonely with Viv so far away.

Viola felt the brush of a new kind of dread.

"Oh, that was lovely, Mr. Sparrow, thank you," she gushed when the applause had dwindled. "I don't think Mr. Waller himself could have played it better."

Mr. Sparrow lowered the lid over the keys, then poked his head around the aging grand piano to give her his dear lopsided smile. "You know that's not true, Lala," he said wryly, "but I appreciate the sentiment." Mother would never have believed how Mr. Sparrow spoke to them in private, so easy and familiar. It was only her teasing that made his shy streak come out. "I'm lucky if Fats gives me the time of day."

Mr. Sparrow had become a regular at the after-hours joints favored by Harlem musicians, black performers who weren't allowed to patronize the whites-only clubs they played. A friend had taken him to one of the basement bordellos where the *real* show began, after the well-heeled went home, and he'd been hooked ever since. At first, he'd kept to the shadows, seeing how he felt like a traitor in their midst. But Viola was sure he'd won them over, even if he wouldn't say so, because Mr. Sparrow had all the charms of a young child in a man's body and wouldn't hurt a fly. And you couldn't hide something like that, could you.

"Well, it's only a matter of time before you're playing The Savoy. Did you ever hear back from that Hoagy gentleman?"

Mr. Sparrow laughed, scraping back on his piano bench so he could lean against the wall. "Mr. Carmichael has better things to do than look at one of my songs."

If only Mr. Sparrow had a little more confidence. It was something of a fault. Viola glanced over at her sister, whose furrowed brow still betrayed her distraction.

"Poor Babs," Viola said a little too loudly to the room at large. "What do you suppose happened to her?" She blushed, violently, not being accustomed to such crude attempts to ferret out information.

"It is obvious, child," Madame Koslova said in that husky, muscular tone that seemed to proceed from the back of her throat. She settled her girth into her overstuffed chair by the potted palm. "The little minx has engineered her own abduction in a plot to obtain the ransom. Brilliant, really. I would not have thought her capable of such initiative."

Viola gaped, shocked. Imagine, Madame Koslova endorsing such a scheme!

"Such nonsense, this," Miss Sphinx said, with an offhand laugh as if the matron had, of *course*, been joking. Madame Koslova grunted and shifted over to the other hip. "I am sure my worthy friend will agree," the poetess went on, sitting cross-legged in the Empire Revival chair with the gilded armrests, "that the woman would not be capable of the . . . the . . . how do you say," she snapped her long fingers, "the Machiavellian tact*eecs*." Miss Sphinx accent did so remind one of Mother's except for that roundness around the vowels and the way her mouth pouted on the ends of words. Poor Madame Koslova, what could she say? Even Viola could see how Miss Sphinx had cleverly branded her nemesis as a schemer while absolving Babs in the same stroke, even if it was by virtue of stupidity. Oh, it was hard, wasn't it, but then Viola couldn't help but feel Miss Koslova needed to be set down on occasion.

It was at about this time that Vivian perked up. She too had considered that Babs herself might be behind the abduction, but even if she were capable of such a ploy, why would she do it? Was she really that hard up for money? Her career might be on shaky legs, so to speak, but at least she was dancing. And if Ziegfeld really was the father of her baby, why would she extort *him* for ransom? For though she hadn't yet gotten her hands on definitive proof, she was simply sure about the existence of a child. Had Babs and Ziegfeld fallen out? Was it some kind of twisted revenge?

"Miss Le Roy's behavior is indicative of ze poorly formed ego, yes?" Dr. Weber offered with just a trace of the staccato style that marked him as German born. "It has made her susceptible to manipulation, particularly by ze men who are substitutes for an absent father." For some reason, Dr. Weber always sat nearest to the door of whatever room he happened to be in, though Viola refrained from subjecting this behavior to the Freudian analysis the good doctor favored. "It is logical to assume she has fallen prey to one of her suitors," he finished through a cloud of smoke as he flourished his pipe, "perhaps someone who has formed a fixation on her because she reminds him of his mother."

It was not a bad theory, Vivian thought, although Dr. Weber's speculations were generally like a one-note horn. But when one considered Babs's chosen profession and her long line of suitors, one could not help but suspect she might be vulnerable to exploitation. But by whom? Luigi Luciana? Had the gangster used her to squeeze money from Ziegfeld, his longtime rival, the very man who had stolen his gal? Or maybe it wasn't even about the money, and the abduction itself was the mobster's retaliation for having been spurned. Ziegfeld was famously short on cash, so he seemed a strange target for a ransom demand. But then, he was almost as good as Madame Koslova at procuring more funds when needed for one of his ailing shows. Could there be another man in the picture? Vivian had not forgotten about Babs's afternoon visitor. Who was he, and how did he fit in?

"If you ask me, that mug Luciana is behind it," Al said from the alcove where he sat, tucked behind the spider fern. Al had a way of blending in, and his sudden pronouncement startled them all. "Somethin' ain't right, and I've a mind to go tell Owney all about it, if'n it weren't bad form to go rattin' on one's associates."

Vivian sat upright on the divan, unsettling Viola from where she slumped against her. Yes, Luigi Luciana. If nothing else, he might be easy to eliminate as a suspect, clearing the field. There was only one way to find out more, and Al would be the perfect escort.

"What's *your* theory, Viv?" Mr. Sparrow said, still leaning back against the wall, one lanky leg crossed over the other, hands clasped in his lap. Vivian looked over to find herself strangely unmoved by the twinkle in those deep blue eyes. There was no denying Mr. Sparrow's charms, but at 28 he was rather too old to be mooning over, now, wasn't he.

Vivian caught Al's eye through the spiky fronds of the palm plant. "I think a visit to The Fair Lady might be in order. What do you say, Al?"

A silence descended on the room at odds with the tenants' usual patter, for they had even now been engaged in a multitude of conversational asides. Shiva and Deva, the piano room canaries, stopped chirping.

Mr. Sharma cleared his throat. "Miss, ahem, Miss Vivian," he began, carefully, "I d-do not think that would be, er, wise. There are forces of . . . of evil at work here of which, perhaps, you have no c-c-concept." The sageness of this remark, coupled with a haunted wisdom in his eye born of deep experience, gave even Vivian a moment's pause.

But a moment passes quickly.

"Dear Mr. Sharma, you needn't worry," Vivian said, flashing the smile that had once caused Tommy Parker to tumble into the ocean from the spectator sloop at the annual regatta. "With Al as our escort, what could possibly go wrong?"

CHAPTER FOURTEEN
Dreams and Schemes

Vivian was too young to truly appreciate the phrase "famous last words," which came into popular usage after Civil War General John Sedgwick remarked, "They couldn't hit an elephant at this distance," just before being shot dead by a sniper.

Consequently, she woke up Monday morning full of workmanlike zeal.

"Rise and shine, Lala." She pounced on her sister's bed before the sun had fully risen. Viola sat upright, ripped straight from a dream in which she and Grampy Cornelius had been strolling arm in arm beneath a crimson sun along the banks of the River Nile. Nothing had made sense, even in the dream. Hadn't there been something about a statue? Or was it a gold medallion? Seven cows had trailed them along the embankment, cooling them with seven, giant fans (although just how the poor cows wielded them escaped her recollection), and all the while, seven vultures circled the heavens, looking for a meal.

"Counting Father, I suppose *we're* the seventh," she said blearily, unaware that the sounds her lips were forming held meaning.

"Honestly, Lala, the things you say," Viv complained, absently, for she had already wandered off to the bathroom where she was applying just enough rouge that it could not be seen. Mother could not abide makeup, being beautiful enough to disdain subterfuge. "Now, you can't let on to Mrs. Lurch. You know she'll just scare all those mobsters off, and then where will we be?"

Vivian had explained the plan to her sister in the wee hours of the previous night. Al would be their sole escort to The Fair Lady. If anyone at the club raised an eyebrow, he'd say he was giving the girls an illicit taste of New York's infamous night club scene.

"The best lies contain a kernel of truth," Vivian had explained, quoting wisdom so widely observed it could not be attributed to anyone. "If we go in disguise, we're sure to be found out. But if we pretend we've pestered Al into indulging our girlish curiosity—well, who's to say it isn't true?"

"But Viv," Viola had protested, "what if something goes wrong." She'd been thinking about how comforting it would be to turn to Mrs. Lurch in their time of need.

"Don't be a worrywart," Vivian scolded. "Nothing ever happens on a Monday. Besides, Al will protect us if the local riffraff start throwing chairs."

Viola wasn't so sure. Dear Al was a wily one and known to disappear on a dime. He couldn't be blamed for his formative years, during which time he'd studied the success of wharf rats, evading death by sheer dint of stealth.

"Come on, Lala. Let's search Babs's room before the others are up."

This was another scheme Vivian had hatched in the dark of the night. Sighing, Viola dutifully complied, rising to don a mauve rayon day dress that brought out her eyes. Protests would be of little use. Vivian had emerged from yesterday's funk determined to take the case by storm, so there was nothing else for it but to uphold the Twins' Code and hope for the best.

Twenty minutes later, Vivian knelt before the turret room door, wriggling her trusty pocketknife in the lock as Viola hovered behind.

"It's just a matter of tricking the lock into thinking you're the key," she murmured now, which sounded to Viola suspiciously like something she would say. "Hold up that lantern, won't you?"

The gas lantern fizzled in complaint as Viola hoisted it high. Contorted shadows danced across the chiseled stone, deliciously creepy, like a scene from the Spanish Inquisition.

The lock gave way with a decisive click.

Vivian stood. "Now for the police tape," she said, as if contaminating a crime scene were all in a day's work. "And it isn't a crime scene, Lala," she snapped, picking up Viola's stray thought. "Babs's room isn't where the abduction *occurred*."

This reasoning seemed scanty, even to Viola who was known to deduce a picnic from a pile of bird droppings.

"There," Vivian said with satisfaction, squeezing her lithe form through the "X" formed by the tape. "And no one's the wiser."

Viola followed suit, and soon they were poking about the room in the rosy dawn light that infused the stained-glass windows with a supernatural glow.

"Oh, it is rather like my dream," Viola murmured, stopping to admire the glowing glass mosaic that overlooked the park, distorting its trees and bushes into the dunes and pyramids of a vanished time. "And this one," she said, softly, moving on to another, which transformed midtown into the scalloped hillside of an Incan temple, perched impossibly at the top of the world.

"What are you doing over there, Lala," Vivian hissed. "Look in her dresser drawers. There has to be *something* they missed."

They rummaged around for a good ten minutes more, confirming that the baby rattle inscribed with *F & B* was nowhere to be found. Then, Vivian gave a small cry of satisfaction which, true to form, managed to sound both savage and sublime.

"Voilà!" she gloated, holding up a small black volume she'd found wedged into the pages of a gossip rag, which in turn had fallen between the magazine rack and the stuffed chair. It looked like an address book. "Really, I would have thought Sergeant Kowalski to be a bit more thorough than that." It was the first time she'd said his name aloud, and the sound of it was strangely embarrassing.

"You can't blame that dear sergeant for the work of his flat-foots, can you," Viola pointed out. "Why, he and the detective were only up here for two shakes of a lamb's tail before they commenced with giving us the third degree." This use of police slang was not entirely accurate, as it generally implied violence used to extract a confession, but Viola could not resist taking license.

"So be it," Vivian said smugly. "Their loss, our gain."

"But aren't we all after the same thing?" Viola said on a note of despair. She was already worried about withholding their knowledge of Babs's gentleman visitor. "And, well, isn't this all, well, *illegal?*"

"It's not like you to be so literal, Lala." Vivian ducked back beneath the police tape, prize in hand. "Are you feeling quite alright?"

"Of course, I am," Viola said, her voice edged with something that surprised them both. "I just don't feel right about it, Viv. Babs's life could be in danger!"

Vivian carefully closed the turret room door behind them, taking care not to damage the tape, then turned her full attention to her twin. "Think about it this way, Lala—we're all on the same team, it's just that some of us don't know it. I wish there was another way."

"But why don't we ask—"

"If we can help, pretty please? Come, Lala, you know that's nonsense. We're just a couple of girls, they'll say, good for nothing more than wearing lipstick and walking around with candelabras on our heads."

Vivian said this with a good deal more heat than she'd intended, which vexed her because, after all, she didn't want to be one of *those* girls, the ones who hung around in cafes, sporting cropped hair, smoking cigarettes, and wearing trousers. She didn't want to be *strident.* And she certainly didn't want to be branded a *feminist,* accused of being unnatural, or hating men, or taking jobs that rightfully belonged to all those poor, out-of-work chaps who sold apples on corners.

Did she?

It was all a muddle, which made her cranky. But she forced her foul mood aside. She could see that tact was called for.

"Look, Lala, I'll make you a deal. If our leads don't come to anything in . . . in . . ." she chewed her lip, "oh, let's say a week, we'll come clean to the police about our findings. Deal?"

Viola was taken aback to be fielding deals while possessing no known collateral. Except for, maybe, twinship.

"Deal," she said with a shy smile.

"Good, that's settled." Vivian turned to hurry down the spiral staircase that had lightened with what promised to be a sunny fall day. "We'd better hurry along. We've got just enough time to give this little black book a thorough going-over before breakfast."

"Can you tell what it is?" Viola inquired, padding silently after. She was feeling better now that the "two minds" provision of the code had been formally invoked.

"An address book, I think." Vivian flipped through the pages as they wended their way down, squinting at the sloppy script. "Oh, that is perfect, Lala. As soon as we get to our room, let's see whose name is listed under the letter *F*!"

CHAPTER FIFTEEN
Fair Ladies

The page in Babs's little black book devoted to *F* yielded only three results, none of which were Florenz. Oh, Mr. Ziegfeld was in there all right, but under Z for Ziggy Wiggy, a remnant, no doubt, of a more affectionate time.

"Frankie Morgan. Hmm. It can't possibly be the other two, Edith Fairbanks or Francine Bates," Vivian mused, more decisively than she felt. The idea that the baby rattle they'd spied in Babs's room might have been merely a gift for a pregnant friend was not to be borne. "There's simply no order to these entries. If I've said it once, I've said it a million times, that woman is a slob."

Indeed, there were F names to be found throughout the address book: first names, middle names, and surnames strewn about according to whim.

"Here's a Fink," Viola said, having picked up the book after her twin tossed it aside. "Written right next to Hector Howard, which is crossed out." She flashed Vivian a mischievous smile. "What can he possibly have done to deserve that?"

"I can't imagine," Vivian said, returning Viola's sly look as she rose to neaten her hair before they were due downstairs. "Leave off for now, Lala, and help me decide what to wear tonight."

The rest of the day dragged on and on, which was only to be expected with a night of danger and excitement dangling before them like the proverbial apple. Cookie was grumpy, having burned the morning porridge. The maids, Dixie and Dolly, were late to work (a fortunate distraction as Mrs. Lurch had been eyeing the twins rather more than usual all through breakfast). And old Horace broke his second to last remaining tooth attempting to eat a raw potato just before going out to mulch the hydrangeas. Mistress Dubois would talk of nothing but the trial of Chicago gangster Al Capone all through Latin and French, obsessed by the question of what sort of business required a man to put his associates "on ice." And no one said a word during dinner because Mother and Father had clearly had a spat. By the time the girls got up to their room, they were plum worn out.

"Is she gone yet?" Viola asked distractedly from her bed where she had *The Scarlet Letter* propped up on her knees, pretending to read while secretly debating whether the preacher Dimmesdale was an honorable man or a coward—or maybe both, seeing how he could never make up his mind. She did so want him to be happy, and the idea of him sailing off with Hester Prynne and their love child for foreign shores simply reeked of romance, if only he hadn't had God frowning down on him all the time. It really was a pity.

"There she goes," Vivian said with satisfaction as the stolid figure of Mrs. Lurch cleared the front stairs and turned up Central Park West, headed for the new movie palace over on Broadway. Monday was her evening off, and tonight she was off to see Buster Keaton's new feature film, *Sidewalks of New York*. Mrs. Lurch was a sucker for slapstick. "And off we go," Vivian said, turning from the curtains with a gleam in her eye. "Now, Lala, put that silly book away. You'll wrinkle your dress lying there like that."

Viola snatched off her eyeglasses and rose. Even wrinkled, the twins were a sight to behold, Vivian in a sapphire blue, calf-length frock with a matching crop jacket and white gloves, Viola in a silky, floral dress with a wide lace collar and petal-like sleeves. With their flaxen hair coiffed neatly and their hats pinned on, they looked as fair as the namesake of the club they were about to infiltrate.

"Not a sound, now," Vivian cautioned as they eased out of the bedroom door and tiptoed downstairs, creaking as softly as possible across the wide hall to retrieve their coats. Once on the front doorstep, Vivian heaved an audible sigh of relief. "Now, we've only to nip around the corner, and Al will whisk us away."

Trusty Al was waiting, as promised, at the corner of Columbus Avenue and West Sixty-Fifth.

"Well, ain't you ladies lookin' fine," he said, flicking his cigarette butt away and hitching up the wide lapels of his heavy coat against a wind that was whipping up the avenue. There was a hint of frost to the air, and the cast-iron streetlights were framed by little halos of light. "I've got to say, Miss Vivian, I don't think this here is such a good idea, friskin' Luigi's place, what with him and me bein' on, er, *formal* terms of late."

"We take the responsibility entirely upon ourselves, Al," Vivian said, crooking her arm in his as they all struck off down the darkened street, the headlights of oncoming cars cutting through the mist.

"It ain't quite like that, if you don't mind me sayin'. I may be a bootlegger but that don't mean I ain't a gentleman, if you see what I mean."

Viola came alongside to take his other arm and give it a friendly squeeze. "Just think of it as research for my novel, Al. How can I capture that underworld *je ne sais quoi* if I don't experience it for myself? Great writers must risk life and limb for their art." This was all hogwash, of course, but it seemed to impress Al, and he gave a considering grunt. Fatalistic by nature, Viola had come around to their adventure and decided to take the glass half full, even if what was inside the glass killed her.

Al flagged down a cab and they all piled in, the twins side by side facing forward with Al opposite, jiggling his hat on his knee. They passed the drive to midtown talking about the lamentable decline of ethics in Al's professional milieu.

"It's the snatch racket that's brought us low, I'm tellin' you girls. Time was even mugs in Sing Sing offered their services to the coppers, if you can believe it, just to nab that rat who snatched the poor little Lindberg baby. And now? You got snatchin' rackets all over the place." He swept an arm wide in his zeal, causing the girls to recoil against the cracked leather seat. "This here is how it works. You got the Peddler behind the scenes—he's the idea man, see? He's the guy as shops his mark around to the highest bidder. Then you got the Finger who's the brains of the operation, and the Spotter—he's a nervy type, and good with a heater. He leads the actual snatchin', see? Leavin' the negotiations to the Voice—*that's* the most dangerous part of the gig . . ."

Al seemed to know an awful lot about the nefarious practice of kidnapping wealthy New Yorkers for ransom, which had spiked since the days when the world wrung its hands over little baby Lindburg. Viola could see it pained him to witness the depths to which his associates had fallen.

"But none of that applies to Babs's case, does it," Vivian cut in. "What good is she as a ransom mark? She barely has enough money for her rent, and her roots are an awful fright. Why, I think she can hardly afford the cheapest kind of peroxide." She chewed her lower lip, thinking. "And if Ziegfeld is the ransom target, he's not much better, is he? I read that *Smiles* was a disaster, even with Fred and Adele Astaire on the playbill. Ziegfeld barely scraped enough money together for *The Follies* after—" She broke off with a gasp. "How thick of me! Lala, tell me again, exactly what does that ransom note say?"

Viola cleared her throat. "'You have made your fortune by turning floosies into fantasies and trinkets into treasures,'" she recited, dutifully. "'Now you must work your magic once more unless you wish to pay the piper and see all your illusions undone.' It is rather a mouthful, isn't it?"

"And that's the whole of it? Why, the note doesn't even demand a particular sum! It just says, 'you must work your magic or pay the piper,' whatever that means. And at least there's been no mention by the police of a follow-up demand. What if it's not a ransom note at all?"

This bombshell rocked all three of them, but they had just pulled up outside The Fair Lady and had little time to explore the ramifications of Vivian's new theory. Mind you, there wasn't anything to see but the darkened window of a diner beneath a striped awning, and beside it, a rickety old staircase that disappeared downward into the gloom. Down those stairs, behind a narrow door with a peephole was a whole new world for those that knew the password.

Al looked at his watch. "It's only ten o'clock. It'll be crickets in there until at least eleven." He turned to the girls as the cab drove away behind him. "I got a bad feelin' about this. What do you say I take you two home and just do a little snoopin' myself? This ain't no place for two fine ladies."

Viola's heart swelled with hope for the briefest of moments, almost eclipsing her dread. But it was not to be.

"Al, you're being frightfully dramatic," Vivian scolded, taking his arm to drag him toward the darkened stairwell. "We're here now and we're not leaving until we've had a chance to meet this Mr. Luciana for ourselves. Now—lead the way.

CHAPTER SIXTEEN
A Fight to Remember

Inside, The Fair Lady was all but deserted.

A fat man in an apron greeted them from behind the long mahogany bar, upturned glass in hand as he swiped a bar towel around its rim.

"What'll it be?" he drawled, twirling the toothpick in the corner of his mouth with a deft flick of the tongue.

Al, who had delivered the password through the peephole, still looked jittery, rattling change in his pocket with one hand as he reached up with the other to take off his hat and tap it against his thigh.

"Sure, er, I'll take a whiskey, and, er, a couple of soda waters for my, er, guests here."

They settled at a round high-top in the corner to wait for their drinks, draping their coats on the extra stool. "Al, what exactly happened between you and Luigi," Vivian asked in a low voice. "You're making me nervous."

Al opened his mouth to reply, spasming with surprise as the bartender came up from behind to plop their drinks on the table and turn with a long, slow look and amble back toward the bar.

"I don't feel exactly welcome," she added when he had gone.

Al leaned on his forearms, slumped over his drink, and gave her a sheepish grin.

"I tried to tell you, Miss Vivian. Luigi has concocted a slight confabulation in his mind, see, that I slipped his joint some bung liquor a while back when I was running samples from a new booze mill—which *ain't true*," he hissed, pausing to look again over his shoulder. "But once Luigi's got an idea, he ain't keen to part with it."

"I see," Vivian said, thoughtfully. This could be a help or a hindrance, depending on how it was played. High emotion was volatile, but it did sometimes impair judgment, which could come in handy for taking Luigi off his guard.

She patted his hand. "Leave it to me, Al," she said, then turned to sweep a look around the club. "And where is the inestimable Luigi?"

Patrons were beginning to trickle in. A well-dressed couple sat down at a white-skirted table by the corner stage where bar hands were setting up a drum set and adjusting the microphone. Oh, it *was* lovely to be out on the town, even if it were all in a night's work.

"Oh, he'll be here, all right," Al said morosely. "He ain't never missed a night fraternizing with the customers. It's why he's still in the business, ain't it, when you got joints shuttin' down right and left nowadays."

"I thought you said Babs used to dance here," Vivian remarked, "but I don't see where. A person would fall off that stage before they'd taken three steps."

"Yeah, well, Luigi's a sentimental guy, see? He changed up the place after Babs gave him the boot. Said it pained him to look at all those skirts flashing their legs and bosoms when not one of them was his Babs."

Vivian gave him a dry smile. "Sentimental, indeed." She looked over to her twin, whose gaze was fixed on the ceiling. "Lala, what on earth are you looking at?"

Viola's gaze snapped down. "Oh, sorry, it's just so terribly interesting, isn't it? How there's a whole secret world lurking under floors and behind closed doors." Actually, she was thinking again about Hester and tragic Dimmesdale, and how they'd had to hide their love from prying eyes and could only show their true selves in the shadows of the deep, dark wood. "Viv, why do you suppose people are ashamed of who they really are?"

"Well, *I'm* never ashamed, so I wouldn't know," Viv said, and of course she believed it, poor dear. She wasn't putting on airs, and after all, people couldn't help but lie to themselves, especially where the heart was involved. But it wouldn't do to rattle her confidence.

"I say, Viv, do you suppose—" Viola began, intending to guide the conversation to safer ground when a guttural roar issued from across the club.

"You gotta whole lotta nerve coming into this joint after whatch you done," said a great bear of a man, coming around the end of the bar like a prizefighter entering the ring. "Why I oughta—"

"Mister *Luciana*," Vivian gushed, turning in one smooth motion to glide off her stool and onto her high-heeled feet. She perched one toe behind her, like a dancer getting ready to shine. "Can it really be you? Why *Al*," she turned to give Al's arm a playful swat, "you said he was handsome, but I had no *idea*."

This patter struck Viola as a tad transparent, vulgar even, but, as usual, Vivian had judged her target well. A chameleon by instinct, she had become something the gangster could relate to, a high-class tart, maybe even a gold-digger, someone who could look after herself.

Truly, Viv was brilliant, which made Viola all the more nervous. What if she played her role a little too well?

"Well, don't just stand there." Vivian crooked her forefinger, beckoning, then gave Al a not-too-gentle push off his stool before patting the seat. "Come sit and let's have a little . . . chat."

Luigi had stopped cold in his tracks, his wide, red face more puzzled than beguiled. But now he stood up a little taller, unclenching his fists to straighten his tie.

"Don't mind if I do," he said, sauntering closer. As he pulled out his stool, he turned to Al, leaning in close to put a fingertip on the end of his nose. "You and me got business . . . *later.*"

Al smiled ingratiatingly. "Luigi, Luigi, youse killin' me. How many times I got to tell you, that hootch was—"

"*Later,*" he said again, removing his finger to waggle it back and forth, just once. Straightening, he turned to Vivian, who had slipped back onto her stool and was now leaning on one elbow, chin in her palm. "Now," Luigi said, "who might *you* be?"

If Vivian was rattled, she didn't show it. Whatever else Luigi was, he was clearly not a fool. Amused enough to go a little farther down the garden path with Viv, he was already on the lookout for thorns. Viola was just noting this when her attention was quite distracted by a rat-faced man, hovering beside an enormous, potted palm nearby. No, not rat-faced. *Weasel*-faced. She gave a shiver.

"My name is Vivian," she said to Luigi, popping her chin up to extend the hand, elbow still planted on the table. It was a charming gesture, and the gangster smiled as he took her hand, his amused look shifting slightly to interest.

"Enchanted, Vivian, to be sure," he said, inclining his head with mock formality. His accent was 50 percent Italian, 50 percent New Yorker, and 100 percent gangster. "So, tell me, Vivian, what brings you to my humble establishment. Ain't you a bit young to be patronizing such a place as this?" He cast a look over each shoulder in mock apprehension. "You got any coppers standing by to render assistance to a young lady in distress?" When he looked back to her, there was steel in his eyes.

"Maybe," Vivian said, not missing a beat. Frivolity would not occupy this man. He wanted real repartee. It struck Vivian suddenly that there must be more to Babs than met the eye. "Do you know any distressed young ladies?"

He narrowed his eyes, as if taking her stock, then relaxed again, smiling without humor. "I do not think that I do, Miss Vivian." He leaned back against the stool back, apparently taking her at her word. "Let me guess, you and your sister here," he shot a sideways glance at Viola, "who, appearances aside, is a different kettle of fish altogether, you is out on the town to see how the other half lives. That about it?"

"I am driven by curiosity, Mister Luciana," Vivian said, quite truthfully.

He nodded sagely. "Fair enough, fair enough. And how do you know *this* mug." He yanked his head Al-wards, not bothering to look.

Now they were getting to it. "As a matter of fact, he's a boarder. Father decided to take in boarders, you see, after the crash." Luigi's eyebrows shot up. Honesty was definitely the best policy with this one. He could smell a rat a mile away, but up close, it was anyone's game. "Yes, Mister Luciana—"

"Luigi."

Vivian paused for the breath of an instant and smiled. "Yes *Luigi,* I can see you understand quite well. We Society types can get a little bored uptown, even those of us who are a tad," she gave a delicate shrug, "down on our luck. Honestly, I don't know what we'd do without our tenants, Viola and I. We'd simply die of boredom." Luigi was smiling again, enjoying the gag as Vivian spoofed the spoiled debutante. Now, to drop the bombshell, when he was least expecting it. "Why, when Babs Le Roy took up residence in the turret room, I absolutely could not believe our luck—"

Down came Luigi's palm on the table, rattling the glasses. "Babs Le Roy lives with you?" he said, dropping the game. "The dancer Babs Le Roy?"

"Is there any other?" Vivian was studying Luigi's face for signs of panic, guilt, or any vestige of some similarly damning emotion. But frankly, he just looked like a wounded puppy dog.

"You got Babs Le Roy living at your house." He shook his head back and forth, slowly. "Go figure."

Vivian felt her brow wrinkle and quickly smoothed it. The genuine love she glimpsed now in the mobster's eye gave her pause. Babs had always seemed a tad unremarkable, truth be told, though she hardly would have *said* such a thing. And yet, that sweet, tortured light in Luigi's eye gave her an odd twinge about the stomach, as if she might have missed something important, might, in fact, have missed the whole *thing*. Who was this woman who could soften the heart of a hardened man? Vivian flinched, recalling her jokes about the starlet's grammar, her slovenly habits, her, ahem, fledgling intellect. She supposed, now, that it was all rather unkind. No, decidedly unkind. But worse than that, Vivian suspected suddenly that it was she who'd been proved the simpleton.

Gathering herself, she pressed on. "Lived, at our house, Mister—I mean Luigi. Babs *lived* at our house, but of course, ever since she went missing the room is quite—"

"*Missing?*" The guttural roar was back. Vivian flinched back. "Babs Le Roy is *missing* from your house?" He stood, pushing back from the table so that his stool crashed to the floor. "You been playing games since you got here, little lady. So, tell me," he lowered his voice, placing both hands on the table to lean in, "just what exactly do you mean by saying Babs Le Roy, *my* Babs is," he roared the last word, "*missing*! Whatch you done wit' her!"

Collecting her wits, Vivian wiped a bit of Luigi's spittle from her cheek and likewise stood, eye to eye with the gangster. "Mister Luciana, I don't know exactly what you're insinuating, but I assure you, I have nothing to do with Babs's disappearance. Quite the opposite, in fact. I am doing everything in my power to determine what has happened to her since—"

The crash of breaking glass, followed by a loud volley of cursing brought all their heads around. The table behind them had gone over in the heat of a fight between two young men who had clearly had a few too many drinks. Back and forth, they pushed each other in the chest, while a third man went for his gun, waving it at the ceiling and yelling insults that were slurred beyond recognition. Down came a stool on the gunman's head as the brawl spilled out, pulling in patrons from the table beyond as the bartender rushed across the floor, bat in hand.

Where had all these people come from? So absorbed had she been in her conversation, Vivian hadn't even noticed the nightclub filling up with tuxedo-clad gentlemen, whirling their dates across the floor as the fledgling notes of the jazz trio suddenly went sour. Someone was thrown against the stage amid a cacophony of cymbals and shrieks while, above it all, the voice of the bartender boomed out, calling for order.

But Luigi Luciana had a mind for only one thing.

"So, you part of some snatch racket, that it?" he said, ignoring the melee to grab Vivian by the shoulder to turn her roughly back to face him. "That mug Diamond send you over here to fix me up for the ticket, eh? Maybe see if I's gonna pony up some dough for Babs? That it?" The first roil of fear surged up from Vivian's stomach, but she pushed it down, hard. Where was Lala? Vivian twisted her arm from Luigi's grasp to survey the chaos. Al was long gone, naturally, but Lala would never run out on her twin. Fear for her twin drove up from her gut, gripping Vivian's throat, just as Luigi accosted her, spinning her around to pin both arms behind and say menacingly in her ear, "If you done anything to hurt that sweet, beautiful girl, I swear, I's gonna—"

But whatever Luigi was *gonna* do was forever lost to posterity. Vivian felt the great bulk of his body ripped away and turned just in time to see a solid right hook laid across his jaw, sending the gangster to the black-and-white checkerboard floor.

Luigi rolled onto his side, swiping a fist across the corner of his mouth.

Sergeant Kowalski did not waste a single moment on words. Grabbing Vivian's hand, he dragged her across the glass-strewn floor, skirting punches and handbags and bodies flung across their path until they reached the door.

Vivian pulled away on the threshold, looking back. "Lala!" she cried.

"Outside! Now!" Sergeant Kowalski shouted as he yanked her out the door.

CHAPTER SEVENTEEN
Tête-à-Tête

"But what about *Lala*!" Vivian yelled, ripping her elbow from the sergeant's grasp. "How dare you just whisk me away, as if I didn't have everything under—I don't have time for this." She turned back toward the club door. "My sister is in there, and I'll be *damned* if I'll stand by while—"

"Viv, for goodness' sake, I'm over here."

Vivian twirled around to see her twin, looking bedraggled as she wiped dirt off her hat before pinning it back on. She looked up from under her elbow as she struggled with the hat pin. "Oh, Viv, it really is a pity about our coats."

"Our *coats*. Lala, how can you worry about our coats at a time like—"

"May I suggest we discuss this elsewhere?" Sergeant Kowalski gazed back over his shoulder. "Luciana won't follow, but I'd rather put some distance between us, if it's all the same."

"Won't foll—but why on earth *not*?" Vivian said, remembering the sergeant's solid right hook.

He looked back to her. "Because I'm a copper. Now—" He swept an arm forward. "Perhaps we can talk around the corner."

The way he said *talk* said it all. He was planning to give Vivian a talking *to.*

"Some copper," she muttered as she walked a pace ahead. "Why didn't you just raid the place?"

This comment was expertly designed to get under the sergeant's skin, but he only replied, "Because I was busy saving you." He let this sink in for a moment, then added, "Besides, Luigi's place is generally one of the better joints. We have bigger fish to fry."

"Oh, you mean your sterling detective is on the take?"

That would get him.

"I mean, apart from the Volstead Act infractions, you generally won't find any murder, mayhem, or rackets behind the scenes. Luigi runs a clean place."

Insufferable! And she was supposed to be getting under *his* skin.

"This looks good," he said, stepping into the circle of light beneath a lamppost. Cars were whizzing up Broadway, headlights blurry in the mist that still hung over the streets. "Now, why don't you tell me just what you girls were up to, although I'm pretty sure I know."

"I am not a *girl*," Vivian seethed, although, technically, she was. But there was something about hearing the sergeant say it that was decidedly enraging.

"Viv, you could at least thank him," Viola said, joining them from where she'd trailed behind.

"For what," Vivian said, taking this moment to unpin her hat and examine it for damage. "I had the situation well in hand."

"Luciana had *you* well in hand," the sergeant said with a note of humor that brought Vivian's gaze smack up to his.

"I would certainly have gotten *out* of hand," she began, then, "I mean, out of *his* hand, I mean—I would have gotten the situation under control."

Surprisingly, the sergeant said nothing, merely holding her gaze until it was Vivian who looked away, pretending to be busy with her hat.

"I believe you would have," he said finally, in a matter-of-fact voice, but Vivian did not judge it safe to look up again. "We had already determined that Luciana was not the kidnapper, you know."

This brought her gaze up. "But—but how could you be sure?" She had ruled him out after judging his reactions, but not everyone had her instincts.

The sergeant shrugged. "Solid policework. You know, interviewing witnesses, following money trails, questioning motives, that kind of thing."

Was that irony? Was he patronizing her? Vivian eyed him a moment longer, noticing that the glint in his eyes, while playful, did not tend to insult. Indeed, there wasn't much about his appearance that tended to offend, what with his brown hair, slightly scruffy where it showed beneath his fedora, and that jag in his nose where someone must have punched him once, and a considering look in his eye that once more made her look away.

"Viv, you said *damned,*" Lala said with a giggle, out of the blue. Vivian looked over at her sister, who was clutching her bare arms in the cold. She'd been prepared to scold Lala for being silly, but when their eyes met, she couldn't help the smile that cracked the corner of her mouth.

"Damned if I did," she said, and then they both broke down.

"Look, I'm on foot," Kowalski said when they had mastered their laughter. "Let me catch a cab here to see you girl—*ladies* home," he said, catching himself with a wry glance at Vivian. "You can tell me all about your big sting on the way. Deal?"

Five minutes later, they were settled into a cab heading back the way they'd come just a couple of hours before. But for Vivian, it might as well have been a lifetime. Lala sat beside her on the cracked leather seat, but instead of Al's wiry form opposite, there sat Sergeant Kowalski, seeming quite large by comparison with his long limbs and athletic frame. Was that why it seemed so crowded in here? Why was it so blasted hot all the time? Vivian found she'd really rather not talk at all and stared out the window instead.

After a moment or two of awkward silence, Viola cleared her throat and stumbled into the breach. Vivian was not known to leave the recounting of her exploits to others, but an explanation must be made.

"You see, Sergeant . . . well, actually . . . Vivian and I were just . . ." she fumbled into her handbag, which she had miraculously retained in the melee. "Would you like a stick of Dentyne?" When Kowalski shook his head, she fussed the bag closed again. "As I was saying, well, Vivian was rather thinking that Mr. Luciana . . . well, and I—"

"Why were *you* at the club anyway, Sergeant Kowalski?" Vivian snapped, turning from the window where she'd been leaning against the glass on her bent arm. "Were you spying on us?"

He examined her steadily. "Was I doing my job? Yes. You were keeping something from us, so I've been keeping an eye on—"

"Spying. Exactly. *After* hours, I take it? Or are you on the clock, Sergeant?"

Inexplicably, he laughed. The sound of it, the way it animated his face, and the quick, sideways look that accompanied it, took Vivian completely off her guard. She turned back to the window.

"If you must know, yes, off the clock. You're not the only one that has instincts, Miss Van der Beeck," he said, as if he'd read Vivian's thoughts. "Now, we'll soon be getting to your house, so if you don't mind, I'll take the facts about now."

Somehow, Viola muddled through an explanation. Vivian's suspicions about the gangster weren't really *news*—she had already told the detective about them on the occasion of his visit to Canary House. It was simple enough for Viola to convey the details of tonight's escapade without betraying anything, well, secret. She knew she was still bound by the Twins' Code, and even if she'd had half a mind to tell the nice sergeant all about Babs's mysterious visitor, about the rattle with its inscription and Babs's little black book, or even about how Vivian suspected the note wasn't a ransom demand after all—well, none of that was hers to tell.

When they got out of the cab, the sergeant was still studying Vivian, as if she were a nut he had not yet cracked.

"It was bad form of me not to have thanked you, Sergeant," she said, offering him her hand at the front door, to which he had escorted them. What was it about Viv's apologies? Her moments of humility stood in such stark contrast to her force of personality that one couldn't help but feel gratified, as if the queen had deigned to offer you crumpets with your tea. And yet—Viola could hear the distance behind the words.

Sergeant Kowalski seemed to hear it too. "No need," he said, with similar reserve.

Oh, dear. There would be no living with Viv for some time yet.

CHAPTER EIGHTEEN
Crumbs

Like Vivian, Johann Van der Beeck had possessed a stubborn streak that disposed him to outbursts of unpredictable behavior. This quirk is best illustrated in the recounting of a certain incident that took place at the University of Leiden in 1641. Young Johann was a student of philosophy, studying in the shadow of such luminaries as René Descartes, who had briefly attended the university not long before.

Johann was not suited to a life of study. He spent most days arguing obscure points of philosophy at the local tavern. Quintessentially Dutch, he liked his drink and suffered from a kind of schizophrenia that one might call the good-angel-bad-angel syndrome. How to be both wealthy and modest? How to meld the excesses of such festivities as the *kermissen*, that age-old drinking festival, with the Calvinist strictures of economy, piety, and above all, restraint? These were the forces that split the Dutch character in two, creating a fissure that ran like a seam down the years—and nowhere more so than in the Van der Beeck line, fated (or cursed) to tread a narrow path, much as Grampy Cornelius would centuries later cleave to an Andean crest in the company of a llama named El Malandrin.

And the most quintessentially Dutch characteristic of all? Curiosity.

Johann Van der Beeck craved novelty even more than good Dutch ale. When summer came to Leiden and the weather grew too hot for the laying open of cadavers, the university would open its anatomy theater to the exhibition of "curiosities." The wide arena with its serried benches was transformed into a repository for skeletons, botanical specimens, and relics that had come into the university's possession in the name of scholarship.

Johann was particularly captivated by one such acquisition.

For one thing, it was gold. For another, it was *old*. And for a third, it looked as mysterious as the words etched neatly on a label beneath its domed bell jar: Pizzaro's Folly.

Equally mysterious was the relic's disappearance that very same day, sparking a frenzied investigation by local authorities that coincided perfectly with Johann's decision to book passage for New Amsterdam on *Den Eyckenboom, The Oak Tree,* a *fluytschip* due to set sail within the month.

Strangely enough, Viola was thinking about treasure the morning after the twins' ill-fated visit to The Fair Lady.

"I say, Viv, do you suppose this is a treasure map?"

Vivian had dragged her sister up to the attic for an impromptu cleaning spree to clear the mind. She left off cataloguing various Van der Beeck artifacts to look over her twins' shoulder at the sprawling diagram with its faded nomenclature.

"Rubbish, Lala. It looks like somebody's nursery school scribblings. You know how this family simply cannot throw anything away."

The attic testified to this statement, crammed to the rafters with boxes and crates, vases and valises, old dolls, letters, books and baubles, all collected in the years since Johann Van der Beeck had made landfall at the Great Dock of New Amsterdam.

"All the same, I think I'll keep it," Viola murmured.

"You can tuck it in the diary," Vivian said wryly. "Maybe it's a clue to the mystery of the curse."

Viola liked this idea, though surely Viv was right, and the map was just the childish fancy of some young Van der Beeck of yore.

"I don't know how much more of this I can take." Vivian plopped down to sit, smearing away a strand of flaxen hair that had escaped her charmingly domestic head kerchief. Never let it be said that Vivian Van der Beeck failed to dress the part. She had thought organizing the attic would make her feel better after last night's debacle, but the enormity of it did overwhelm one.

"Ahem, pardon ladies, but I was, er, wondering if you would like to partake of these here refreshments." Al poked his head up through the floor hatch, a plate in hand, piled high with Cookie's scones. "I can leave these here if youse hungry."

Vivian gave him a withering look over her shoulder, then shrugged. "Do what you like, Alastair. You always do."

Viola flinched. Poor Al. The use of his full Christian name was rather uncalled for.

"Aw, come on Miss Vivian." Al set the plate down to scramble out onto the dusty attic floor. "How was I to know there was only one copper? I judged it, er, inadvisable to remain on the premises. Ain't I told you it was a bad idea casin' Luigi's joint like that?"

"You certainly did, Al," Viola said reassuringly as she frowned at her twin. "Viv remembers the conversation perfectly well. And I seem to remember her reply was something along the lines of 'we take responsibility entirely upon our—'"

"Oh, have it your way," Vivian groused and gave a yank of her head hither, indicating that the peace offering of scones had been accepted. "Have a seat, Al, and help yourself to a scone." She sighed, heavily. "I'm afraid I'm not hungry at the moment."

Al perched himself on a nearby crate and offered a scone to Viola, taking one for himself before setting the plate aside. "I's sorry to hear that, Miss Vivian. If it's any consolation, you was something else last night. Youse tougher than a gun moll, and that's sayin' somethin'."

This softened Vivian somewhat. "Well, Al, I do what must be done. But I'll tell you, this case has me stumped."

"Seems to me your confidence has just got a little roughed up," Al said with a sympathetic nod. "When that happens to one of my boys, I tell them just get right back on that horse and go knock off a jug or somethin'," he said, encouragingly.

"That means 'go rob a bank,'" Viola explained.

"I know perfectly well what it means, Lala," Vivian said with a grateful smile for Al. "And Al's absolutely right. This is no time for moping around." She got to her feet, dusting off her old calico day dress. "Come along, Lala, it's time we initiated phase two of our investigation."

The scone in Viola's stomach rebelled. "Are we only in phase two?" she said, a tad mournfully, but then got to her feet with a dutiful sigh, dusting crumbs her from pale yellow culottes (that looked quite fetching paired with a striped sailor blouse). "Onward, soldier. Far be it from me to stem the tide of progress."

An hour later, Vivian had convened a special meeting in the conservatory with what tenants happened to be around that day. Mistress Dubois was laid up at home with swollen ankles, leaving the girls at leisure; hence, Vivian's campaign to organize the attic. But now that she'd shaken off her funk, she saw that what really needed organizing was something else entirely.

Her list of clues.

Mr. Sparrow was holed up in his room, deep in the throes of a new composition, and Mr. Sharma was out, most likely researching his new project for the New York Historical Society. This was a pity as Vivian had come to rely on ignoring his good judgment. Madame Koslova was also out, lunching with fellow Theosophist Harold Waldwin Percival, whose ideas on being conscious of the consciousness of consciousness had so captivated the aging philanthropist that she had organized several charity drives on his behalf. Her absence left Miss Sphinx in a receptive frame of mind, and with Dr. Weber and Al to round out their tête-à-tête-à-*tête*, the discussion promised to bear fruit.

"Let's begin with what we know," Vivian said. She scooted her wicker chair away from a brood of chickens who were clucking loudly over a pile of vegetable peels.

"There's the baby," Viola offered, helpfully. "We can infer its existence from the rattle, as well as from Babs's prolonged absence and her attempts to hide the existence of her parents' country home, where the infant may be secretly residing," she added, channeling her sister's chain of logic.

"Well done, Lala," Vivian beamed. She turned to the others to fill in the gaps. There had been conversations here and there with the tenants on the subject of Babs, but it was hard to keep track of who knew what. "For those of you who may not recall, we're nearly certain that Babs left the limelight because of an illicit pregnancy, which leads one to the question of parentage. *Whose* baby is it? Answer that, and I believe you're one step closer to the culprit. Let us begin with the letter *F*, inscribed on the rattle."

"*Florenz* Ziegfeld." Viola said. "But perhaps that's too obvious."

"Precisely. Why make himself the subject of a ransom—or extortion demand? But we'll leave that aside for the moment."

"Is it possible that ze showman has devised a clever ruse?" Dr. Weber posited, striking a match along the bricks of a nearby planter to light his pipe. "He has only to pretend to be ze victim in order to deflect suspicion, while raising ransom funds from others for ze safe return of his star. If he is also ze blackmailer, he keeps ze money for himself, yes? It is just like ze mechanism of transference, wherein ze subject projects his needs onto others to avoid responsibility."

"Excellent, Dr. Weber. According to *The Scribbler*, Mr. Ziegfeld is in a hole after his last flop."

"But you say the ransom demand may not be so in reality?" Miss Sphinx inquired. "For it does not make the . . . how you say . . . command?"

"Demand, yes, that's right. The message on the note doesn't specify a ransom demand but instead implies it. Why?" So far, the tenants were remarkably cogent, which might be marked down to that second urn of coffee Cookie had brewed after old Horace drank the first down to dregs. "But before we get to that, let's catalog other suspects whose names start with *F*."

"There's Frankie," Viola chimed in. "From Babs's little black book." They'd let the tenants in on their illicit find. After all, Al wasn't likely to betray them to the coppers, and the rest of the tenants were either too loyal or too absentminded to cause any problems.

"It ain't widely known, but Luigi's real name is Flavio," Al offered. "Flavio Luciana. He's that big shot Lucky Luciano's cousin, only he kept the old Sicilian spelling of the family name, just so as to stay mum about his connections, see?"

Vivian did see, having read an account of the recently concluded Castellammarese War in which Lucky had engineered the killing of Guiseppe "Joe the Boss" Masseria in a Coney Island restaurant in order to be installed as a crime boss in his own right. If Luigi were indeed bent on decent racketeering, as Sergeant Kowalski had intimated, he might well want to distance himself from his more violent relatives.

Momentarily distracted, Vivian brushed the image of the sergeant's steady, sidelong gaze from her mind like a persistent fly.

"That's two established connections to the letter *F* with Florenz and Flavio, then" she said, doggedly turning her mind to the matter at hand. "With a possible third, depending on the identity of Babs's afternoon visitor, who might be Frankie Morgan. A jilted lover perhaps? One can't forget the way he stormed out of Babs's room—and out of the theater too . . . *before* intermission."

"Don't forget the preacher," Viola added. "He was there too." Vivian gave a perfunctory nod. Lala was only preoccupied with him because of that dreadful book, of which she'd become entirely too fond. "We don't know his name," Viola continued, "but I suppose if Dimmesdale can father a child out of wedlock, so too can a poor, downtrodden fanatic. Oh, it is hard to be under God's thumb all the time, don't you think?"

"Quite so, Lala," Vivian affirmed, feeling magnanimous. "Okay, the preacher goes on the provisional list, along with the mysterious afternoon caller, a.k.a. Frankie Morgan. Now, for the note. Lala, refresh our memory as to its contents."

Viola, gratified to be singled out for commendation, looked up and to the left where her mental library was shelved. "'You have made your fortune by turning floosies into fantasies and trinkets into treasures. Now you must work your magic once more unless you wish to pay the piper and see all your illusions undone.'"

"It is very poetic, this note," Miss Sphinx said in breathy tones. "The alliteration with the floosies and the fantasies, the trinkets and the treasures, the paying and the piper—it is clearly the work of a poetic mind."

Vivian crumpled at the brow. She hadn't even thought of the words themselves as clues.

"Of course, more *F*s," Viola said excitedly. "Didn't I tell you, Viv? The *F* might not even stand for someone's name."

Vivian wasn't ready to follow Viola off *that* cliff, not without exhausting the terrain. "Let's keep our moorings, shall we, Lala? Remember, the inscription on the rattle said, *That which binds us. F & B forever.* It's just like something you'd scratch into a tree trunk."

"The Piper," Al murmured. "That's Luigi's old nickname, ain't it, before he decided to clean up his game. They used to call him Luigi 'The Piper' Luciana on account of his playin' a flute at the funeral of those guys he'd bumped off. You know, it was Babs that decided him to turn over a new leaf."

"And then there's that old saying: 'He who pays the piper calls the tune,'" Viola quoted, handmaiden that she was to all things medieval. "It harkens from the days when the king, who paid the piper, also made the laws, although I don't see how that applies here."

"The simplest answer is most often correct," Vivian countered, quoting her own wisdom from that Franciscan friar cum philosopher of yore, William of Ockham. "Most likely it just means that Ziegfeld will have to pay up or suffer the consequences." Privately, Vivian had ruled the mobster out, and Lala's courtly reminiscences were beside the point. But another idea was forming, just barely in reach. "Let's assume, for the moment, that Ziegfeld is the intended target of the note. He's frightfully good at raising money, even when he doesn't have any of his own. Working his magic, as the note says. But why would he pay a ransom just to get back—forgive me—a rather washed-up star that won't help his bottom line one bit?"

"But Viv, remember, Ziegfeld might be the father of her child!" Viola protested.

"Exactly, Lala, but unlike you, he's not the sentimental type. And his wife is perfectly fed up with his philandering. *The Scribbler* is absolutely definitive on that point. One more out-of-wedlock baby and Billie Burke will pack up her star-studded suitcase and go. And you know it's only her Hollywood career that's keeping them afloat."

"I think I see what ze young lady is getting at," Dr. Weber mused, through a cloud of smoke that drifted up toward the soft-lit ceiling panes. "Ze ransom note is itself a ruse."

"Well done, Dr. Weber," Vivian said, truly impressed. She was feeling more and more confident about her developing theory. "Babs disappears, so naturally the police assume it's a ransom situation. Meanwhile, the note is actually an attempt to blackmail Ziegfeld in plain sight with language only he will understand."

"Oh, Viv, you *are* clever," Viola said admiringly. "So, the malefactor is threatening to reveal the existence of Babs's secret love child to Ziegfeld's long-suffering wife."

"And in order to place pressure on ze showman," Dr. Weber said, picking up the thread, "ze blackmailer delivers his threat in ze guise of a ransom for ze starlet's safe return, ensuring that all eyes will be on Mr. Ziegfeld. He cannot go behind ze scenes, if you will forgive ze pun, in order to make ze threat go away. No, he must work his magic or else raise ze suspicions of all ze world."

"It is sad, though," Viola said, a tad crestfallen. "Do you think Mr. Ziegfeld is really such a scoundrel? I rather thought he lived in desperate fear for his erstwhile love."

"Make no mistake, Lala. Mr. Ziegfeld is a businessman, first and last."

"But who then is behind this heartless blackmail?" Miss Sphinx asked, stroking her heavily ringed fingers across one cheek. "Who is this criminal with the deviant mind and the poet's tongue?"

That Vivian did not yet know, so she started with what she did. "Someone who knows about the baby," she said, slowly. "The baby whom we surmise is just now masquerading as yet one more sibling in Babs's extended family brood. And you know what that means, Lala." She shot her sister a look.

Viola sighed. "That phase two of our investigation is about to begin?"

"Precisely. It's time we made a little visit to the family farm."

CHAPTER NINETEEN
A Mother's Intimation

Preston Hollow was the largest hamlet in Rensselaerville, so named for the colony founded in 1629 by Dutch patroon Kiliaen van Rensselaer. A jeweler and former director of the Dutch West India Company, van Rensselaer never ventured to his namesake manor, situated near present-day Albany, New York. An ocean away, he sat in his comfortably appointed home office on the Dutch canal known as the Keizergracht, writing long letters in order to enlist settlers on his behalf.

He also sent a certain Adriaen van der Donck to manage his affairs as *schout,* or sheriff, of the fledgling settlement. Van der Donck was charged with collecting pelts, enforcing contracts, and ensuring that the colonists congregated on Sundays to invoke the Lord's name—in approximately that order. The young schout set sail for Rensselaerswyck in 1641 on the square-sailed *Den Eyckenboom* along with a cargo of tar, pitch, oakum, brandy, yarn, coal, and twenty bales of French canvas—as well as a handful of settlers bound for New Netherland.

Johann Van der Beeck was among them.

The intertwining of fates that was to knit these lives together had in fact begun some years before when the young van der

Donck's maternal grandfather volunteered the services of his peat boat to Maurits of Nassau in a daring Trojan Horse operation to reclaim the Castle of Breda from Spanish invaders. Said grandfather was deeded a house, named harbormaster, and lauded down the years to generations of Dutch school children.

Sound familiar?

Some tapestries are meant to be woven. The threads fray and separate, only to tangle once more into a strange brocade, knit by forces only dimly understood.

It was to the outskirts of Preston Hollow that the girls drove the following Saturday, accompanied by the redoubtable Mrs. Lurch.

"Oh, it is wonderful to have you with us, Mrs. Lurch," Viola said, delirious with relief. "I was dreading phase two until I knew you'd be beside us to help gird our loins."

"Really, Lala, I positively detest that phrase," Vivian complained.

"I don't know why, Viv. If Elijah can gird his loins to run before Ahab to the entrance of Jezreel, surely there's nothing untoward about it."

Viv was just out of sorts again, ever since her forced confession of their recent exploits, which Mrs. Lurch had obtained through the application of silence and other forms of torture.

"Nearly there," was all the worthy housekeeper said now, turning onto Route 145 at the little town of Cairo. What was once a three-day sail north from New Amsterdam now took just over three hours, at least the way Mrs. Lurch drove—or would have done, had it not been for the sad condition of the family Packard. In 1924, the Single Eight had been a top-of-the-line luxury vehicle with eight cylinders and all-wheel brakes, but in five short years, Father had turned it into a jalopy that even the creditors would not touch.

It was nearly noon when they pulled up before the picturesque hill upon which Appleby Farm was perched.

"What a dump," Vivian said.

Privately, even Viola agreed, although the ramshackle house with its sagging porch did possess a certain tragic charm. And the environs were suitably bucolic, what with the sad-eyed cows chewing at their cud.

"It's well-staffed," Viola offered on the bright side. Indeed, the porch seemed to be sagging under the sheer weight of children, dangling their legs through rickety slats, hitting each other with sticks, examining each other's heads for lice. "They're only braiding each other's hair," Viola chided, sensing her twin's train of thought. "Really, Viv, you *are* a snob sometimes."

"I'll just be over here, girls, in case there's a kerfuffle." Mrs. Lurch had already pulled her folding chair out of the car and set up under the shade of a chestnut tree. She opened her dog-eared copy of *Les Misérables* and settled in for the duration.

"Can I help you?"

The voice brought both the twins' heads around, back to the house where a woman stood, flanked on both sides by the grubby children, now lined up solemnly behind the porch railing. If the girls were expecting some caricature of the country "bumpkin" (a term derived from the Middle Dutch *bommekijn* meaning "little barrel"), both were chastened by the woman's quiet dignity, standing there in her calico housedress, an infant on her hip.

"About six months old, wouldn't you say, Lala?" Vivian said in a quiet aside. Vindicated in her calculations, she could not help but feel a little smug. "Excuse me, ma'am," she called out, beginning the long climb up the hill. She had worn her sports outfit today, high-waisted trousers paired with a red jacket—and, of course, her canvas sneakers. The October sky stretched overhead with that startling blue that sometimes graces the heavens just before winter. "I'm terribly sorry to trouble you, but may we have a moment of your time?"

Viola traipsed behind, a tad mulishly. This was her least favorite part of investigating crimes, sticking her nose into other people's business when she'd prefer to keep it buried in a book, thank you very much.

"What kin I do for you girls?" Up close, the girls could see that the woman might once have been as beautiful as her daughter, in a robust kind of way, with her large-boned, buxom frame. But there was that same glamour about the cheekbones and lips, the charm of the button nose, and the wide-set blue eyes that were Babs's trademark feature.

"You must be Babs's mother," Vivian said, with a touch of surprise. The resemblance was just so striking.

"Babs?" The woman took a step back, cinching the boy closer—for it was a *him*, a cute little lad with a questing gaze and dimpled smile. The woman's sky-blue eyes narrowed slightly. "Just what is it that you two is lookin' for, if you don't mind me askin'. You ain't with the police, surely, and besides, I've told them every—"

"Oh, so they *have* been to see you. What a relief! Mrs. Appleby," Vivian began, making a reasonable guess at Babs's real last name. "We're friends of Babs, and we're concerned about her welfare. We'd like to talk to you about her disappearance."

So direct were these words, so earnest their delivery, that Viola almost believed her sister sincere. Could she really be seeing a new side of her twin? Oh dear—and how ghastly that she felt so glum about it when it was wonderful, surely, her darling Viv, shining through just now without an ounce of guile. It was just such a jarring change that for a moment, Viola's breath was quite robbed—by panic or wonder, she could not tell.

Babs's mother seemed disarmed by Viv's frankness as well, which eased Viola's stomach, somewhat. Maybe it was just another tactic, after all.

"Well, yes, I see. That is kind, young miss," she equivocated, gratified, yet clearly reluctant to say more. "The whole thing has shaken us up, I won't say it hasn't. We've always wanted what's best for our Barbara, and the whole thing, well . . ."

What *whole thing* was she talking about, Vivian wondered? Her daughter's disappearance, of course, yet something in the woman's demeanor spoke of deeper trouble.

"Yes, the whole thing is rather beastly," Vivian echoed, studying Mrs. Appleby closely. "It's so hard to hang onto them, isn't it, with all the temptations of city life. I want you to know that Babs—that is, *Barbara*—hung up that picture you gave her, that charming one of the farmhands at table. Why, it was positively the first thing she did when she moved in. She was our boarder, you see."

Mrs. Appleby's eyes suddenly swam with tears. The rigidity that had propped up her polite demeanor slipped for a moment, revealing despair so deep, both girls felt the pang. She disengaged one hand from the baby's bum to wipe her eyes.

"I suppose you'd like to come in?" she said with a touching note of deference. "I ain't got much to offer, but there's a chance Alfred ain't polished off the brandy."

"That would be lovely, Mrs. Appleby," Vivian said.

They climbed the steep stair to the porch, the children scattering at their approach, then closing ranks as the screen door wheezed closed behind them.

"Sit, if you please," Mrs. Appleby said in her best parlor-ese, bending with effort to set the youngest Appleby gently on the floor. She nodded toward a faded floral sofa. "I'll just see about the brandy."

With that, she disappeared down the hall, leaving the little boy plunked squarely on his cloth diaper, staring at the twins with wide eyes while he gnawed on his fist.

"Cute, little fellow, isn't he?" Viola said.

"The resemblance *is* striking," Vivian agreed. "But then, Babs does have that baby doll look about her."

"Oh, yes, what with her eyes and that button nose, I quite agree—oh, Viv, look!" Viola pointed to the mantle over the white-washed, brick fireplace. "The *rattle*," she hissed.

There it was, displayed among the knick-knacks between a chipped Dutch china doll and a basket of apples.

Vivian hopped to her feet. "Well *done*, Lala." She stepped nimbly over the battered but well-polished coffee table. Slacks *were* liberating, weren't they? Crossing to the mantle, she picked the rattle up in her slender fingers, turning it to the light to read again the chiseled inscription. She was just on the point of setting it down when Mrs. Appleby returned, a small tray in hand.

Viola drew in a sharp breath, but Vivian merely took her entrance in stride.

"What a charming, little rattle, Mrs. Appleby," she said—then, astonishing her twin with the boldness of her new approach, "I do believe we saw it in Barbara's room some days ago."

The stout woman froze. For a moment, Viola feared she would drop the tray, but then she took a couple of steps forward to set it carefully on the coffee table, straightening to clasp her hands tightly under her sagging bosom.

"It was a gift," she said carefully, "from our Barbara, to . . . to . . . celebrate the arrival of the little one."

This was addressed to Vivian, who held Mrs. Appleby's gaze with such frank understanding that Viola was seized by the urge to bare her *own* soul, if Viv hadn't already known everything worth knowing. Indeed, her twin had no need to utter a word; it was all there in her eyes which said, loud and clear, that she knew that Mrs. Appleby knew that she knew that Mrs. Appleby knew that—well, something like that. It was all a muddle except for the knowledge that the cat was out of the bag.

"He's an adorable child," Vivian said.

Mrs. Appleby blew out her cheeks, then shuffled over to sink into a threadbare stuffed chair as if her age had caught up with her.

"We all thought it would be better if the tyke stayed here," she said with a canny look up at Vivian, who still stood by the mantle. "The city's no place for a child, even if Barbara were able to . . . to care for him. And besides, it wouldn't be good for her . . . career." The carefully chosen words did nothing to mask Mrs. Appleby's grief and confusion, the portrait of a woman who was out of her depth. "And then that Parson Rathbone feller was always fussin' around, houndin' her about the child, though I don't rightly know why she put so much store by his learnin'. Always seemed to me there was something off about the man. Why, last time he come callin' I had to send him packin'.'"

Vivian frowned. She could feel Lala's pointed stare but refused to meet it. Parson Rathbone, was it? So, that was his name. Honestly, Lala had been an absolute *tyrant* about that fellow. The last thing they needed was fuel for the flames.

"Was he . . . a friend?" Vivian asked, after some consideration.

Mrs. Appleby harumphed, shoulders shrugging as she gazed off to the side. "Our Barbara surely thinks so, though she's such a kind heart, that one. Never did have much sense. That old coot had her convinced her soul was downright *soiled*, which ain't one ounce true, no matter what she's done. Why Barbara wouldn't hurt a fly, and to my mind *that's* what the good lord sees."

Vivian liked the woman's spunk. "Quite right. I couldn't agree more, Mrs. Appleby. I take it that's why you sent the man *packing*, as you said."

Mrs. Appleby seemed to take pause, perhaps wondering at how freely her tongue was wagging. She shrugged again and reached over to take up one of the brandy glasses, downing it in one gulp. "Sometimes it ain't perdition that scares a mother half so much as salvation," she said, and there was such an undercurrent of dread beneath her words that even Vivian blanched. "But be that as it may, Barbara stands by him, and we stand by our Barbara. Come girls, drink up."

Vivian joined her twin on the couch and they each took a small, dutiful sip of the apple brandy. It was good for homemade stuff, though neither girl was a drinker, with the exception of eggnog at Christmas and the occasional cordial when Cookie took it into her head that their blood was thin. Mrs. Appleby rambled on about this and that, steering clear of hazards in the road. Vivian judged her an honest woman at heart, and indeed, nothing she said was an outright lie. But then, why should she trust two young women that she didn't know from Adam—or more to the point, Eve?

"It seems that Barbara was absolutely meant for the stage," Vivian said, after hearing an anecdote about Babs's childhood debut at the county fair. Warm remembrance had loosened Mrs. Appleby's tongue once more, and instinct told Vivian that the pastures were fruitful, though she best tread carefully. "It does take its toll, though, city life. Why, my sister and I detest the coal smoke. And to leave all this," she swept her hand around, sure that Mrs. Appleby would cast the shabby but clean environs in their kindest light. "The fresh air, the cows at their cud, why it's charming, there's simply no other word. Do you know, she told us that when she was a girl she was quite the tomboy, romping up and down the farm, climbing trees—"

"With her brother," Mrs. Appleby burst out, putting a fist to her mouth to stifle tears, then pulling it away with a gasp, as if unable to hold back the words. "He tried to bring her home, our Eddie did, said he was gonna set her straight, and if anyone could talk her out of this nonsense, it were our Eddie, them being the best of friends and all, but—oh!"

Emotion overcame her, and she could say no more. She required a few moments to master herself, and when she did, the mask of civility was firmly back in place. Her jaw hardened with resolve as she reached down for the babe who sat beside her feet, hauling him onto her lap and hugging him tightly so that he began to fuss.

"Eddie, yes, I see," Vivian said, eyeing Mrs. Appleby as Viola eyed her twin. Viv must be concocting some story even now, just to draw the woman out. After all, she'd be bursting to know whether this Eddie was Babs's mysterious afternoon visitor. But instead, Vivian merely rose from the sofa, gathering her jacket, which she'd neatly laid aside. "I can see this is a private matter, Mrs. Appleby. We are so sorry to have upset you. We're just so anxious to help in any way we can."

Again, Mrs. Appleby's face softened, though the years of steady hardship lingered in her gaze. Her grip on the babe eased, and he settled with a happy burble.

"I appreciate that, young lady. I surely do."

Viola rose as well, joining her sister by the mantle.

"Please, don't get up, Mrs. Appleby, we'll see ourselves out," Vivian said. "You've been more than gracious, and I think the little tyke could use your attention right about now."

The woman gazed down fondly at the bald head as the child played with one of her buttons. It was clear the baby soothed her.

"Well, now, you've been lovely guests, I must say. And if you learn anything of our Barbara, you'll let us know, won't you? Those policemen have a lot to do without coddlin' those of us as can't help but worry."

The abject humility of this statement so moved Vivian that she worried momentarily for the state of her priorities. She was becoming entirely too sentimental. Luckily, what was best for her interests in this instance was also best for Babs. She must get her hands on that rattle.

"Of course, we will," she said with an earnestness that surprised even her. "We are doing everything in our power to bring your Barbara home. Speaking of which, there is one small thing you could do to help us in our inquiries."

Mrs. Appleby looked up from the babe and gave a firm nod. "You have only to ask, dear."

Vivian gestured toward the mantle. "The rattle. Could we borrow it? I don't know if it's connected to Babs's disappearance, but I'd like to study it in greater detail."

Mrs. Appleby appeared startled but nodded again. "Surely, take it dear, I've no real use for it. Seems a bit too fine for the little one. I always supposed Barbara sent it along to us for safe-keeping, her having such a trial with housekeeping, if you must know."

Vivian and the woman shared a glance, a silent moment of rueful bonding. Babs *was* a slob. And yet, it was as though the starlet Vivian had thought she'd known had begun to materialize only since her disappearance, first through the love in a gangster's jaded eye, and now, through a devoted mother's account of a dreamer, a worker, a loyal sister with a playful streak and kindness in her heart. Babs, *Barbara*, was a person who brightened the lives of those around her.

It was . . . humbling. Yes, that was the word. Beastly, but there was nothing else for it. Vivian feared she had been rather a fool.

"We'll take good care of the rattle," she said, reaching over to pluck it from the mantle and slip it into her jacket pocket. "Thank you again—we'll be going now."

With a small wave, they headed back out through the creaking screen door. The children on the porch scrambled aside, once more closing in behind so that Viola felt rather like Moses, parting the Red Sea. The twins turned at the bottom of the stairs to find them staring back for a count of one, two, three—and then all hell broke loose, with sticks flying, and shrieks of laughter, and one little boy leaping onto the back of his brother, who pelted down the stairs and across the hill.

When they got back to the Packard, Mrs. Lurch was fiddling under the hood. "Well, that was enlightening," Vivian said.

"What do you suppose all that talk about perdition and salvation was about?" Viola said as she climbed into the front seat beside her twin, snugging the door closed as they watched Mrs. Lurch through the windshield, elbows bent as she dug about with a wrench.

Vivian could just *feel* Lala sniffing about. "So help me, Lala, if you bring up Reverend Dimmesdale one more time, I'll positively disown you."

Viola scooted away from where she'd been slouched against her sister's arm. "I don't know what you mean, Viv. It isn't my fault that the preacher keeps showing up in our investigation. And it does so remind one of Dimmesdale standing in the wild wood," she couldn't help adding, "wondering what little Pearl would think of him, even though she was his own love child, and then tragic Hester unpinning that wretched A from her dress, only to have to put it on again later when poor Dimmesdale's heart quailed. In light of that, I don't see why the little tyke couldn't be the love child of Babs's preacher. It only stands to reason."

Vivian sighed. Reason had nothing to do with it, but she had to accede the point. It would be folly to rule anything out.

"He's on our list, Lala," she said in a placating tone, slipping her arm through the crook of Viola's elbow with a little squeeze as they sat there side by side. "Speaking of the list, let's go back over our suspects. You know how Mrs. Lurch is once she gets her hands dirty. There's no telling when she'll let up."

CHAPTER TWENTY
Something for Something

Viola found herself musing on *The Scarlet Letter* all the way home. She had a dim notion that Boston, home of the fictious Hester Prynne, lay somewhere to the east as the Packard choked and rattled back to New York, suffering under the ordeal of Mrs. Lurch's lead foot. Indeed, if a seventeenth century crow, perched in the upper branches of the Appleby's chestnut tree, had unfurled its black, ragged wings to fly 161 miles to the east, it might have settled on the steepled rooftop of some colonist's house. The Appleby's chestnut had even been a sapling in those days and, in the years since, had survived fire, axes, and the constant onslaught of the Appleby children—only to fall prey to a blight first detected killing trees at the Bronx Zoo.

Over the next few days, the twins were kept busy with their studies and occasional expeditions to the attic. And yet, Viola could not stop thinking about Dimmesdale, Hester and little Pearl, even in the midst of reading Keats, whose works and brief, tragic life were close to her heart. If only that Bristol-bound clipper had counted among its passengers the star-crossed lovers and their dear child! But even without Chillingworth to spoil their happiness, that *pall* was already there, hanging over the scene like perpetual dusk. One simply knew that nothing would work out as it should. Perhaps that's what was bothering her, a feeling of doom that lingered, even after she had given up on Keats and put the book away, as if closing it could likewise silence her thoughts. She *knew* this feeling. It was like an old wound that kicked up every now and again, when the weather blew in.

It was a full ten minutes before Vivian looked up from muddling through her own tome, excerpts from the *Book of Optics*, penned long centuries ago by the medieval Arab scholar known as Alhazen. Viola's book lay discarded on the sofa beneath the "nursery" windows, as they still fondly called the second story room. Her twin was nowhere to be seen.

"Where on earth can she have wandered off to," Vivian groused, marking her page with a tassel before setting the book aside. "If she's gone off looking for Old Horace again, I'll positively..." She trailed off, aware that she was mumbling aloud, but *honestly*, her twin needed more looking after by the day. Horace had become Viola's newest charity project, though to Vivian's mind, the old man was beyond help, what with mistaking the hydrangeas for intruders and booby trapping the kitchen garden with tactics adapted from his time as a Civil War recruit, fighting for the 2nd Vermont Brigade.

After an exhaustive search of the house, she finally found Viola in the east wing of the third floor, which had been mothballed for almost two years.

"Lala," she huffed, joining her sister on the threshold of the connected rooms. They were the mirror image of their own chambers, directly below, except that here, instead of toile quilts, the narrow beds were shrouded with canvas, and the windows were draped, not with chintz, but with black cloth to shut the world away. "You're being insupportably morbid, you know you are," she chided, but with a gentleness that surprised even her.

"Oh, Viv," was all that Viola could manage. She could almost see them, phantoms cavorting at the edge of sight. Teddy and Titus as tow-headed ten-year-olds, bouncing on their beds, then hauling Vivan and Viola up to bounce along with them. Teddy and Titus at fifteen, heads bent together in whispered conference as they sat, shoulder to shoulder, concocting new ways to pester Cookie in her larder. Teddy and Titus, fresh back from college on an unscheduled break that no one had bothered to explain, their eyes too bright, their speech too rapid, their complexions fevered, though no illness plagued them—at least none that the doctor could name.

"*Viv,*" Viola said again, her voice cracking on a note of despair that nearly broke Vivian's resolve to take a firm hand. "Why do you suppose they did it? Was it the curse, after all?"

This was a shade too far. "Perfect nonsense," she said, though less sharply than she might have done. She felt oddly shaken, though it *was* perfect nonsense. After all, life invariably failed one, so it was only to be expected. People died, people left, people let you down at every— "You *know* they were always high-strung, Lala," she said, interrupting this unwelcome train of thought. "The signs were there from the start, and there's nothing to do but face up to it. Of *course*, they were unruly and brilliant and magnificent and we loved them like—" and then her own voice inexplicably broke, and for several moments, she could not speak. "We—we loved them like our own hearts," she managed, finally. At this, Viola looked up into her sister's eyes as they clasped hands. "It's only what one can expect, feeling a little sad about it," she soldiered on. "We were always looking up to them, weren't we, being five years the younger. Always looking up until one day—"

"They weren't there," Viola finished, quietly, with a squeeze of her twin's hand before releasing it to wipe her cheek as she gazed back to the empty room. Her sister's distress had sobered her. For her own part, going through the thicket of despair was all in a day's work, but she could see that her twin was pressed to her limits. "I do hope they're in heaven, though," she said with a shuddering sigh as the grip of her own grief gave way. "You know what devils they were, Viv."

Vivian could not help a garbled chuckle as she reached up to surreptitiously dash a tear from her own eye. The knot in her stomach eased. "More rot, Lala. Utter nonsense. I'm not even sure heaven exists, except as the mess most people make of their lives. Besides, if it does exist, I'm sure that God has better sense than to oust two poor scamps like Teddy and Titus."

Viola shot her sister a sidelong glance. Good, her "nonsense" had done its work, though she wondered how long Viv could carry on this way, holding her grief like a suitcase, the contents of which escaped her. Not everyone could walk through the shadow of the valley of death without succumbing to its evils. She would have to keep a close eye on her twin.

Luckily, a distraction was on its way in the form of an unexpected caller. Later that afternoon, as the twins were each immersed in their respective reading, Mrs. Lurch stuck her head in through the nursery door.

"That sergeant is at the door," she said, matter-of-factly, and if she noted Vivian's sudden flush, she gave no sign. "Where do you want him?" she continued, as if oblivious to the effect of this strange formulation, though Viola suspected she was having a bit of fun.

"In the—well, let's see, yes, in the parlor. Do see him in," Vivian finished firmly, her face a slightly florid mask of self-possession.

Moments later, they entered said parlor to find the sergeant already settled with one of Cookie's scones and a cup of tea.

"What an unexpected pleasure," Vivian said, a bit stiffly. Viola thought the sergeant seemed awkward as well, rising slightly from the floral divan to acknowledge their entrance. He *was* a gentleman, flatfoot or no. "So, *ahem*, tell us, Seargent, what may we do for you?"

"My apologies for barging in unannounced," he said. Perhaps it was a trick of the afternoon light, but Viola though she detected a flush in his cheek, as well. "I've been thinking that we ought to turn over a new page here. After all, we can be of more use to each other as allies than enemies, don't you think?"

"Hardly *enemies*," Vivian said, her own color deepening. "I don't know what I've done to give you that impression, Sergeant, but I do apologize."

The young man raised his steadfast gaze to hers, and it was only then that she realized he'd been avoiding her eye. "Good," he said, as if he genuinely meant it. Vivian fanned her face, then quickly dropped the hand to her lap. Beastly awkward, talking with strangers. "Perhaps we can engage in a bit of quid pro quo," Sergeant Kowalski said.

This unfortunate phrasing sent a jolt down the back of her legs.

Vivian cleared her throat again, determined to restore order. "I'm sorry, Sergeant, but perhaps we should carry on with our separate investigations. I don't know with what you could possibly expect to barter."

Viola flashed her sister an exasperated look. She could see that Viv had lost all awareness of the words coming out of her mouth. To his credit, the sergeant did not greet this statement with the laugh it clearly merited.

"How about information?" he said, stating the obvious, but so mildly, one could hardly take offense. It was rather fine of him to hold out the olive branch, Viola thought, if only Viv weren't such a mess. "We've had a ransom demand come in, this time with hard figures—$50,000 in cash for Babs's return."

This revelation did the trick. Vivian slid to the edge of her chair, the hem of her plaid skirt falling away from her thigh in a way that would have spurred Tommy Parker to new heights of poetic verse. If the sergeant noticed, he gave no sign, though Viola thought his cheek might have deepened a shade.

"*Really*," she said. The breach of protocol implied by the sergeant's disclosure was not lost on her. "Can you . . . can you tell us anything more? Has the miscreant proposed a drop?"

Kowalski also seemed energized and set his plate aside, dusting his hands free of crumbs. He leaned forward, elbows resting on his knees and fingers laced, then paused, as if to evaluate his options. "Yes, a drop is specified, although I can't reveal the details. But we've had someone step forward to volunteer as an emissary to deliver the ransom. A Pastor Rathbone, who has a small parish by the docks, over in—"

"Babs's preacher!" Viola cried. "Oh, Viv, didn't I say?!"

"You certainly did, Lala," Vivian said, approvingly. "Bravo. It appears he means to be Babs's savior, perhaps in more ways than one? Tell me, Sergeant, have you ruled the preacher out as a suspect?"

Kowalski's eyes narrowed. "A suspect? On what basis?"

Vivian threw off the urge to look away from those thick-lashed brown eyes. If the sergeant was moderately attractive, what of it? She had entertained the infatuations of much more handsome young men than the sergeant without a single heart flutter.

"I didn't think it worth mentioning because, well, Lala does get *ideas* sometimes—sorry, Lala, but you know it's true. But now, it appears there was something to it. You see, she observed what might have been a rendezvous on a streetcar between Babs and this gentleman. And we both saw him outside the theater the night of Babs's disappearance, *raving*, if you must know."

The sergeant's brow knit. "Is that so. It fits with what he's told us. As it turns out, he's been ministering to her for some time. But it's worth taking note of." His gaze cleared, coming back to

Vivian's with a frank intensity. The corner of his mouth turned up into a rueful smile. "Thank you for telling me, Miss Van der Beeck," he said, with a touch of softness beneath his voice. Good lord, why was this room so intolerably warm? Cookie must have stoked the furnace with the October chill coming on.

She returned his smile, though it still felt stiff. "Think nothing of it, Sergeant. While we're at it, I suppose I should also come clean about another detail that I, well, that I wanted to keep for myself. You can't blame me for that, can you?"

The sideways smile gave way to a laugh. "No, I don't believe I can."

Vivian sighed. "Right. Well, as it happens, Miss Le Roy had an afternoon caller a week or so before her debut. A young man who left in high dudgeon. I was under the impression that they had *words*."

The smile slipped as the sergeant's brow knit once more. "And did you happen to *catch* any of these words?"

"Not really, no. But Babs was quite distressed after he stormed out. And then . . . well, we saw him at the theater the night of her disappearance."

Unaccountably mortified, Vivian felt her cheeks flame. The sergeant's gaze darkened a moment, his eyes never slipping from hers. Then, he shook his head with a kind of resigned chagrin.

"Any other things you haven't told me, Miss Van der Beeck?"

She sat up a little taller. Why should she feel guilty, just because she was clever enough to have gathered a few clues?

"There may be a couple of other small observations." There was nothing else for it. She kept picturing Mrs. Appleby's haunted eyes, which was such a distraction when one wanted to focus on the facts at hand. If there was even a *chance* the sergeant could be helpful, she'd have to tell him at least *some* of what she knew. "I have a theory as to the identity of the afternoon caller— or rather two theories, although one has come to the fore since—"

she stopped herself before going into the details of their visit to the Appleby farm. No need to risk another *talking to.* Better to cut to the chase. "I believe the caller may have been Babs's brother, Eddie."

Viola turned to her with an excited clap. "Well done, Viv. I was thinking the same thing. He must have come here to talk her into coming home with him. Do you suppose that's why he came to the theater too? To try again after failing so miserably the first—"

"I'm afraid that would be impossible," Sergeant Kowalski interrupted, draining his teacup and setting it on the drop-leaf table. "Eddie Appleby is dead."

"Dead!" both girls said as one.

The sergeant rose, reaching for his overcoat, which he'd draped over a nearby chair. "Dead. He was killed in a hit-and-run accident the night of September 26 while—"

"Walking on the sidewalk, down Broadway in the middle of the—oh, how *could* I have forgotten!" Viola clasped a hand to her mouth, then slowly let it drift down to her lap. "It was in the newspaper, don't you recall, Viv? That paper you nabbed from Babs's room after we ransacked her poor heart for—" Viola's gaze latched onto the sergeant's, and she cleared her throat, "—after we looked in on Babs and her afternoon caller. 'Speeding Auto Careens onto Sidewalk: Man Killed,'" she quoted, verbatim.

"My sister has a good memory," Vivian explained, frowning as she considered this new turn of events. She'd been so certain she was onto something! But, of course, this explained why Mrs. Appleby was so distraught—her son, *killed* while en route to bring her errant daughter back into the fold! "September 26, you say? So, Babs must have only recently found out about it when we saw her." Was Lala right? Was Babs's visitor perhaps not the cause of her distress, but rather attempting to comfort her? Why then had he stormed out?

"I'll tell you more about the accident on our way to the station," Kowalski went on. "We should have you both look over some mug shots for a possible ID of this visitor of Miss Le Roy's."

Vivian nodded and rose, so distracted as she headed toward the doorway that she bumped right into the sergeant. Startled, she looked up into his face as he reached out reflexively to put a hand on each of her arms, setting her back a bit. Perhaps it was just that they'd been taken off guard, but they *did* stand there a tad longer than was necessary, Viola thought, until the sergeant's hands dropped away, and the spell was broken.

"Dreadfully sorry," Vivian murmured as she took another step back, dismayed that the heat had returned to her cheeks.

"Think nothing of it," Kowalski said wryly, echoing her previous words.

CHAPTER TWENTY-ONE
A Crowd

The district office was a warren of oak desks and file cabinets, bustling with activity. Officers in their gold-buttoned uniforms came and went. Clerks navigated the aisles behind teetering armloads of paperwork. Doors lining the perimeter burst open as voices hollered things like "Hey Mac, get me that file on the Brewster case, pronto!" And the noise! Above the murmur of voices, telephones rang and typewriters clacked, joining the blare of horns from the street just outside the bank of tall, narrow windows.

Vivian watched it all, eyes shining as they darted from sight to sight.

The sergeant watched Vivian with a strange look on his face, as if he were puzzling out a sum that would not add up.

Viola watched them both. Oh, dear, she thought. Clearly, it *wasn't* just Viv.

"I see you've never been to a police station before," Kowalski said, putting one hand on Vivian's back as he gestured forward with the other and inclined his head to Viola, as a gentleman might do, so as not to exclude.

They had not taken two steps when a familiar voice reached them from across the room.

"Kowalski! In my office, stat! And bring those interview transcripts from the—"

Detective Flanagan fell silent, emerging from a doorway just beyond the last row of desks to put his hands on his hips. One eyebrow shot up, joined shortly by the other, just before both brows scrunched together then plummeted down—as if his face were giving a special reenactment of his thought process for the benefit of the viewing public. How *did* he conduct interrogations, Vivian wondered. The man possessed not one ounce of guile.

"What are *they* doing here?"

These words might have struck Viola as rude, but then, Aunt Lavinia had shamefully traumatized the poor dear, hadn't she. And here they were, crowding him on his own turf, trailing the aftermath of his ignominy like a skunk's musk. Hmm, that was rather good. She would have to jot that down.

By now, Kowalski had escorted them around the far desk and led them to Flanagan's door. "They've come to look over some mug shots for a possible ID—a visitor of Miss Le Roy's who was spotted at the theater the night of her abduction," the sergeant said, catching Vivian's eye in a moment of sympatico. His use of the passive voice smoothed over her omission without hiding it, striking that balance between pragmatism and integrity that the young sergeant exemplified. If Vivian felt a small burst of admiration somewhere in the vicinity of her heart, it was easily mistaken for indigestion.

"Hmph," the detective said. He looked them over, then seemed to soften, perhaps recalling that their assistance had been the one bright spot in a grueling interview. "All right, then. When you've finished up, bring me those transcripts. There's been a new development since the ransom demand was—" This time, it was the detective's words, not his brows, which betrayed him.

Perhaps Auntie was right about the old curmudgeon. He was simply out of his league.

He cleared his throat with a series of grunts. "Well, yes, ahem, you know the one I mean, Kowalski." He hemmed and hawed a bit more, then turned with a nod and retreated to his office.

"Is he always so—" Vivian checked herself, "brusque?" She'd been about to say obtuse, which struck her as a bit high-handed.

But the sergeant seemed to know her mind. "You're not the first person to underestimate Detective Flanagan," he said as they walked, three abreast, toward the double doors at the far end of the room. Holding one of the frosted glass doors ajar, he flashed Vivian that canny, sidelong look she had noted on their first meeting. "He's decent," he said as they passed through, "which puts him at a disadvantage when he's up against people like Detective Broderick. But he gets results. And I'd trust him with my life."

High praise, indeed. Vivian was inclined to reserve judgment on the matter, but she was glad she'd pulled her punch. She wouldn't want the sergeant to think her uncharitable, not that she cared unduly what he thought, only it wouldn't do to alienate her new ally at this tender—

"Sergeant!"

They turned to see a young woman burst through the double doors, waving a file as she click-clacked down the tiled hall. Her dreadfully plain blouse with the point collar and dark skirt marked her as a secretary of some sort—though Vivian had to admit the clothes did suit her lithe, athletic frame. She had a dark-haired vivacity about her that was fetching, even striking, especially when she fixed Sergeant Kowalski with a brilliant smile that seemed to be meant for him alone.

Blasted stuffy in here. Vivian felt a bit out of breath as she stepped to the side to make way for the energetic newcomer. One really ought to open a window or two.

"This'll save you having to grab that file yourself," the young secretary said in a voice that struck Vivian as entirely too familiar for the address of a superior. "I happened to overhear Flanagan." She gave a wink that said, *Who wouldn't overhear him.* Passable banter, Vivian supposed, indicating some modicum of intelligence, though it was better reserved for one's typing pool mates. What *had* she eaten at lunch? Vivian hardly recalled, though just now it was giving her a horrid spot of heartburn.

Kowalski was leafing through the file, then snapped it closed and hefted it.

"Thanks, Jane," he said with that relaxed grin Vivian had glimpsed on one or two occasions, the one that seemed to come out either by accident or when he felt entirely comfortable. "One less thing for him to harp on," he added, with a wink of his own.

The secretary turned on her heel, casting a wave and smile back over her shoulder. "That's the idea, Adi. That makes two you owe me now," she called just as she passed out of sight.

Adi.

That stuffiness was frankly overwhelming. Vivian fanned her face with one hand as the sergeant turned back to them with a smile, extending the file to suggest they continue on their way. *Adi.* The sound of it rather stuck in one's head. Imagine, calling your superior by a nickname! Not that *Adi* seemed to mind. The two of them appeared to be on a first-name basis—a *nickname* basis, when it came to it. And what was this *first* favor that the upstart of a secretary had conferred? What kind of standards did they maintain in this workplace?

"Viv, it's *this* way," Viola said gently, running a few steps to retrieve her sister from where she'd wandered past the door which the sergeant now held open. She slipped her arm though her twin's with a squeeze. Poor Viv—though it wouldn't hurt her to at least *tune* a second fiddle. In fact, it might do her good.

"You ladies can sit here." Kowalski pulled out two chairs from a dented and gouged wooden table that ran the length of the room. "I'll be right back."

Vivian sat, smoothing her plaid skirt over her knees. Viola settled beside her, strangely at a loss. She abhorred awkward silences, and an awkward silence with one's twin was the loneliest sound in the world.

"Here we go," the sergeant said, ducking back in from the side room with one large book in hand and two others tucked beneath his arm. He laid the first before them, opening it to reveal rows of photographs, portraits taken full face and in profile, some with a number-bearing placard held chest high.

"I don't believe we'll find a *thing* in these books," Vivian complained, privately, for Lala's ears. "But I suppose the sooner begun, the sooner done."

Moods aside, Viola thought her sister might be right. For the first half hour, she half expected to spy Babs's preacher, staring up from the book with a spooked expression, his visage snatched from some prior life as a petty criminal or a con artist or even just some poor day laborer who was down on his luck. Now, *Hester's* preacher, Dimmesdale, had always maintained the highest moral standards—well, except for that *once*. But there was the dastardly character of Hester's estranged husband, Roger Chillingworth, who led a double life for no other reason than to feed a spiteful nature. Perhaps Babs's preacher—Pastor Rathbone, she corrected herself—was *also* not what he appeared to be. But as the pages flipped past and the hour wore on, Viola was forced to admit defeat.

There was no sign of Babs's afternoon visitor either, but on the last page of the last book, Viola put her finger down on a picture in the third row.

"That man?" Kowalski said with interest, placing one hand on the table to lean across Vivian to where the book was laid. Vivian scooted her chair out and rose, stepping away.

"By all means, Sergeant, sit if you like," she said in a voice that sounded tense, even to her ears. Really, she ought to be getting more sleep.

Sergeant Kowalski tried to catch her eye, but she was wretched tired. She looked away, affecting a yawn that she fancied was on its way.

Still leaning on the table, the sergeant turned his attention to Viola. "That's Mack Macavoy. Are you saying that's the man who visited Miss Le Roy?"

"Oh, dear me, no," Viola said. "I wasn't being clear. I have seen him though, at Mr. Luciana's place. Is he a hardened criminal?"

Kowalski stood, running a hand through his hair, then letting it flop to his side. "Well, it makes sense that you saw him there. He's not one of Luigi's associates, strictly speaking, but he's in the game, mostly on the gambling side." He sighed. "I guess that was a bust, then."

Was it? Viola peered down at Mr. Macavoy's wizened features, remarkably like the Chief Weasel from *The Wind in the Willows*. It wasn't for nothing that the Chief Weasel was the leader of all the baddies. And hadn't this fellow been loitering close at hand, perhaps even eavesdropping?

But even Viola knew that such theories would hold little sway outside the pages of her imagination.

A moment later, Sergeant Kowalski held the door open to let them into the hall.

"You remember the way out?" he said with a nod to Viola. He ducked his head a bit to catch Vivian's eye, but she was busy fussing with her purse.

"Of course, quite, thank you," she said when she'd gotten the blasted thing settled. The latch was absolutely acting up these days. "Do let us know if there's anything we can do." She allowed her gaze to drift up for the briefest of moments to where the sergeant, *Adi*, was studying her, his brow once more slightly knit.

"I certainly will, Miss Van der Beeck," he said, "You do the same."

Oh, dear, Viola thought, noting the formality that once more edged his voice. Make no mistake, Sergeant Kowalski was not one to run after anyone. Viola had best prepare herself for another long organizing expedition, which *did* cut into her reading time.

"Goodbye, Sergeant," Vivian said with a stiff nod, turning up the corridor. "Come along, Lala, don't be all day about it. We've got our work cut out for us. That attic is a frightful mess."

CHAPTER TWENTY-TWO
Disasters and Diversions

The next few days came and went in a flurry of organizing and cataloging, mostly in the attic where the twins' burst of industriousness would not raise Mother's elegantly penciled eyebrow. Not that Mother cared unduly what the twins got up to, as long as they kept their hands clean. Before long, Saturday had rolled around—and not just *any* Saturday.

It was their eighteenth birthday.

Unfortunately, the party was a disaster. Cookie and Mrs. Lurch did everything right, mind you. They set up extra tables in the conservatory, each with a centerpiece culled from the fall garden. They sequestered the chickens in their makeshift coop so they wouldn't peck at the birthday presents, and even created a dais in the corner where Mr. Sparrow could entertain them all with his clarinet. But then, the sky above the glass roof began to darken well before nightfall, heralding a storm that fairly shook the panes before it was done. Madame Koslova lost her pince-nez among the potted ferns, ushering in a search which ended with a dreadful *crack*. Mr. Sharma suffered a nervous attack when a thunderclap startled Al into accidentally discharging his pistol—

into the bougainvillea, thankfully, no harm done. Mrs. Lurch was able to cure most everything, settling Mr. Sharma with a draft of brandy and banishing Al to his room after delivering a few choice words, but even Mrs. Lurch was not a miracle worker.

For the worst thing to happen is what *didn't* happen.

Mother and Father didn't show.

"Och, kittens, 'tis certain they got caught up at the club, they did," Cookie said in her kindly manner, blinking rapidly. She always blinked when she lied. "There be so much traffic around these days, what with those newfangled automobiles runnin' 'bout. Gor! Don't get me started."

"Thank you for being kind, Cookie, but we all know that's perfect nonsense," Vivian said matter-of-factly. There was nothing for it but to meet the beastly thing head on. "They weren't *caught up,* they simply forgot, and that's all there is to it. Most likely they're enjoying a marvelous night out on the town. Remember, Viola and I are eighteen years old, so you needn't coddle us."

Viola could see the strain of being brave was wearing on her twin. As for herself, she thought one couldn't miss what one had never had, and Father and Mother had always been a *twosome,* hadn't they. It was only natural that they would forget.

"It's what comes of all that gallivanting!" Auntie cried suddenly from behind the mandevilla trellis, where she'd lain, half-forgotten, tucked into the reclining wicker rocker. "Gallivanters" were not to be borne, ever since Grampy had disappeared on a Tuesday night with little more in hand than a battered suitcase and a map of Bhutan. "Next thing you know, they'll be sending us postcards from Timbuktu!"

Viola could see a diversion was needed. "Here's what—why don't we play a game of charades," she suggested. "Oh, Mrs. Lurch let's *do* call Al down. I'm sure he's learned his lesson, and he's such a ham at charades."

And so, it was decided. The tables were moved aside, the chairs set in rows, and old Horace was sent off to retrieve Al on the condition that he leave his gun locked in a drawer. Dr. Weber was a tremendous sport, acting out *The Hound of the Baskervilles* on all fours, Mr. Sharma felt sufficiently recovered to enact *Tom Thumb,* a surprisingly whimsical choice, and even Madame Koslova and Miss Sphinx teamed up for a go at *War and Peace.*

"I do believe they're trying to lift our spirits," Viola whispered into Vivian's ear, feeling a tad verklempt.

But when they got up to their bedroom later that evening, Viola could see it was all for naught.

"Now, Viv," she said, sitting her twin down on her bed. "This can't go on. You've simply got to snap out of this *mood,* or poor Babs will languish in peril to who knows what dreadful end. It's time we made a plan."

This sort of stern pep talk from Lala was a new thing, but Vivian supposed it was an implied obligation under the Twin's Code. And it was true, Vivian had been feeling unaccountably dour for days now. It was high time she got a talking to.

"Well done, Lala, spot on," she said, straightening her shoulders. "I've been a perfect bore, haven't I. Right then—pull up a chair and we'll get down to it. I've been thinking about who next to eliminate from our field of suspects. It's been staring me in the face, I tell you, but that's what comes of being glum. I have no one to blame but myself."

"It's only natural, Viv," Viola said as she pulled over the French cane-back chair from the writing desk. Now that Viv had snapped out of it, she rather feared she'd overdosed her on bitter medicine. "Being a sleuth *and* a girl *and* only eighteen—why the world is positively set against you. 'Every man has his secret sorrows that the world knows not,'" she added, quoting Longfellow.

"And *woman,*" Vivian said, approvingly, feeling eighteen was a creditable age to assume the title.

"Well?" Viola pressed. "Who shall we eliminate next? Oh, come now, Viv, wipe that grin off your face. You're simply playing with me, you know you are."

"Very well, Lala," Vivian relented. "How would you like to take another trip to the theater?"

Apart from this teaser, Vivian would say no more about phase three of their investigation, and it would be several days before they'd be able to implement it. There was still school-work to be done, a reminder that although the twins were now eighteen, in the eyes of Mistress Dubois they were very much children.

"Arma virumque cano, Troiae qui primus ab oris italiam," Viola said, reciting the first verse of *The Aeneid*. "Arms and men sing," she began her translation, "of Troy who first from the mouth of Italy—my, that is awkward verbiage, don't you think?" She looked over at the governess, who was busily mashing a ball of wax. "I say, Mistress Dubois, that likeness is uncanny."

The elderly woman glanced up from her creation, which looked remarkably like the head of a cyclops, with one eye protruding from the lump. "Do not worry your head about the arms and the mouth, ma petite," she said. "Voilà!" She held the wax ball aloft. "Behold the eye, blinded by Ulysses's sword. He is so proud! And yet, is not his pride itself the monster? Who is it that is truly blind? This is the question."

"It's certainly a question, two, in fact," Vivian noted dryly. "Absurde quaestio, if you ask me," she added in a barely audible grumble. "Besides, I thought we were talking about *The Aeneid*, not *The Odessey*."

"I don't think it's absurd at all, Viv," Viola protested, tilting her head to consider the lump. She had recently begun to suspect that Mistress Dubois was in fact a genius, disguised as a bumbling crone, just like in those old fables where the sage tested the wanderer by pestering him for a drink of water and some gruel. "Besides, I'd much rather talk about *The Odessey* and poor

Ulysses's dreadful plight, wandering from shore to shore, only to confront the monsters of his lamentable existence. Why, I do believe everything in both poems is a symbol, so why should the mouth and arms and eyes be any different?"

Vivian suppressed an eyeroll. Mistress Dubois's flights of fancy were surpassed only by Lala's own, although one had to concede the point. The poem could be read literally or figuratively, which was why it put her in a foul mood.

"Well, *I* think it's utter nonsense. And as for Ulysses, he's just survived the sack of Troy. If he's seeing monsters, it's probably because he has a dreadful case of shell shock."

Viola caught her sister's eye, and for a moment, they were both quiet. The mention of shell shock put them in mind of Father, which invariably felt like the floor falling away under their feet.

"This is enough of both the Latin and the Greek for today," Mistress Dubois said with a canny look at the twins. She set her wax aside and clasped one hand to her back to rise. "We will take a constitutional, oui?" Ever since they'd whisked Mistress Dubois away in pursuit of Babs, the governess had conceived a fascination with the morning constitutional as a cure for every ailment. "It will clear the head and work the arms and the legs while giving the eye les vignettes à regarder," she added with a wink.

"Oh, that *does* sound fine," Vivian said, snapping out of her slouch. "You do have your moments, Mistress Dubois," she said, surprised by the note of fondness in her own voice.

Perhaps Mistress Dubois heard it too, for she was flushed as they passed into the hall, then made their way down to the front hall to bundle up.

Outside, it was a dreary day of high clouds and brisk winds that chafed the face. The first few days of November had proved to be unseasonably cold, but the twins didn't care. Freedom was in the air.

"I know, Mistress Dubois, let's take a field trip to the library," Vivian said, pausing on the sidewalk before they'd even finished the block. "I'm just desperate to do some research about the French Revolution."

Mistress Dubois's mouth started working mightily, as if she were chewing taffy instead of trying not to smile. It was a small tic that revealed itself whenever she was especially pleased.

"Ah, ma petite, finally, you have taken the interest in that most momentous of events! It is a day to rejoice, non?" She reached up one pudgy hand to remove her turban and fling it skyward. The twins giggled. What had gotten into the old dear? A little carpe diem with her coffee? Holding her back to bend over, Mistress Dubois retrieved the hat with some effort, tugging it over her still jet-black hair, which was smoothed, as usual, into a low bun. "But it is too long a walk for an old lady. We will take the car of streets."

The twins shared another glance. At this rate, they'd be downright fond of Mistress Dubois by day's end, and then who would be left to torture? It was a sobering thought.

"Right, then," Vivian said crisply. "But let's take a bus instead. It'll be faster than traipsing all the way over to Third Avenue."

Turning, they ventured across the avenue and into Central Park, strolling past leaf-bare trees, past mothers pushing baby carriages and young couples, arm in arm. Once, a dapper older gentleman thrust out the tip of his cane in greeting. Mistress Dubois covered her mouth shyly with one hand—which wasn't at *all* like a paw, Viola thought, especially clad in that attractive black glove. They'd been horrid toward their governess, and she mustn't blame Viv for it, at least not entirely. Twins' Code or no, Viola had begun to think she'd been all too willing to follow blindly where her sister led.

This thought was sobering too, and Viola pushed it away, falling instead to comforting musings about *The Scarlet Letter* and whether Babs's preacher was more like Dimmesdale or Hester's ghastly estranged husband, Roger Chillingworth. She wasn't sure just when this notion had taken hold except that her glimpse of the poor man outside the theater had suggested a character too morose to be saintly.

Vivian drifted off into her own thoughts too as they boarded the double-decker bus that would take them down Fifth Avenue to 42nd Street. The broad avenue was clogged with afternoon traffic, boxy Vauxhalls and snub-nosed Hudsons and Chevrolets all honking and swerving around the occasional police officer, planted bravely in the middle of an intersection. The park fell away, replaced by the plate-glass storefronts and awnings of the shopping district, then the St. Thomas Church with its chiseled arches, and finally row upon row of brownstones with their neat, cast-iron fences.

As the bus rattled southward, she reflected on the true object of this little field trip, a bit of intelligence gathering in advance of phase three—her planned visit to the offices of none other than Florenz Ziegfeld Jr. It was high time they determined whether the showman was indeed the father of Babs's secret love child. If he wasn't, Babs most likely was just the victim of a snatch racket, just like Al had said. Had Vivian made things too complicated with her theory that Ziegfeld was being blackmailed? Sometimes a ransom note was just a ransom note. And if Ziegfeld wasn't the father of a secret child, what was there to blackmail him with? Vivian hated to concede an error, but if her extortion theory was flat out wrong, there was nothing for it but to face facts.

That was just the beginning of what she had in mind for Ziegfeld's interrogation—though he would never know that's what it was. It would be a challenge, though, what with Ziegfeld's legendary secretary guarding the citadel. Perhaps a review of old society pages at the library would spark ideas for a strategy. Vivian was just mulling on this difficulty when the marble edifice of the library came into view, covering an entire city block.

"I'm sorry, Mistress Dubois, what did you say?"

So occupied had Vivian been, she'd barely heard the governess spouting bloody facts about the French Revolution.

"And so, the king, he tries to escape his dreadful fate. For the guillotine, it is chopping the heads off to the right and to the left, chop, chop, chop!" She demonstrated with the edge of her palm, repeatedly beheading the seat back before her. The passenger seated there had long since fled for the front of the bus where he now sat behind the driver, casting furtive glances at Mistress Dubois's rabid reenactment of the First Terror. "And the king, he does not wish to say au revoir tête, non non! He has need of the head! But do you think he makes it across the border?" The governess fixed her with a crafty smile.

Vivian was tempted to say that, no, Louis XVI would not secure his freedom but would instead be recognized, in an age before photographs, by his profile on a gold coin. But she couldn't quite bring herself to steal the old lady's thunder—a terribly bad sign.

"Goodness, I don't know, Mistress Dubois!" she humored her, with a note of irony she felt sure would be lost on the good matron. "But . . . hmm . . . if he had escaped, surely the revolution would not have been successful."

The governess beamed, her small, dark eyes alight, like those of a mole that sensed the end of the tunnel was nigh.

"Tu as raison!" she said, raising one finger triumphantly only to slice it across her neck. "And the king and his head were soon parted!" she cried, ushering in the rapid departure of the nervous passenger as the bus came to a halt at its stop.

"New York Public Library," the driver droned.

"That's our stop," Vivian said, rising briskly and ushering a flustered Mistress Dubois up the aisle. The governess was hopeless with transitions. "Lala, come along or you'll end up in the Bowery, for goodness' sake," she scolded.

Viola snapped out of her reverie, inspired by a glimpse of the newly built Empire State Building, towering above its neighbors. "Coming," she said, hurrying forward and out the door just before it snapped to.

After some difficulty getting across the busy street and then coaxing Mistress Dubois away from the marble lions that flanked the wide staircase, the three of them were finally standing in the midst of Astor Hall, which was much too grand to be called a lobby. Vivian could see she'd have to get away if she were ever to conduct her research in the periodicals section.

"I say, Lala, weren't you saying that you wanted to show Mistress Dubois the Judaica Collection?" she said breezily, already turning to go.

Viola had fully expected to be stuck on governess-sitting detail, but she found it bothered her less than it once might have done. And she appreciated that Vivian had selected a topic close to Viola's heart: the plight of the Jewish people, for whom she'd always felt an affinity. It was deplorable how they got left out of the best circles—a bit like the Van der Beecks, now that it came to it—and for no other reason that Viola could see than their superior determination. The Old Guard was frightfully snobby about bloodlines and all that rot, which had, conversely, made Viola embarrassed by her own lineage.

"Come along, Mistress Dubois. Viv knows perfectly well where the best books about the French Revolution are kept, and I would so like to show you a divine tome on Yiddish Theater," she said with genuine enthusiasm, taking the governess by the arm. "Ta ta, Viv," she said with a wave before Mistress Dubois could protest.

Vivian cast a grateful look over her shoulder before disappearing into a crowd of patrons that were sweeping up one of the marble staircases. Viola steered Mistress Dubois firmly toward the other one, up to the first floor where the main reading room stretched in all its grandeur. She paused to relish her first sight of those two long columns of tables with their green-shaded reading lamps. To each side, walls of books beckoned below tall windows, gauzy with light. Chandeliers dangled from the high paneled ceiling. And the smell! Old paper and leather and the musty odor of cozy, familiar rooms mingling somehow with the tang of intrigue, the mystique of distant places, and the bittersweet yearning for home. Oh, to live in a library! And to think, there were people who did just that! Why, the superintendent of this very building lived in a seven-room apartment, somewhere on the mezzanine floor!

Viola fell into a fantasy that revolved around a midnight frolic with the superintendent's children through darkened chambers, the headlights of passing cars slicing across the walls through high windows. It was hard to pull herself away, even with Mistress Dubois jabbering beside her—until she spied something that gave her slender frame a jolt, from the top of her blond head to the tip of her size six shoe.

Babs's preacher! *There*, just a few tables away, sat Pastor Rathbone, hunched with great concentration over a pile of books. Oh, it *was* a coincidence—only Viola didn't believe in coincidences, not with the allure of fate, tempting her at every turn. Just then, the man frowned up at the ceiling, then bolted to his feet, rushing to a nearby wall to scan titles as he proceeded toward the back of the room.

"Mistress Dubois, wait here just a moment," Viola said, detaching the governess's arm to walk quickly over to the pile of books the preacher had been poring over. She felt rather giddy with the excitement of it all as she kept an eye on the preacher, who was still examining titles, his back turned away. When she reached the table he'd abandoned, she looked down, flipping over the open book to spy the title etched on the front cover.

Pyrotechnics: The History and Art of Firework Making, by A.S.A. Brock.

Pyrotechnics? Babs's preacher was a fireworks enthusiast? It seemed unlikely, and Viola was just on the point of turning to the other books, strewn about the table, when she cast a glance in the preacher's direction and saw him turning back toward her, a new volume clutched in his thin hands.

Luckily, Viola was good at being invisible. Long practice with disappearing into books had given her the ability to be wraithlike at will. She ghosted back to Mistress Dubois's side and was soon escorting her down the center aisle.

"Come, Mistress Dubois," she whispered, her heart still thumping madly as she strove to sound natural. "There's a positively engrossing volume about the diaspora that you simply must see."

CHAPTER TWENTY-THREE
Ruses and Revelations

"Who may I say is inquiring?"

Mr. Ziegfeld's secretary had the sharp features, shrewd eye, and small, convulsive movements of a crow, protecting its brood. She had clearly spent long years fending off journalists, aspiring starlets, con men, and creditors, and was not one to be duped.

Little did she know she had met her match.

"Vivian and Viola Van der Beeck, representing the Van der Beeck estate. He should be expecting us."

The Van der Beecks had been extravagant patrons of the arts back in Grampy's day, and the name still had a *ring* in certain circles—as long as one didn't pick up.

The secretary quirked an eyebrow, then made a show of studying her appointment book. "I don't see you listed here." She looked up with a thin smile. "There must be some mistake."

Their fieldtrip to the library had been productive, particularly the hour Vivian had spent in the periodicals section, examining everything from gossip rags to—of all things—golfing magazines.

"No, you wouldn't see it, would you. We ran into Flo at

the—" She stifled a gasp. "Why, you're *that* Miss Dix, aren't you? I say, congratulations on your tournament win. I'm an absolute fan, really I am. I never miss an issue of the USGA's newsletter. I recently came across that article about—"

"You golf?"

One would not have thought a crude appeal to vanity would prevail. But Vivian had judged the aging secretary well and knew she lived for two things: her employer and amateur golf. This theory had been bolstered by the assortment of small trophies, photographs, and golfing memorabilia sprinkled about the secretary's otherwise immaculate desk.

"Poorly," Vivian quipped. "But I love to watch. And that course at Van Cortlandt is lovely, isn't it? That par 5 on the second hole is a doozy!" She laughed lightly. "But look at me, taking up your time. Honestly, Flo said he would inform you of our little pop-in, but that's Flo for you, juggling ten balls only to drop eleven."

Miss Dix appeared to waver. "The Van der Beecks?" she repeated, perhaps swayed by the family name, which was only disreputable to insiders. Even gossip was kept strictly in-ranks.

"I'll tell you what, just have Flo put his head out here for a moment, and I'm sure he'll recall the whole ghastly thing. It's a financial matter, you see, and Father sent us over to, well, you know, help the cause." Vivian was betting that once Ziegfeld recognized them from that night in Babs's dressing room, he'd be curious enough to usher them in.

The whiff of remuneration must have carried the day. "Well, I suppose it won't hurt to disturb him briefly," Miss Dix said with a wink, pushing back from the desk and clicking across the outer office to a large mahogany door. Cracking it, she thrust her head inside. The girls heard the murmur of voices, and then Miss Dix stepped back as the scowling visage of Florenz Ziegfeld Jr. emerged.

"Just what is the meaning of—humph." The tirade was cut short before it was begun. His gaze snapped from Vivian to Viola, then slipped sidelong to his secretary, who had returned to her desk. Trusted or not, it appeared he wished to keep this matter private, even from her. "Ah, yes, the Van der . . ." He faltered on the last syllable.

Vivian came to the rescue, striding forward to whisk through the door. "Nice to see you, Flo. Come along, Viola," she called back, just before disappearing into the inner office. "You know how Flo hates to be kept waiting."

Once inside, they pulled two chairs up to Ziegfeld's desk, which was piled high with all manner of papers, designs, photos, and broadsides. On the wall behind him, a montage of framed prints paid homage to the female form. And there, on the corner of his desk, was the infamous gold-plated telephone, the ultimate symbol of his excesses, much like his hundred-word telegrams, the cost of which was rumored to run into the thousands. No matter how broke Ziegfeld was, he never stinted, giving him a reputation for luxury that packed theaters even as it drained his bank account. It was ironic, really. The instinct for glamour that had ensured his success might well prove his undoing.

And to look at him, the strain was taking its toll.

"You're the girls from the theater."

"That's right, Mr. Ziegfeld," Vivian said, dropping the "Flo" act. "We're friends of Babs's," she fudged. After all, they'd all been fond of each other, hadn't they? "I'll get right to the point. I know you're a busy man."

Vivian's straightforward approach seemed to be paying off. The tightness around Ziegfeld's oddly smushed-looking features relaxed, and the faint, smirking smile he habitually wore settled in more firmly. With a weak, square chin and wide-set eyes, Ziegfeld had a face destined to remain behind a desk, not in front of the cameras and crowds his starlets favored. Oh, certainly, he had charisma, a restless vitality—though at the moment, he seemed genuinely *unwell.*

As if on cue, he coughed and tucked a finger into his collar to stretch it out, craning his neck. "I like your style, kid. Okay then, get to the point."

Vivian gathered her thoughts. The trick was to interrogate Ziegfeld in such a way that he'd be likely to play along. A pretense was called for, and what pretense would be more plausible to the famed opportunist than self-interest?

"You see, Mr. Ziegfeld, the thing is, Babs brought us in on your little *secret*," she began, with just a hint of innuendo. If he had been blackmailed, there must be *some* kind of secret, and it stood to reason that Babs was involved. "I just want you to know, it's safe with us."

She held her breath, waiting to judge the effect of her words. The hint of a smile evaporated as Ziegfeld leaned back in his chair, knitting his fingers together.

Bingo.

"I see. What did you say your name was, kid?"

"Vivian."

"Look here, Vivian, if you're looking for money, you've come to the wrong place. I'll be lucky to scrape together Babs's ransom."

"Nothing like that," she assured him. "As I said, we're merely friends of Babs's. We're only concerned for her welfare."

The smirk was back. As Dr. Weber might have observed, it was human nature to project one's own motives onto others, and Ziegfeld had clearly marked her as an opportunist, just as she'd intended.

"Of course, of course," he humored her, gesturing broadly with an open palm. "Please, how can I help."

Now for the tricky part. So far, Ziegfeld's reactions tended to vindicate her theory that he'd been blackmailed. But how to get him to divulge the *nature* of his secret, now that he thought they were already in the know? She'd start with the only real clue they had—Babs's baby. After all, that was the most likely secret Ziegfeld was hiding.

"Well, to begin with, perhaps you can clear up a little matter for me. Did you give Babs that little keepsake?"

He frowned. "Keepsake?"

"The baby rattle."

The frown persisted. Vivian judged it to be genuine. No, Ziegfeld hadn't sent Babs that rattle, lovingly inscribed. But did that mean he wasn't the father of her baby? Vivian decided to gamble boldly. It meant divulging a piece of sensitive information, but maybe she could startle the truth out of him.

"Let's be frank, Mr. Ziegfeld. We know about Babs's baby."

The man reared back in his chair so comically, Vivian was hard pressed not to laugh.

"Baby!" he cried. "What baby?" Almost immediately, the machinations of his mind played across his features as he appeared to put two and two together. Vivian chewed her lip. Whether or not Ziegfeld was actually the father of Babs's child was beside the point. He clearly did not know of Babs's illicit progeny which meant it was not the secret that had been used to extort him—if any such secret existed. Yet, Ziegfeld's reactions seemed to validate that blackmail was involved, and Vivian's gut told her there was a secret.

So, what was it?

"That little fool," he muttered angrily as he settled back into his chair. "For God's sake, who's the father?" His eyes snapped up to Vivian's.

She raised one eyebrow.

"What are you—are you saying—the very idea!"

"Your reputation does precede you, Mr. Ziegfeld."

"That's never how it was with Babs! My heart is spoken for."

The obvious implication was that his wife, Billie Burke, had claimed this dubious prize, but from the papers, Vivian suspected another contender—Marilyn Miller, the one starlet who seemed to defy his attentions. Regardless, Vivian found she believed that when it came to Babs, it wasn't like *that*.

Her smile was equal parts charm and chagrin. "Forgive me, Mr. Ziegfeld. I couldn't help playing with you just a bit."

Relief seemed to disarm him somewhat. He'd battled rumors of infidelity all his life. A note of admiration, even affection, entered his eye.

"You're an interesting creature, Miss Van der Beeck. Vivian, wasn't it? Any interest in the stage?"

A wave of revulsion gripped her stomach. What had happened to the girl who could not get enough of Marlene Dietrich's eyebrows?

"I'm afraid not, Mr. Ziegfeld," she managed, mastering her face so that it betrayed only gratification. She was scrambling for her next move when Viola piped up unexpectedly.

"I suppose you really *have* made your fortune turning trinkets into treasure," she mused, absentmindedly. All the broadsides plastered about the room had put her in mind of poor Babs, just a girl from the country, heading for the big city with nothing but a suitcase full of dreams. My, that was nice, wasn't it. Oh, where was her journal when she needed it?

Ziegfeld lunged forward, planting both hands on his desk.

"Luigi can't know about that! For God's sake, he'd have my hide. And the statue is a perfect replica—why, it's *better* than the original!" he eased back into his chair, hands spread wide in appeal. "Where's the harm, I ask you? What is gold but an idea? As far as Luigi is concerned, the debt is paid!"

A *statue*? And a fake gold one, at that! So, this was Ziegfeld's secret?

Still reeling from the revelation Lala had shaken loose, Vivian fumbled for words. "Now, now, Mr. Ziegfeld, far be it from us to extort you like that horrid blackmailer." She used the word purposefully and was satisfied to see it vindicated in his face. What to ask now? She had a million questions, but before she could cue up even one, Ziegfeld burst out, as if still unable to contain himself.

"And of course, the rat could be anybody." He flung a hand up only to bring it down on his desk, ruffling his papers. "Who's even *heard* of Betty Boone?"

Betty Boone? Vivian certainly had not. And what did Miss Boone have to do with the identity of the *blackmailer*? But Vivian didn't want to appear too ignorant, not when she was supposed to be in Babs's confidence. Still, maybe one question . . .

"Were there, well, any other clues as to who might have perpetrated this dreadful ploy?"

She knew the words were a mistake the moment they left her mouth. The showman seemed to snap back to himself, perhaps recalling that she and her twin already knew too much. Why should he further illuminate them?

His eyes narrowed. "Look here, Miss Van der Beeck," he said, back on formal terms, "let's quit this game. Why don't you just tell me what it will take to keep you quiet. I can't have the police nosing about this little matter, for obvious reasons." He gave her a strained smile and blinked. Truly, it seemed he was almost spent. "Do we understand each other?"

Clearly, she would get little more from Ziegfeld now that he was on his guard. A shrewd man by nature, stress had made him careless, but the gig was up.

"Well, there is one small thing you can do for us."

"Name it."

"Perhaps we're not too different Mr. Ziegfeld. We both want to keep the police out of our business, even while we sometimes need their help," she began, with the quirk of a smile at the corner of her mouth.

The smile he returned seemed a tad less weary.

"Go on . . ."

"My sister and I are curious sorts, you see, and we'd rather like to observe the ransom drop. Not to interfere, mind you. Just call us . . . amateur sleuths. Now, the police have told us about the drop, but naturally, they can't divulge the details. Do you suppose you could fill us in? As I said, we promise not to interfere."

Perhaps honesty truly was the best policy—or at least the most effective.

"Is that all?" he said, his relief palpable. "Grand Central, next Friday, 5:00 p.m. sharp—rush hour. The exchange will be made near the newspaper stand in the main concourse."

"And Babs? She'll be released?"

Ziegfeld nodded wearily. "That's the idea. What choice do I have? I'm calling in every favor I've earned over the last decade for this one. It's that or . . ." he fixed them with a rueful gaze, "pay the piper."

Out of the corner of her eye, she spied Lala, jerking her head toward Ziegfeld's cluttered desk. What was she getting at?

"You know, Mr. Ziegfeld," she fussed with her purse nonchalantly as she rose before fixing him with her most direct gaze, "you can trust us to help. Do you truly not know who this dastardly blackmailer might be?"

Ziegfeld snatched a large sheet of paper off the pile on his desk and thrust it into her hands.

"Take it, please. For God's sake, if you can nab the rat, I'll be the first to thank you. It's bound to be someone who has taken up with her, but beyond that, your guess is as good as mine. And I can't ask the cops to go snooping around. I don't need that trouble, not with Luigi breathing down my neck."

Vivian gazed down at the broadside, advertising in bold strokes the debut of Betty Boone to the Follies stage. So, this is what Lala had been getting at.

She returned his gaze with a wink. "Understood, Mr. Ziegfeld. Your business is our secret. We'll see ourselves out."

CHAPTER TWENTY-FOUR
Two and Two

"**S**ometimes a dream is just a dream. You know, Lala, you really ought to stop eating Cookie's pimento-stuffed puff cakes before bedtime." Vivian gave a final flourish to her nose, snapping her compact shut and placing it on the vanity before rising to turn.

But Viola was unmoved. "I tell you, Viv, Grampy was rambling about gold something-or-other. I remember because he brought it up just as we were waving to that nice Egyptian fisherman who had captured seven silver sardines with his net of jeweled barnacles. And then the cows started mooing in harmony, and I woke up forgetting all about the details until yesterday in Ziegfeld's office when he mentioned that gold statue, and then it hit me!"

"*What* hit you, Lala."

"There's a secret in *our* history too, Viv," Viola whispered. "And it has something to do with gold—a statue or maybe an icon or a coin, or perhaps a lump of some sort."

Even Viola had difficulty making sense of the words that had come out of her mouth. When she was channeling information, it was all a jumble.

Vivian took three steadying breaths. "Fine, Lala," she said, smoothing down the close-tailored, pin-striped dress she'd chosen for the day. There was nothing for it but to humor her twin. And who knew—if it turned out that once again Lala's gibberish held the seeds of genius, Vivian would be the first to admit it. "We'll look into these deep, dark family secrets as time allows. Does that satisfy you?"

Viola was silent for a moment. There was something else she wanted to talk to Viv about, something that concerned the sergeant, but she didn't know how to broach it. "Have you given any thought to the preacher's library book?" she asked instead, feeling somehow both relieved and ashamed. Really, she ought to have a little more backbone.

"Oh, that," Vivian said distractedly as she turned to pass out of the bedroom, leading the way downstairs. She'd scheduled another meeting with the tenants, and it was bad form to be more than, say, twenty minutes late to one's own debrief. "I imagine he's just interested in the subject, Lala. Preaching must be dreadfully boring. Maybe fireworks are a kind of hobby on the side."

"A hobby, hmm," Viola repeated, slowly, as if trying to find the idea persuasive. Vivian felt a pang of remorse. Regardless of whether Pastor Rathbone was a legitimate suspect, she wanted to distract her twin from the subject. Lala was so suggestible of late, and that dratted book had filled her head with all manner of nonsense.

"Perhaps the tenants will have some ideas about it," Vivian added, comfortingly. "We've only got Madame Koslova and Mr. Sharma today, but beggars can't be choosers." Privately, she held out little hope that the spiritualist would prove cogent, and Mr. Sharma's advice was invariably cautious to a fault. But it wouldn't do to cancel the meeting for low attendance, what with Mr. Sparrow being so busy all the time, and Miss Sphinx preoccupied with her newest cycle of epic poetry. And then Dr. Weber had positively let them down at the last minute, citing some nonsense about how Thanatos had driven a former patient to the edge of ruin. As for Al, he came and went as he pleased. Vivian hoped to make them all regret their absence by holding a smashing good meeting that Madame Koslova would hold over their heads.

The worthy madame was already settled in the parlor when the twins arrived, wedged into the needlepoint chair that Mother had been trying to get rid of for years on the sly, only to be thwarted by Auntie at every turn. The girls had just taken their seats on the sofa when Mr. Sharma rushed in.

"Sorry to k-keep you waiting," he said, hurrying over to sit close to the fire in the "junior chair," a holdover from Father's youth. Mr. Sharma was always cold.

"Oh, that's alright, we only just got—ow!" Viola tucked her wounded toe behind her other foot, giving her twin a rare frown.

"Not to worry, Mr. Sharma," Vivian said graciously. He needn't know they too had been late. A little remorse made for good conversation. If he were trying to appease them, Mr. Sharma would exert every effort to be useful. "Now, let's do get started with what time we have left," she added for good measure.

Honestly! Viv had been an absolute tyrant lately, ever since that young secretary had put her off Sergeant Kowalski. Whatever fears Viola had entertained as to the betterment of her twin's nature had been laid to rest.

"Fine," she said, so pointedly that all three of them turned to stare.

"Are you feeling quite alright, Lala?" Vivian deigned to inquire.

"Quite," she said, resolved to keep her helpful comments to herself, thank you very much.

"Right then," Vivian breezed on. "Let's begin with a recap of our extremely illuminating interview with Mr. Ziegfeld. Lala, would you care to fill us in?"

"No . . . thank you," she managed, torn between the pleasure of being asked and her determination to make a stand.

Vivian proceeded to pick up the slack, creating such a captivating account of the visit to Ziegfeld's office that Viola rather forgot that she'd been there. It was a trial harboring resentment. Perhaps Vivian would notice soon and put the matter to rest.

But at the moment, Vivian's thoughts had strayed far from any consideration for her twin's feelings. "Therefore," she finished, "we can categorically remove Mr. Ziegfeld from the list of potential fathers for the *love child*, as Lala would say—although, in the process of eliminating him, we have completely transformed our understanding of the case."

Madame Koslova grunted loudly, giving them a start. "So, the old rascal is being blackmailed, after all," she said with an appreciative cackle as she shifted to the other hip in her endless quest to ease the discomfort of her voluminous frame. "Already, the secret doctrine reveals its nature and its workings," she added, cryptically. "The wisdom of the first hermetic philosophers teaches us that all barriers are illusory."

For a moment, all were silent. Then, Mr. Sharma cleared his throat. "Perhaps the g-good madame will elaborate?" he said in his neat, civil voice.

Madame Koslova groaned as she shifted hips. "The truth will out."

"Indeed," Vivian agreed, anxious to herd the conversation toward more fruitful pastures. "But I suppose it wouldn't hurt to help it along. Let's revisit what we know, shall we?" The gathered acolytes nodded their approval. "Firstly, and perhaps most importantly, Babs has been the victim—not of a simple snatch racket—but of a blackmail attempt. Ziegfeld was intended to grasp the *real* threat, encoded in the language of the ransom note, and the real threat was that Luigi would find out about the fake statue. Ziegfeld would then, quite literally, pay "the piper," that being Luigi's former nickname. Although this was a blackmail attempt, the *appearance* of a ransom situation would both give him a pretense for complying with the demands encoded therein, and also lend his efforts a public urgency."

"But at first there *was* no ransom demand," Viola objected, forgetting her resolve.

"Quite so, Lala. The initial object of the blackmail effort was to gain some non-monetary benefit from Mr. Ziegfeld which was presumably communicated after the fact."

"Betty," Viola murmured, recalling Ziegfeld's words. "Who *is* this Betty Boone?"

"That is the first question," Vivian said with a nod. "Which leads invariably to the second." She looked about at the circle of faces, unable to resist a little pedagogy.

"Who c-c-cares about her," Mr. Sharma said quietly.

"Precisely," Vivian agreed. "Who cares enough to see her planted on Ziegfeld's stage, yet is greedy enough to be ultimately unsatisfied with her debut—"

"—as payment for whatever sins Mr. Ziegfeld has c-committed," Mr. Sharma finished, his voice subdued.

"Do you suppose it's just greed?" Viola pondered aloud. "That changed his mind, I mean. If he was greedy to begin with, why wait?"

Vivian shrugged. "Remember, Lala, we don't know for certain that the blackmailer is a man."

"We don't?" Viola had completely forgotten her grievances in light of these developments.

"Desperate circumstances call for desperate action. And Mrs. Appleby has many mouths to feed."

"Viv! You're not suggesting—"

"That she might have engineered her own daughter's abduction?" Vivian raised an eyebrow, lending a sinister aspect to her angelic visage. "Not without her daughter's help."

"Viv!" Viola cried again. "Now you're just playing with us. You don't honestly think she would do such a thing!"

Vivian didn't, but the integrity of the investigation demanded rigor. "What I think is beside the point. It would be folly to rule them out, Lala. A detective's creed is a brutal one—as is the subject of her craft."

"The c-c-criminal mind knows no gender," Mr. Sharma agreed solemnly. "But so far, if I am not mistaken, er, no clue c-connects Miss Le Roy or her family t-t-to this Betty who has taken Miss Le Roy's place on the stage. And, ahem, as you said, Miss Vivian, if the mother desired money to feed her family, why should she make the ransom demand after the f-f-fact?"

This was more than Mr. Sharma had ever said at one go, and Vivian felt chagrined at having underestimated the diplomat. If Mrs. Appleby simply had mouths to feed, why begin with a concession to replace Babs on the Ziegfeld stage? Unless it was a strategy to get Babs back home where she belonged. It wasn't half bad as a theory, except that Vivian could hardly imagine Mrs. Appleby conceiving such a ploy.

"Well reasoned, Mr. Sharma. There's the deceased brother, Eddie, as well. Perhaps he was the brains of the operation until he met his untimely demise." She frowned, paused, and made an entry in the small notebook she had brought to the meeting. She'd quite neglected the matter of the hit-and-run, which might or might not have been accidental. "Regardless," she said, looking up, "let us conclude that Babs and her family are second-tier suspects. Now, there is the matter of the statue."

Madame Koslova had been so quiet that Vivian suspected she was napping. Suddenly, she hefted out of her slump, her eyes popping wide.

"Ah, the statue! Mr. Ziegfeld is an alchemist, as surely as Paracelsus of old. Turning trinkets into treasures—this was the phrase that prompted his reaction!" She chuckled, huskily. "The old devil has repaid a debt to his little gangster friend with a statue, a valuable statue that had no value at all."

"A fake," Vivian agreed. She couldn't help but hear the note of admiration in the good madame's voice, of one charlatan for another, she supposed. In the name of philanthropy, Madame

Koslova knew how to run a good con. Who better to plumb the depths of the criminal mind? "Mr. Ziegfeld is suspected to have taken loans from all sorts of disreputable sources. And Luigi isn't the sort of creditor you default on. The question is, who wanted this Betty Boone to have a shot at stardom *and* knew about the statue? Answer that and you have your list of—"

"Blackmailers and k-k-kidnappers," Mr. Sharma cut in. Gracious, he was outspoken today, though it struck Vivian, somehow, that each time he opened his mouth, he intended to say something else. Now and again, she caught him eyeing her as if he were rather working up his nerve.

"So that's why he was lurking around," Viola burst out, slapping one delicate hand to her forehead, then looking around at their questioning glances. "The Chief Weasel," she explained. "I mean, Mr. Macavoy. I'll bet he's the blackmailer." She looked down, frowning as she thought of the ransom note. "Though he hardly seems to have the poet's touch," she mused, quietly.

"Based on what, Lala," Vivian said, trying to keep the exasperation from her voice. She knew perfectly well that her twin had relented from her pique and had no desire to ruffle her feathers. After all, soothing Lala's feelings detracted from her line of inquiry.

Viola considered summarizing the general plot details of *The Wind in the Willows* for her twin's benefit, seeing how Vivian had likely stricken the book from memory. Viv frowned on talking animals.

"Remember, I saw him at Luigi's place," she began instead, determined to sound reasonable. "And I'm nearly certain he was listening in on our conversation. And . . . didn't Sergeant Kowalski say he's in the gambling racket? What is blackmail, I ask you, but a colossal gamble? And. . . and. . . " she grasped for some acceptable way to suggest the gangster's resemblance to the leader of all the baddies. "And he has a crafty face," she finished, lamely.

Vivian was a tad disappointed that Lala's reasoning was so thin. She'd hoped to add another solid suspect to her list. Still, it wasn't entirely outside the realm of possibility that this Macavoy was involved.

"Excellent, Lala," she said, though it was mostly to atone for being so beastly in recent days. She wasn't sure what drove her to it. "We'll see what else we can find out about this Macavoy character. We still have several days until. . . " Her gaze drifted to Mr. Sharma, who did not *appear* to be listening. Their plans to shadow the ransom drop had been discretely omitted from today's agenda, and the diplomat was sure to disapprove. "We have nothing at all planned for the next few days after lessons," she said instead. "And while we're at it, we can look into the matter of Frankie Morgan. I've completely left him out."

Viola frowned, thinking of the *something else* she'd wanted to talk to Viv about. It was high time they involved the police in their investigation. But it was painfully obvious that this whole sergeant matter was clouding her twin's judgment.

"See here, Viv," she began quietly, shooting a look at Madame Koslova, whom she was fairly certain had actually fallen asleep this time. Mr. Sharma was still sitting in his miniature arm-chair, staring into the flames as if to divine the tortured reasoning that spurred men to evil deeds. Viola hoped to keep this con-versation between her and Viv. "You did promise to bring the sergeant into things if our leads didn't go anywhere. And even though, well, they have gone somewhere—well, that's rather the point, isn't it? Don't you think this could all get a little danger-ous?"

"Now, Lala, haven't we fended perfectly well for ourselves so far?"

"But think of The Fair Lady, Viv," Viola persisted. "Now, I know you think the sergeant overplayed his hand, but I tell you, I was positively relieved when he landed that punch. You don't know what would have happened," she finished grimly, determined to make her point.

Vivian knew perfectly well where all this was headed. Lala thought she was avoiding the sergeant because of some foolish romantic notion. Nothing could be further from the truth. Oh, perhaps Vivian had softened to his peculiar charms at the first, but he had revealed his true character that day at the police station. A ladies' man, through and through. No, thank you. Vivian van der Beeck was nobody's mark.

"Very well, Lala," she said, watching with satisfaction as her twin blanched with surprise. "We'll visit the sergeant tomorrow and come clean about everything *except the drop.*" Vivian could see the best way to lay her sister's fears to rest was to meet the thing head on. Besides, she had already concluded that official resources would be needed to ferret out the blackmailer's identity. "But I absolutely won't lose this chance to spy on the ransom exchange, and you know perfectly well that the sergeant would be obligated to dissuade us."

This concession was more than Viola had hoped for, and she nodded mutely before mustering a reply. "Well, alright, as long as we can take Mrs. Lurch with us for the actual spying expedition. I won't accompany you without our Juno to guide us." She narrowed her eyes, breathing evenly through her nose to stave off fainting.

Really, Lala was becoming harder to control by the day. "Fine," she said, judging herself beaten. "We'll bring Mrs. Lurch in on the ransom drop, but if she ends up forbidding us to go, I'm telling you right now, I won't miss it, I simply won't."

The standoff continued a moment longer, then Viola extended her hand. "Deal," she said, the knot in her stomach easing so that she felt dangerously lightheaded.

"Well, I suppose that's it for today," Vivian said, rising, only to find Mr. Sharma fixing her with a troubled gaze. She cleared her throat. "You've both been frightfully helpful. And Madame

Koslova, perhaps you can fill the others in on our revelations. I just know they'll appreciate it."

The good lady had woken and was struggling to extract herself from the needlepoint chair. Mr. Sharma was still gazing at Vivian, his lips parted as if he meant to speak. Drat, she hoped he hadn't overheard their plans about the ransom drop. The man was a dear, but he took entirely too much upon himself.

But the day was still young, and they had time for another go at the attic before resuming afternoon lessons. High time to wrap things up.

"Oh, let's do," Lala said, picking up on Vivian's train of thought as if she'd spoken aloud. The one benefit of Lala's obsession with this family curse nonsense was that she couldn't wait to get back to the attic. "I've just stumbled upon an old crate and I'm simply bursting to see what's inside."

CHAPTER TWENTY-FIVE
A Meeting of the Minds

Sergeant Kowalski wore a crisp white shirt, sleeves rolled up to the elbow, first button undone against the loose knot of his navy-blue tie. The white of the shirt, ironed and spotlessly clean, contrasted with the tan of his skin and the untidiness of his hair, the natural wave of which defied order, despite its attractive trim. His coat was hung over the back of his chair, and his vest was taut against the broadness of his chest as he leaned forward over his desk to clasp roughened hands in the space between piles of paperwork.

If Vivian noted all these details, it was only long habit that drove her to it. A true detective left nothing unobserved.

"What can I do for you ladies," he said with careful civility that was slightly at odds with a glint of interest deep in his brown eyes.

"I believe the question is what we can do for you," Vivian said evenly, relieved to find she was quite unmoved by the roundness of his voice, which had the strange quality of being almost like a touch. Yes, clearly she had sorted herself out most admirably. There was nothing that a bit of effort, coupled with iron-clad reasoning, could not accomplish. "Or, perhaps, to be fair, what we can do for each other."

She could not help but feel a small flash of heat at the unintended nuance of these words, which the sergeant appeared to register as well, his gaze deepening almost imperceptibly.

But then, he leaned back in his chair, clasping hands behind his head, and the moment was broken. "I see. Please, proceed."

Vivian cleared her throat. "Yes, well, I believe it's our turn to offer quid pro quo. Some new information has come to our attention, and it seemed to Lala that law enforcement might be best positioned to help us follow up our leads. But first . . ." She reached into her purse to take out Babs's little black book and slid it across the desk, inadvertently brushing the sergeant's hand with the side of one finger. "You should have a look at this."

Vivian had been mulling over how best to broach the subject of the book without revealing their impromptu search of, *ahem*, the crime scene. She wasn't about to lie, but she was equally loath to come clean. She hoped Sergeant Kowalski's utilitarian brand of decorum would prevent him from prying.

He flipped through a few pages, then looked up. "Interesting," was all he said, though his eyes said considerably more.

Viola was feeling rather like a fifth wheel, or more technically a third wheel since there was only the three of them. She could see that all sorts of conversation was being had between the two of them with the language of the eyes, which was a favorite device of hers in novels. But she was sure Vivian would disown the exchange if pressed.

"I suppose we also ought to tell you about the rattle," Viola blurted suddenly, surprising them all. She hadn't expected to involve herself, but the words had come out all on their own. "Because of the initials," she explained in a quiet aside to Vivian, as if she'd interrupted a joint session of Congress.

"Yes, the initials," Vivian repeated, narrowing her eyes slightly at her twin. "I was getting to that. You see, Sergeant Kowalski—"

"Adam. Please, call me Adam."

A thrill went right down the back of Vivian's legs. Her eyes snapped back to the sergeant's, only to find him eyeing her steadily, as if to gauge her reaction.

Or Adi, she thought, before she could help it. *I could call you Adi.* But "Adam" was heady enough for the occasion, and she steeled herself against its charms.

"As I was saying, *Sergeant Kowalski,*" she repeated, mortified that her cheeks still betrayed her, "Lala and I happened to see a keepsake in Babs's room when she first joined us that may prove illuminating."

The sergeant's brow betrayed his own discomfiture, if ever so slightly. He chewed the inside of his cheek, a gesture that threatened to undo all Vivian's hard work. On she plunged through her account of the rattle with its inscription and initials, its disappearance from Babs's room, and the presumption that it had been mailed to the family farm for safekeeping—though she kept their visit to the farm to herself. And there was no need to divulge that the rattle was in their possession.

"Of course, we surmised that the initial *B* must stand for Babs, leaving the F for the name of the suitor," she finished, torn between regret and satisfaction. Her rebuff had clearly left him unsettled, but the determination had not left his eye.

He flipped again through the pages of the book, then looked up cannily. "Frankie Morgan?"

"I see you've already hit upon it," she said, appreciatively. It certainly hadn't taken him long to parse the contents of that book.

"It's the only one that fits," he agreed. "Right, okay, I'll see if we can bring him in for questioning. Will that be all?"

The flash of disappointment caught Vivian off guard. Was he quite ready to be done with them? "Oh, we're just getting started, Sergeant," she said firmly, quashing the feeling at once. "You see, we ran into Mr. Ziegfeld the other day."

Vivian had spent considerable time pondering their visit to Ziegfeld's office, attempting to massage it into an acceptable frame. Surely the sergeant would not approve of their expedition, not after the *Luigi incident*. But more importantly, there was sensitive material involved, facts they had promised Mr. Ziegfeld that they would not reveal. And yet they must broach the issue if they were to marshal official resources to the cause. How to impart that the showman had been blackmailed, that this was not a simple ransom situation, without landing him in hot water?

How much could she rely upon the sergeant's discretion?

Eyeing him closely, she made her way through the account like a burglar stealing in under cover of night. If their eyes had been talkative earlier, now they were positively voluble. There was the darkening of the brow as the sergeant processed that the twins had not merely "bumped into" Ziegfeld, the intimation of worry and frustration, astonishment at the revelations of their interview, the digestion of certain, necessary omissions, and at the last, a reluctant but strangely profound flash of admiration in his gaze that sorely tested the back of her knees.

"Interesting," was all he said.

But Vivian could see that it was done, that the sergeant knew precisely enough what had happened, that he'd evaluated what he could and could not reveal and had already begun to plan what came next. He clearly understood that approaching Mr. Ziegfeld directly on this sensitive matter would only alienate a valuable asset and detract from their progress on the case. It was more than she could have hoped for, and it struck her suddenly that she had never had so much success communicating with anyone but her twin. An aura of intimacy hung over the exchange, which she could neither bear to be with, nor bear to part with.

Really, Vivian, she schooled herself, *get a grip.*

"As I see it, Sergeant," she concluded, "we must get to the bottom of this Betty Boone nonsense. We must evaluate who might have knowledge of the, well, *object of interest.* And now that we know the ransom is the blackmailer's *second* demand, we must proceed with great caution. Clearly, we are dealing with someone greedy at best and desperate at worst. Lastly, we must reevaluate what relevance the father of Babs's child may have to the case as the illicit pregnancy clearly was not the true object of the blackmail."

The sergeant nodded, matching her step for step. "I'll still bring Frankie in. Would you like to observe the interview?"

Somewhere in the silence between them, a "we" had emerged without her even knowing it. She was now a partner on the case. Vivian almost yearned for the firm footing of combat.

"Oh, yes, well, that would be, um, lovely," she fumbled, fuming at the lameness of her reply.

But the sergeant seemed to neither notice nor care. A new note had entered his eye, a gleam of deep interest, of excitement, though whether it was about the case or something else, Vivian could not say.

"I'll put a patrolman on it today. With any luck, we'll have him in some time tomorrow. I'll call you then with an update," he said, rising to escort them to the door. Her breath caught at the brief, light pressure of his hand on the small of her back.

"Thank you, Sergeant," she managed. "We look forward to future developments."

CHAPTER TWENTY-SIX
Twins and Triangles

"Look, Viv, here's *another* set of identical twins—Clara and Catherine, born in 1710 on Ann Street only to die in each other's arms of smallpox when—goodness, Viv, they were only twenty-one."

"Lala, you truly are becoming downright morbid," was Vivian's sole reply. They were sitting in the front hall, on the bench beside the mansion's only telephone, just in case the sergeant called with news of Frankie.

"I'm simply following the clues," Viola complained. She didn't know what Viv had against this particular mystery, except that it concerned their own history, which had more tragic chapters than a gothic novel. As the reigning family historian whose job it was to maintain custody of the diary, it was Viola herself who had entered the deaths of poor Uncle Teddy and Uncle Titus into the rolls when they'd jumped from the rooftop of the Ansonia Hotel, not long after their unexpected sabbatical from the ivied halls of Columbia. "Come to think of it, *they* were twenty-one too . . ." she mused now, half to herself.

"What was that, Lala?" Vivian said, but Viola could see she was miles away, probably strolling on some imaginary riverbank with you-know-who—though that was more her own style. Viv was most likely explaining to herself how perfectly blasé the sergeant was, how immune she was to his charms, which amounted to the same thing. If only life were like a book, each moment a scene captured for all eternity that one could visit and revisit at one's leisure. Why did everything have to change?

"Never mind, Viv."

Viola knew better than to bring up Teddy and Titus, though it irked her of late that the family never spoke of them. They'd been twins too, and only five years the senior of Vivian and Viola, more like brothers than uncles, really. They'd romped around the mansion half-wild, despite the combined efforts of Cookie and Mrs. Lurch, and an occasional outburst from Auntie Lavinia. Even Father had treated them more like sons than brothers after Grampy had absconded with the mystic, seeing how Teddy and Titus were only a year old at the time, and Father was all of fifteen. It was hard to imagine Father in that role, though—of, well, a *father*. He'd left for the war when she and Viv were only four, and after that things were . . . different. But by all accounts, he'd been both a father and mother to the rambunctious twins, their real mother, Grampy's beloved Pearl, having died giving birth to them.

Sometimes, history was a burden.

These days, Father was lucky if he could look after himself. "Maybe you're right, Viv," she said, sitting upright on the bench where she'd been slouched against her twin's shoulder, thumbing pages. "I'm probably just disappointed that nothing was in that old crate except for a bunch of dusty old china."

"Not every treasure hunt uncovers a trove," Viv said, reassuringly, trotting out another of her original phrases. At least this one was not ghastly, and she was so trying to cheer Viola up, as only Viv could. Viola flashed on that morning's tête-a-tête down at the police station—for that's exactly what it was—an envelope of secrecy descending on the sergeant and her twin that sealed Viv away from her entirely. And to think, it was Viola herself who had driven Viv back into the—well, not exactly *arms*, but at least the thoughts of her would-be lover! She simply couldn't bear to see her twin unhappy. But what if Viv's path to seventh heaven lay over the trampled remains of Viola's heart? Oh, what would she do without Viv to guide her through the swamps of her lamentable existence? The very thought pierced her deepest soul.

Viola was just turning her head to dash tears from her eyes in pained solitude when she was saved from the mire by the bell.

"I'll get that," Vivian said, hopping up, just as lah-de-dah as you please. "The Van der Beeck residence. Yes, oh, hello Sergeant. Yes. Hmm, I see. We understand. Indeed, thank you." She deposited the mouthpiece back in the cradle. "Come along, Lala. We're expected down at the station within the hour."

Viola sighed, rising to fetch the hat and coat that were already hanging on the stand by the door. Well, on the bright side, Viv might never own up to her feelings. Knowing her twin as she did, Viola thought that as likely as not.

Viv did so abhor emotionality.

It was a quiet afternoon at the precinct with half the desks empty and only a few miscreants and malefactors wandering about in cuffs or being booked and fingerprinted at the front counter. The typing pool was a sparse affair as well, Vivian noted, with no sign of the dark-haired Jane. Most likely, she maintained poor work habits, which would be consistent with her general disregard of workplace ethics.

"There you are. Come on back, ladies," Sergeant Kowalski said with a wry smile, popping his head out of one of the rear offices. "I'm just finishing up a little filing and then I'll take you down to the gallery."

His head disappeared from sight, and Vivian led the way through the maze of desks to the office, her sister trailing behind truculently. Truly, Lala had become morose of late. Vivian might have discretely disposed of that dreadful Hawthorne tome, but with Lala's photographic memory, it would have done little good.

"I say, Sergeant Kowalski, it's positively lonely in here this after—"

Vivian felt the blood drain from her cheeks and hoped that spot of rouge she'd applied before leaving the house was up to snuff.

"I'll be with you in just a moment," the sergeant said over his shoulder with a flash of that smile, the one that Vivian had already divined meant he was happy. "Jane's just helping me finish up my, er—" he shot the secretary a sidelong grin, "assignment, I guess you could call it. You ladies can have a seat if you like."

Vivian sank into one of the hardbacked chairs against the wall. She was feeling peaked today, now that it came to it.

". . . and then, the old curmudgeon asked me if Detective Broderick had ever fudged the record on any of his leads!" From her crouch before the file cabinet, Jane swiveled to flash the sergeant her pearly whites. Vivian supposed some would find her charmingly mischievous. "As if I would know!" the secretary cried.

Sergeant Kowalski's smile was chagrined. "That old rivalry has legs, I'm telling you, Jane. It's all I can do to get him to shut up about it—" His look of chagrin deepened as his gaze flashed over to the twins. "Oh, sorry, ladies. Shop talk."

"Please, don't think of it," Vivian said, arranging her dark, wool skirt over her crossed knee. "Shop talk away." Her voice sounded scratchy to her ears, and there was some tightness around the larynx. She'd have to ask Cookie for a hot mug of ginger lemonade when she got home. It was the season for colds, and she couldn't afford to get sick.

The sergeant seemed to note something in her voice as well and studied her for a moment before returning to his work. Vivian passed the next few moments trying to decide which order of business was most pressing, tracking down Betty's associates, compiling a list of possible confidants for Ziegfeld's dirty secret, or planning the exit strategy for the ransom drop, in case anything went awry. But it was difficult to focus with the patter of conversation between the sergeant and his little helper buzzing in the background. Really, and it was he who had asked them to come down to the station when they had more than enough work cut out for them organizing the attic.

"Thanks, Jane," the sergeant said, finally, rising to dust off his hands. "That should keep him off my back for a while."

"All in a day's work," Jane returned with that pirate's smile of hers that just screamed Adi, even if the word had not passed her well-rouged lips. Cherry Punch by Maybelline, if Vivian was not mistaken. "Let me know if you need anything else," the secretary tossed over her shoulder as she whisked out the door.

Vivian barely suppressed a roll of the eyes. *Need anything else,* indeed. Either the sergeant was a scoundrel or a clod, and the fact that he seemed to be neither was beside the point as it didn't concern Vivian in the least. Why, whatever the sergeant got up to in his free time was entirely his own affair, though one did hope it would not impair his professional judge—

"Or . . . do you need another moment?"

Sergeant Kowalski had placed one hand on her shoulder and was bending down to peer into her eyes with concern.

"Excuse . . . me?"

"Are you feeling okay? Can I get you some water?" he persisted with such earnestness that something seized up around the left side of her chest. *Yet another side of him,* she thought with a flash of despair.

"Oh, she's just been putting in dreadfully long hours," Lala said with gentle confidence, taking her by the elbow to rise as one. "Nothing a good witness identification won't fix, isn't that right, Viv?"

Thank goodness for twins. Vivian glanced over into her sister's eyes in a moment of sympatico. It wouldn't do to have the sergeant thinking she was starting to slip just because she'd drifted off for a moment. There were simply *too* many things to think about.

"Thank you for your concern, Sergeant, but my sister is quite right," she said, with ghastly brightness. "Shall we?" She negotiated the small of her back well outside the reach of Sergeant Kowalski's capable hands, lest he think she still needed support. He needn't have cause to doubt her when she'd only just earned his professional respect.

"The gallery is just down the hall, here," the sergeant said, his voice sounding flatter than it had in the presence of the sparkling Jane. But Vivian could neither confirm nor deny this as all her attention was bent on negotiating a pile of boxes that absolutely *cluttered* the hallway.

He led the way through the double doors and down the long hall, passing the mug book room they'd entered last time, and turning in at the next door. Inside, several chairs were set up before a wide window that looked upon a second chamber, inside of which a line of men were already assembling.

"Please, ladies, have a seat," Kowalski said. Vivian settled beside her sister, then risked a sidelong glance up to where the sergeant stood, running a hand through his tousled hair and gazing fixedly ahead. His face looked different in profile, the jag in his once-broken nose giving him a boyish aspect so at odds with his air of maturity that her throat closed up again. He must have felt her gaze, because he turned suddenly to meet it, a pointed, exasperated determination in his eyes that did rather drive one's heart into one's throat. It was all she could do to force it back down into her chest where it belonged, what with that tightness around the larynx.

She was on the point of saying *something* when Viola burst out with, "That's him! Babs's afternoon visitor!"

Vivian's gaze snapped back to the tinted window as she rose to her feet. Five men stood in the chamber, shoulder to shoulder, the last few just now turning to face the window. And there, smack in the middle, was the bewildered, glum visage of the young man who had stormed out of Babs's room.

"That's him, alright," Vivian affirmed, all other thoughts vanishing from her mind. She turned to the sergeant. "Is that Frankie Morgan?"

Something lingered in his eyes a moment longer, but then he sighed, his brow lifting as he turned back to the window. "Take a moment to be certain, Miss Van der Beeck. Is number three definitely the man you saw in Miss Le Roy's room, and later at the theater?"

"Absolutely, Sergeant. Without a doubt."

He nodded once, gaze still fixed ahead as thoughts worked across his features. She wanted suddenly to say *something* again, though just what this something was quite escaped her. It was so unlike her to be at a loss for words that it only strengthened her resolve to be more vigilant about her health. More sleep, fewer needless distractions, and perhaps a few of Mistress Dubois's constitutionals would put her right, she was sure of it. But when those brown eyes finally slid back down to her face, their gaze still speculative, her throat once more rebelled, and her heart pounded in her ears. If pressed, Vivian would have said the sergeant was making up his mind.

"Right, then," he said, pivoting toward the door. "If that's our man, then let's get him into the interrogation room."

CHAPTER TWENTY-SEVEN
Pressure Points

Frankie J. Morgan had once been the sort of ne'er do well who could sell sawdust to lumbermills, as the saying went, a dubious gift that ran in the family. Most notably, Morgan's second cousin, thrice removed, was serving life in Sing Sing for successfully selling (among other public assets) the Brooklyn Bridge, the Statue of Liberty, and Grant's Tomb to individuals who could not be trusted to tie their own shoes. Of ostensibly Welsh descent, Morgan's line boasted an illegitimate ancestor at every juncture of the family tree. Indeed, unbeknownst to anyone (including Morgan himself) he was of one ninety-eighth Lenape descent, his great-great-great-great-*great*-grandmother having had a fling with a Dutch interloper while hiding from marauding settlers during the Wappinger War of 1643. Said interloper had taken up residence with the Lenape tribe to escape prosecution for breach of contract in the construction of a windmill, having recently booked passage to the new world on a *fluytschip* named *The Oak Tree.*

Sound familiar?

Had Viola known the shifty-eyed Morgan with the movie-star looks was a distant relative, she surely would have entered his name into the diary. After all, kin was kin.

The twins had barely taken their seats in the corner of the room when Detective Flannagan barged through the door.

"Blast it, Kowalski, what's this about a witness changing her tune on that Broadway hit-and—" He drew up, midstride, staring at the twins as if haunted by a recurring nightmare. "What are *they* doing here?"

The sergeant closed the file he'd been reviewing as he sat at the interrogation table, waiting for the suspect to arrive.

"I've asked them to sit in on the interview, sir," he said, turning to place an elbow on the back of his chair. "They observed the suspect on two occasions and may be able to assess the veracity of his statement."

This matter-of-fact reply appeared to deflate the detective's overblown sails. He huffed and puffed a moment longer, then harumphed his assent, pulling out a chair to sit beside the sergeant.

"Good thinking, good thinking, Kowalski." He rubbed his hands together. "Now, who have we got here."

The sergeant flipped the file open for their joint review. "Minor rap list, petty chiseler, mostly cons and scams. Seems to frequent gambling joints and has been scooped up during some busts. Nothing big enough to put him in the mug book."

"Right. And you say he was spotted at the theater on the night of the abduction?" Flanagan shot a hunted look over his shoulder at the twins and cleared his throat. "Reliable ID would you say?"

"Absolutely. And the suspect visited Miss Le Roy's apartment approximately a week before the abduction. They appear to have argued."

Still eyeing Vivian and Viola surreptitiously, Flanagan brightened up at this tidbit, like a child at Christmas.

"Good, good, well, bring him in."

Sergeant Kowalski gave a nod to the officer stationed beside a second door, who cracked the door to slip out of sight. He reemerged a moment later, Frankie skulking behind as if he were the victim of a bum rap. The officer pulled out a chair on the opposite side of the table and Frankie sank into it, shooting daggers for looks at all parties—including Vivian and Viola, whom he clearly did not recognize.

"Frankie J. Morgan," the sergeant began, looking up from the file. "That your name?"

"What do you think, copper?"

Frankie scraped his chair back and thumped one boot up onto the table. From where she sat, Vivian could see his smirk clearly, fouling a face that might have been considered handsome were it not for the bile that animated it. Not malevolent, no, that was too strong a word. Rather, Vivian detected bluster in his injured air, fear, deep in his eye, as of a cornered animal who might be forced to draw blood.

As for Sergeant Kowalski, Vivian could only see his back, broad and muscled beneath his vest, and the ungovernable brown curls at the nape of his neck. Without looking up, he gave the stationed officer a quick nod, prompting him to lean over and knock Frankie's boot off the table.

The sergeant leaned back, lacing fingers behind his head. "Look, Morgan, we've brought you in to ask you some questions, but if you can't behave, we might start to wonder if there's more going on. Are you going to cooperate?"

Frankie tried to glare at the sergeant, but whatever he saw there made him blanch, and his eyes slid away. He shrugged. "Sure, yeah. Whatever."

Kowalski unclasped his hands and leaned forward again. "I understand you know Babs Le Roy."

"Sure, doesn't everybody?"

The sergeant raised his head to fix Frankie with a stare.

"I mean, yeah, okay, we used to be a thing, back when she was hoofing at Delaney's."

Vivian and Viola locked eyes. Delaney's! Where Babs learned to dance down in New Jersey, back in the early '20s, long before she was a star.

Frankie went on to confirm exactly this in response to the sergeant's rapid succession of questions, phrased so casually that the man could not help falling into the rhythm of the conversation. Occasionally, Frankie seemed to check himself as he detailed his relationship with Babs over the years, from their early courtship to their falling out, to his fruitless attempts to win her back. After her success, she was beyond his reach—until recently, that is. The last, troubled chapter of Babs's life had prompted him to believe he might try again. Vivian recalled her impression of the man who had stormed out of Babs's room, overcoat thrown over his arm, face anguished, not hunted and sly as she saw it now. The story rang true, as far as it went, though Vivian couldn't help but reflect on the adage, *the best lies contain the kernel of truth.*

"So, Morgan, tell me about the gambling."

The sergeant's question seemed to take Frankie by surprise, and the detective gave a grunt of approval. That he trusted his young associate to run the interrogation was clear, but as she snatched glimpses of the detective's face in profile, Vivian had to begrudgingly admit that he seemed to be tracking each maneuver, his sharp gaze revealing a depth of thought that surprised her. Perhaps he *wasn't* just a bumbling old fool.

"Sure, yeah, so I play the tables a bit. Who doesn't?"

"Ever play the tables at Macavoy's place?"

Frankie straightened up from his slouch. "Name the place I ain't played," he said with a snicker.

"It's down on Broadway, just across from the New Amsterdam, as it happens. That help refresh your memory?"

"Oh, yeah, yeah, I think I been in that place."

Sergeant Kowalski perused the file for a while in silence. When he spoke again, his casual tone was gone. "Think long and hard before you answer my next question, Morgan. Turns out you've been observed on multiple occasions at Macavoy's place. In fact, the word on the street is that you've been going there for years, that you and Macavoy are on first name terms, although he doesn't always seem happy to see you. We've had a cozy little conversation so far, but here's the thing. You can't be sure what I know and what I don't, and if I catch you out in a lie, the detective and I will have to assume you're up to your ears in kidnapping, maybe assault, maybe blackmail, who knows what else. Bad stuff, Morgan, stuff that could put you away in Sing Sing for a long time. So, tell me, Frankie, how much money do you owe Macavoy?"

The change in the sergeant's demeanor was so striking, so dynamic, that the room seemed suddenly robbed of oxygen. At least it did to Vivian, whose heart hammered in her throat. For the first time, she was beyond questioning the whys and wherefores of her body's reaction, the heat in her face, the ache she could not place, let alone name. It was like she was living in a stranger's body, someone she could not control, someone she did not know.

Frankie licked his lips. "Look, copper, you got it all wrong. Sure, okay, Macavoy and me, we got history. Maybe I racked up a few debts when I was playin' his joint." He snatched a look at the sergeant, then went back to tracing the wood grain in the tabletop with one tobacco-stained finger. "I racked up, oh, I don't know, maybe a grand? Yeah, something like that. But Macavoy, he knows I'm good for it. I'm working on it."

"Well, that's very interesting, Morgan. What kind of work?" The sergeant's casual tone was back, but the threat that underlay it had not budged.

"This and that." Frankie left off tracing eddies in the wood and shrugged. "You might not know it to look at me now, but I got a way about me, sometimes, like a switch I can turn on and off. Macavoy sends me out to reel in suckers who might drop a buck or fifty at his table before they know what's what. That kind of stuff." He shrugged again. "Harmless."

Sergeant Kowalski had closed the file. Vivian did not need to see Morgan shift under that steadfast gaze to know how it felt.

"Harmless," the sergeant repeated, as if the word tasted sour. "Well, that tells me quite a bit about you right there, Morgan. Any other harmless work you're doing for Macavoy?"

The panic in Morgan's face was now evident. "What do you mean? Sure, yeah, sometimes I'm the go-between in a tricky, er, negotiation. All business stuff, maybe not strictly legit, but you know how it is. Ain't you coppers got bigger fish to fry? Why you pickin' on some poor sop who ain't got two nickels to rub together?"

Frankie was working himself up into a real lather, but just when it seemed he might break, the sergeant stood, briskly snatching up the file and tapping it on the table.

"That'll be all for now, Morgan. But we may need to chat again, so don't think about any long trips." He looked over at the officer, still standing by the second door, and yanked his head. "You can take him, Murphy. Make sure you have his new address before you let him go." He leaned forward, knuckles on the table, hand still clutching the file. "No more moving around for a while, huh, Morgan? Pretty sure we're going to need your assistance again."

Frankie got shakily to his feet, looking back and forth between Kowalski and the detective, who also stood now, leaning slightly back on his heels, arms folded over his chest.

"Nice to meet you, Mr. Morgan," Flanagan said wryly. "As the good sergeant said, don't be a stranger."

"Yeah, yeah sure, nice talking to you." Morgan looked over his shoulder as the officer nudged him through the doorway, his expression befuddled and vaguely alarmed. As the door closed behind them, Flanagan turned to his sergeant.

"I give him twenty-four hours," he said with a chuckle.

"Tops," Kowalski agreed with a quick grin for his superior. As he turned toward the corner where the twins were just rising,

Vivian noted how invigorated he looked, then glanced away, arranging her purse on her elbow. "Do you ladies have any insights to add?"

Vivian steeled herself to meet the sergeant's gaze squarely. "He's told the truth, as far as that goes. At least Lala and I could find no discrepancies in his account." She turned to her sister with a quick nod to affirm this presumption. "But he's clearly not telling the whole truth. I assume you've put him at liberty in order to set a tail on him?"

"Very astute, Miss Van der Beeck," Sergeant Kowalski said, with a soft note under his voice that seemed meant only for her ears. Honestly, her imagination was getting out of hand. If she didn't watch out, she'd be reading gothic novels before the month was out. "He's rattled enough to go straight to the source," the sergeant added, turning to his boss.

Detective Flanagan nodded with a pride that struck Vivian as fatherly. "This Macavoy angle is the best we've got. There's nothing to put him in the frame just yet, no contact with Miss Le Roy that we know of, but he's had shady dealings with just about every crooked boss in town. Who knows, he might just be fixing Ziegfeld up for some kind of payout. That man's no angel."

Vivian's eyes snapped to the sergeant's, but he gave a discreet shake of the head. No, of course, he hadn't told the detective about the little matter of blackmail. Vivian had known Sergeant Kowalski all of one month (four days and approximately 16 hours), but already it struck her as inconceivable that he would break his word. It appeared Flanagan had puzzled things out all by himself, which meant he was not a buffoon, after all.

"Right, then," the detective said with a sudden, brusque nod for Vivian and Viola. He clapped the sergeant on the shoulder. "Keep up the good work, Kowalski. And nice work on those files. High time, high time."

And with that, he was out the door.

The mention of the recently organized files put Vivian in mind of the spunky Jane, but suddenly, she felt too tired to get worked up about it all. *Face facts, Vivian Van der Beeck,* she told herself, sternly, *you're downright infatuated.* It had been utter foolishness to deny it, worse still to maintain such obvious airs to the contrary. Truly, she was a fool. There was nothing for it but to admit her feelings. What a relief to see the whole thing with clear eyes. How could she apply the proper remedies if she could not diagnose the disease? It would take more than Cookie's ginger lemonade to set her right.

She must swear off the sergeant altogether, as surely as the reformed drunkard forsakes his booze.

"May I see you ladies out?"

Vivian inclined her head and led the way out of the room, placing Viola as a buffer between her and any courteous actions performed by the sergeant's muscular hands. See, right there, that was part of the problem. Why think of them as muscular? Why think of them at all? She must strike the problem at its source. This conundrum quite occupied her down the hall and into the station proper, where business had picked up considerably.

"Kowalski, that witness on the hit-and-run just came in to amend her statement. You want I should show her to your desk?"

The clerk who had shouted this from the front desk jammed his thumb toward a timid-looking woman of, say, thirty-five who huddled into her dreary gray coat like a mouse shrinking into the shadows.

Kowalski nodded in the affirmative, still guiding the twins toward the front doors that were positively swinging now with the comings and goings of the criminally afflicted.

"That would be a witness on the Appleby hit-and-run, by the way," Kowalski said in a low voice, bending to Vivian's ear as they walked, side by side. Just how she'd managed to lose her buffer escaped her—but *there* was Viola, straggling along behind, clearly distracted by the cacophony around them. What had the sergeant said? Vivian was keenly aware of his presence beside her, which was almost worse than having his hand on the small of her back, the way his height seemed to engulf her in a proprietary way that she could not quite fathom. As if she could only grasp her own true dimensions in his presence. And *drat*, here she was getting flushed again, and they were still twenty paces from the doors.

Then suddenly, Lala was at her other side, drawing her off by the elbow to whisper in her ear. Vivian was on the point of thanking God for twins when she saw the true object of her sister's efforts—not to save Vivian from her own folly, but to discretely point out the tall, slender man dressed all in black who was just now entering the crowded foyer.

"That's him, Viv. Babs's preacher!" Viola whispered excitedly.

"Naturally, Lala," Vivian replied, slightly vexed, for though she wanted to nip Lala's fixation in the bud, there was something unsettling about the man's appearance, a terrible glint in his eye that seemed to cut through the noise and jumble of the crowded station like the voice of God itself. Honestly, she was becoming as susceptible as her twin. "Remember, Lala," she said, reasonably, "he's going to be helping with the ransom drop, as a neutral intermediary, and that's tomorrow, come to think of it. He's likely here to strategize, that's all. You do get carried away sometimes."

But Viola wasn't listening. As Pastor Rathbone pushed through the station door, it was like a page turned in her mind, and she recalled that scene from *The Scarlet Letter* when Reverend Dimmesdale first presents "an apprehensive, a startled, a half-frightened look—as of a being who felt himself quite astray and at a loss in the pathway of human existence." But this man wasn't Dimmesdale, no, not at all. Rather, the image that struck Viola was that of Roger Chillingworth's face, lit by the fire of a passing meteor "with an awfulness that admonished Hester Prynne and the clergyman on the day of judgment." The rest of the line cycled through her mind, like a vulture circling the heavens: "then might Roger Chillingworth have passed for the archfiend, standing there, with a smile and scowl, to claim his own."

"But he *isn't* smiling," Viola murmured confusedly, "and he *isn't* Chillingworth . . ."

"Snap out of it, Lala," Vivian hissed with a shake of her sister's arm. "I can tell you're up to your old shenanigans. Stop gaping, or people will stare." She hated to be stern, but strong medicine was called for when Lala suffered one of her fits—though truth be told, her sister wasn't the only person fixated on the preacher's face. The mousy woman at the front desk shrank as well from his distasteful visage, though she looked the type to jump at any old shadow.

"I guess that's it, for now," said the sergeant, his voice like a firm hand, pulling her out of her thoughts. His gaze was like that too when she looked up, prompting her to wonder how he could touch her without ever lifting a finger. "We'll let you know if anything comes up."

It was her signal to leave and his signal to turn back to his desk where the mousy woman in gray would soon be escorted. But somehow, the moment would not let them go as Vivian warred with the longing inside her—and the panic it inspired.

"Yes, well, Sergeant, thank you for everything."

Yet still, they stood. The lights and movement and bustle of the station, the noise and voices and typewriters clacking—all faded to sepia against the pulse and heat of the sergeant's actual presence, his nearness, the quiet force of his gaze.

"Vivian, I—"

"Oh, look, Viv," Viola said, coming up beside her with her head still turned toward the timid, middle-aged woman who was even now being escorted to the sergeant's desk. "I think I know her from the flower shop on Broadway."

This detail, plucked from the minutia destined to plague a memory like hers, was so mundane it broke the moment, and

Vivian stepped back, as if released from a spell. The soft depth of the sergeant's voice, her name on his lips, the reality of its utterance—it all conspired to undo her completely. She barely had strength to tear her gaze away and turn toward the station doors.

"Do come, Lala," she managed, unable to muster any parting words for the sergeant, unable to do anything but flee. "We must get back by teatime or Cookie will have our ears."

CHAPTER TWENTY-EIGHT
Best Laid Plans

The morning of the ransom drop dawned with all the fire and brimstone of an old-fashioned sermon, at least that's what Viola thought as she and her twin sat on the widow's walk above the east wing, watching the sun rise. They'd hardly slept a wink, what with nerves and a touch of indigestion brought on by Cookie's Irish spiced beef (obtained for pennies on the pound, thanks to her *kleine romantik* with Otto, head butcher at Neumann & Sons). Vivian had brooded as they tossed and turned in their respective beds—until Viola tucked in beside her twin, certain that Viv suffered not from the effects of fatty beef but from les problèmes d'amour.

Even now, Vivian looked to be a thousand miles away. Perhaps Viola could distract her with an exercise in inductive reasoning.

"As I see it, there's nothing to say Frankie and Babs didn't, well, *you know* when he was trying to win her back, Viv. He had opportunity and intent." Viola lingered over her ten-dollar words. "Therefore, we can't rule him out as the father of the love child, and he could easily have purchased the rattle with the proceeds of his ill-gotten gains. He might even have known about Ziegfeld's statue, assuming Babs's somehow knew about it. Pillow talk."

Vivian straightened up from where she leaned against the railing in her pink, woolen pajamas. "Well reasoned, Lala," she said, approvingly, "although I might offer a fact to counteract our budding theory. Timing, Lala, timing. Babs fell on hard times *after* conceiving the child—indeed, it's leaving the limelight in secrecy that tanked her career. And it was only after this setback that Frankie felt emboldened to, as he put it, try again. Still, one can't rule out the possibility of an occasional dalliance rather earlier. He's not a bad-looking fellow, though there's something simply off about him in the eyes. But there's no accounting for taste."

Viola had known Viv would approve of placing Frankie near the top of their list, though privately, she held out little hope he was their homme de mystère. He was simply too much like one of the Chief Weasel's ferrets or stoats, hardly the type to mastermind real devilry.

"Speaking of the Chief Weasel," she said, forgetting herself, "this Macavoy fellow is almost certainly involved, wouldn't you say?"

Vivian ignored her twin's childish lapse. Lala *had* hit upon the likely wrongdoer, if only by dint of whimsy.

"Absolutely. It's a shame we haven't any facts yet to establish opportunity or motive, but my instincts tell me he's our bad apple."

Just what differentiated Viv's "instincts" from her own "flights of association" escaped Viola, but it hardly mattered. For the moment, Viv had forgotten her woes. Viola yawned, covering her mouth with a delicate pat.

"Do you suppose we ought to go dress, Viv? We're going to be simply dragging today, you know we are. And Mistress Dubois simply won't move on from the Reign of Terror ever since you put her onto it. Really, Viv, that was a beastly diversion."

Vivian rose, shaking dust from her pantlegs. "We'll just have to humor her, there's nothing else for it. We simply cannot raise anyone's eyebrows today, what with Mrs. Lurch taking us to our 'ice cream social' later this afternoon." She gave a wink. "Good old Mrs. Lurch. You know, I think she's looking forward to our expedition. That woman is a dynamo."

Beneath her prosaic exterior, Mrs. Lurch was much more a dynamo than either twin knew. Born on an Alberta ranch in 1875, Mary Lurch had run her father's household from the age of 9 when her mother succumbed to prairie madness and took up residence in the chicken coop. But it was not until Mary met and married Constable Lurch of the Royal Canadian Mounties that she really bloomed, fleeing under cover of night to pursue excitement and intrigue in the Queen's service—for approximately three months. The newlyweds were charged with enforcing attendance at the Battleford Industrial School, by force if necessary, removing children from their tribes and homes in pursuit of the government's Policy of Aggressive Civilization. This simply would not do. After defecting from the Mounties, the Lurches led a small, failed skirmish against their former ranks, then lived with the Cree, learning the ways of a vanished time. When Mr. Lurch died of tuberculosis at the age of 42, Mrs. Lurch caught the next wagon train for New York, arriving just in time to answer an advertisement for "superintending housekeeper of a large household" in the *New York Herald*. The rest, as they say, was history.

If Vivian knew nothing of Mrs. Lurch's warrior heart, still, she glimpsed something of its spirit in those slate gray eyes, narrowed beneath the brim of a tidy straw hat.

"Strictly a surveillance operation, girls," the housekeeper said now as they rattled down Fifth Avenue on the same double-decker that had taken the twins to the library the week before. "If it's on the horizon, it's at your front door. Holds for dust storms, stampedes, and a posse of bandits, so keep your distance. Understand?"

The twins assured her they understood perfectly well, and the remainder of the ride passed in silence. They disembarked and walked the last few blocks to the Grand Central Terminal in the gloom of late afternoon. Secretaries and shop girls hurried past businessmen with fedoras mashed low over their brows. Laborers in flat caps and overalls leaned against buildings, congregating to share a smoke. It was life as usual in the city, except for a pall that struck Viola just now as she glimpsed the signs of destitution here and there, crumpled forms sleeping in doorways, the cries of an apple seller, hawking his wares to deaf ears, a sense of desperation that dogged even the well-heeled, hurrying their steps. As Mrs. Lurch led the way across the intersection at Madison Avenue, Viola glanced up to see the newly completed Empire State Building in the distance, towering over its neighbors, its aspect ghastly by virtue of sheer proportion. It seemed indifferent to the suffering around it, spire lit against the gathering dark like a terrible beacon, calling the world to its knees.

"Lala, do watch your step," Vivian groused as Viola bumped into her back. "You heard what Mrs. Lurch said—we've got to look sharp."

"Oh, quite," Viola said breathlessly. She wiped her eyes to dash away her grim vision but could not help a sidelong glance back up at the shining tower. It did so remind one of *something*, though just what escaped her. "The scaffold," she muttered, "that's it," as an image arose of Reverend Dimmesdale, supported by Hester as he mounted the scaffold in the public square, prepared to declare his guilt to all the world, to bare his *own* breast where inscribed upon his flesh was his own, dastardly *A*. "Do you suppose it's the spiced beef?" she wondered aloud as they disappeared into the shadow of the viaduct over the terminal entrance. The effects seemed rather long-lived.

"What are you going on about? Hurry along, Lala. We can't be spotted as we're taking up our position."

They moved down the ramp into the main concourse, where the famous mural of celestial constellations stretched above, drawing Viola's eyes heavenward once more. This did nothing to help her state of mind, nor did the last rays of the sun, slanting through high windows as if to herald a choir of angels. Viola's mutterings got so bad that Vivian was forced to pause long enough to give each of her twin's cheeks a firm pat.

"Snap out of it," she hissed, "or Mrs. Lurch will pack us off for home. You know she can't abide a liability."

That seemed to do the trick, and before long, they were established among the crowd of commuters in the passage beyond the concourse, opposite the newspaper stand with its long counter, crammed with customers. Rush hour was at its height, and the twins had to bob and weave to gain fleeting glimpses of the stand and its contents—newspapers, magazines, and periodicals, bulging from the out-slanting rack above as well as racks that ran the length of the counter. Vivian scanned the scene for any glimpse of the sergeant or his likely associates, visited by a pang of guilt almost as keen as last night's gastronomical distress.

Sergeant Kowalski would not be pleased to find them here.

But that was neither here nor there, as it was none of his business. Vivian tried to strike from her mind the memory of his steady gaze as he'd said her name, Vivian—and just as vainly sought to quell the wondering of what words might have followed had Viola not stumbled upon their moment, breaking the spell. *That's it, Vivian Van der Beeck,* she told herself firmly, *you'll simply avoid him altogether until you're able to act in a rational manner.* Such stern self-talk did help somewhat, but all the same, as Vivian kept one eye trained for the police, she couldn't help noticing it was anticipation, not dread, that guided her eye.

"*There,* Viv, look at that woman. Don't you think it could be Babs under all those clothes?" Viola discretely pointed at an overdressed twosome that was lurking to the side of the newsstand, a man standing behind a woman clad in several layers of coats, her face swathed with a scarf. A lock of blond hair peeked out from beneath her beret. Her arms were clasped behind her—*or are they bound,* Vivian wondered as she watched the man at the woman's back scan the crowd, only his eyes visible above the scarf that likewise hid his face.

"Oh, it just has to be, Lala. I do hope it all goes to plan." The excitement of it all was rather getting to Vivian, and her pulse raced.

The man inched closer to the corner of the newsstand, the bundled-up woman keeping pace in a kind of terrible lockstep. The scoundrel must be dragging her sideways by means of her bound hands, or perhaps he had a firearm, wedged into her back. A flash of outrage surged through Vivian, surprising her in its ferocity. How dare he use her so? How dare they *all* use her, all the pawing, fawning, grasping multitudes, all the men dressing her up and setting her down, all the players and users, trying to stake their claim.

"Good lord, Vivian," she whispered softly to herself, "get a grip."

"Steady, girls, steady," Mrs. Lurch said from where she stood behind. Just then, a slender man in a long black coat passed in front of the couple, obscuring them for a moment. Pastor Rathbone! It had to be. Had he passed the package? And would Babs truly go free? Surely, the police had considered the possibility of duplicity, had likely planted men among the crowd. But just as surely, the blackmailer must have anticipated this.

A portly lady in front of the twins straightened from her stroller, and they lurched aside just in time to see their suspect inching backward. He pushed the bundled woman away from him and turned to flee.

"So, he is going to let her go." Vivian breathed with a relief that surprised her almost more than her burst of rage had done. She was becoming entirely too sentimental.

"But Viv, *look*," Viola cried. Just as the blackmailer vanished into the fray, another man in a plaid overcoat with upturned collar whisked by, grabbing the woman-who-was-surely-Babs by the elbow to drag her into stride. She stumbled along with mincing steps, writhing now, struggling to get free, but in the space to a few moments, her abductor had already grappled her almost to the arched entry that led toward the tracks.

"Not one step, girls," Mrs. Lurch warned, but when they whipped around, her gaze was sharply considering. She pursed her lips as the twins held a collective breath. "Alright," she sighed. "But follow me, and no shenanigans."

They pressed through the crowd, Mrs. Lurch leading the way with a stolid calm that belied their speed. Babs and her abductor were just disappearing around a corner, the gently down-sloping passages branching off toward various train lines. If they lost sight of her for a moment, they'd likely lose her for good. But Mrs. Lurch's trapping instincts guided them truly, and before long, they were following the man and his quarry through a gate and onto one of the train platforms.

"Oh, *drat*," Vivian said, drawing up short. "I do believe we've lost them!"

Tracks ran along both sides of the platform, thronged with people embarking and disembarking from trains on either side. Babs could be on either train already, or well down the platform where it disappeared into shadow. The train on track 32 whistled, signaling its imminent departure, and Mrs. Lurch picked up their pace, guiding them through the moving throng of commuters as the three of them peered from side to side, craning heads to look inside the lit windows. The train to their left lurched into motion with a whine and clang, giving Viola such a jolt, she nearly lost her balance.

But it was Vivian who *did*.

As the train door began to close, a burly fellow jogged by, so intent on hopping aboard that he hardly noticed Vivian, jostling her from behind. She tottered, arms windmilling as she sought to regain her balance near the edge of the tracks where she'd been walking, too focused on the train's interior to notice her position. But now, as the train pulled away leaving only space behind, there was nothing between her and the drop to the tracks below except Mrs. Lurch's sturdy grasp as she whirled about to catch Vivian by the elbow just before she fell.

"Steady, now," the housekeeper said, as if she were soothing a spooked mare. "Easy now, there's a lass."

Vivian leaned forward over her knees to catch her breath as Viola came up from where she'd straggled behind.

"Oh, *Viv*, are you quite alright?"

But Vivian hardly had breath to answer, not so much from her narrow escape but from what met her eyes not fifty feet down the crowded platform.

Sergeant Kowalski.

He was peering into the windows of the remaining train as they had done, moving from car to car. Vivian was just on the point of turning to flee when he looked suddenly back toward the gate, almost as if he'd sensed her presence, and for the briefest of moments, their eyes met.

"I do believe it's time to go, Mrs. Lurch," she breathed, grabbing her sister's hand as she swiveled toward the gate and broke into a brisk trot. *Drat*, she thought again as they hurried out, *I'm really in for it now*, though she wasn't sure if she was thinking about the talking to that would surely follow or the small burst of joy that had entered her heart on meeting the sergeant's eyes.

CHAPTER TWENTY-NINE
Messages and Mysteries

It was not until they were in their pajamas and reclining on Vivian's bed, faces slathered with a thin layer of complexion clay, that the twins finally turned to their post-surveillance debrief.

"Poor Babs," Viola said, fiddling with the silver rattle that did so remind her of Babs's tragic past. "A baby should be an occasion to celebrate life's sweetest pleasures, don't you think? Babs's baby seems to have brought her nothing but woe."

Vivian was lying on her side on the toile bedspread, head propped in her hand. "Really, Lala, I should think that you more than anyone would appreciate that it's not the *baby* who has brought on her woes. Think of Hamlet. Babs is the victim of her own tragic flaws."

"Character is that which reveals moral purpose," Viola acknowledged in a rueful tone, quoting from Aristotle's Poetics. "Or lack thereof. Do you suppose Babs has a noble enough nature to be considered a tragic heroine? I rather think Aristotle might have left her in the chorus."

"Quite right, Lala. You know they were all terrible snobs. Well, regardless, Babs has rotten taste in men. Take this Frankie character—a player, through and through. And Luigi?"

"I don't know," Viola hedged. "He seemed positively *loyal* on the subject of 'his Babs.' I thought it was touching."

Vivian snorted derisively. "Luigi Luciana is touched in the head. Don't you remember his ghastly behavior?"

Clearly, Viv's pride was still smarting over being caught off guard by a riot. A diversion would not go amiss. "Speaking of that, I never told you what that Macavoy fellow was up to over by the potted palms, did I Viv? He was *lurking*, there's no other word."

For once, Vivian was receptive to her sister's flights of fancy. After all, it was only logical to assume that the second malefactor who had snatched Babs away at the train station was Macavoy's accomplice. A brilliant example of the divide-and-conquer tactic. The police would be forced to choose between chasing after the gangster and his package of loot or recovering the kidnapping victim. And if all went well, Macavoy would have *both* prizes.

"Tell me every detail, Lala. Macavoy is up to his ears in this. And if Frankie is indeed the baby's father, he could easily have told him about the statue. As you said, *pillow talk.*"

Viola was only half-listening as she wedged a fingernail into the side of the rattle. "You know, Viv, I think there's a latch here," she murmured.

But Vivian had already climbed out of bed and was headed toward the bathroom. "Oh do leave off that, Lala. You can tell me about Macavoy's lurking while we towel off our clay."

After a fitful night of dreams that plagued both girls, Vivian woke to find that the sergeant had phoned the night before.

"Twice, pet," said Cookie, who had overcome her fear of telephones to venture up from the kitchen and cautiously raise receiver to ear. "Told him it were bloody too late to be calling, I did. Gor! That's exactly what I don't care for. These newfangled devices is always barging in."

"But did he leave any *message*, Cookie," Vivian asked again, fighting the squirm in her stomach. She imagined the sergeant might have had some choice words to deliver on the matter of her recent exploits.

"Only that he had some information for you, dear," Cookie said with a doting smile, hands tucked under her bulging apron. They were chatting in the kitchen where Vivian had come for a snack before breakfast. Bad dreams always left her peckish. "He said you should call down to the station," Cookie recited, as if taking great care over each word. "And that you weren't to think of venturing off on any larks. No, that weren't it." She frowned, looking down. "He had a fancier word, didn't he." She brightened, looking up again. "But it comes to the same thing. Seemed like a decent skin, and he were keen to talk to you, blessed but he were." Turning in one sudden, deft movement, she whipped off her bonnet to swat Fagin, the half-wild tabby, who was scrounging for crumbs on the counter. "Get away wit' ye, blasted wretch!" she screeched, sending the cat yowling off the counter and across the battered wooden floor. Mashing her hat back on with floured fingers, she turned to Vivian with a bemused smile. "Now, what were we saying, pet?"

"Nothing, Cookie, thanks for the scones," Vivian said, thoughtfully, draping a napkin over the plate.

Upstairs, she kicked the bedroom door closed behind her. It was only 6:00 a.m., but already they could hear the distant tinkling of piano keys. "Is he at it already?" Vivian looked up at the ceiling as she placed the plate of scones on the desk, then headed to her closet to rummage for her warmest robe. "It's getting downright frigid lately. I do so hate winter." She popped her head out of the closet to glance at her twin, who was still slumped in bed, an open book propped up on her chest. "You aren't fooling me for one moment, Viola Van der Beeck," she chided. "For one thing, that dratted tome is upside down, and for another, you detest Trollope. You're brooding about those silly dreams, aren't you."

Viola shrank even further into her pillows. "You had to *be* there, Viv. It was ghastly, with all those corpses crowding around, poking me with their bony fingers. Why, one fellow had his head tucked under his arm." She let the book collapse forward, onto her chest, and looked up at the ceiling. "That must have been Edwin Van der Beeck. The diary says he was decapitated by the fourth floor when he stuck his head out of the elevator door."

"If I've said it once, I've said it a thousand times, Lala—a dream is just a dream. Now, let's take our scones upstairs, shall we? Nothing like one of Mr. Sparrow's impromptu concerts to snap you out of this mood."

Viola mulishly complied, taking the robe that Vivian offered and putting on a brave face as she rose. She hadn't told Viv *half* the horrors of her dream, which had ended with a rousing sermon by none other than Grampy Cornelius himself. The dear old man had raved about the *manetuwak*, spirits of a sort, destined to dog the heels of the wicked, and then he'd veered off on a tangent about the power of seven to reinvent the world order by uniting heaven and earth. And all the while, corpses seated to her left and right were nodding their heads sedately as if it all made perfect sense—except for poor Edwin, of course, who had nothing to nod but a bloody stump. Viv would say it was all utter rot, and Viola was inclined to agree, especially now that the details were fading, leaving only the afterimage of Grampy dressed in deerskins as he railed behind a pulpit made of mud, twigs, and beaver pelts.

Or was it Grampy? If the portrait in the library was any indication, the nose was all wrong.

"Hurry up, Lala," Vivian nagged, plate in one hand as she opened the door with the other. "I think he's playing 'Das Veilchen.' I say, he's in a rare mood this morning."

They hurried down the hall toward the main staircase that wound upward through the center of the house, like the twisted spine of some fantastical beast. Mr. Sparrow's chambers were on the third floor, tucked away at the end of a long, dark corridor.

Vivian handed her twin the plate of scones as they came abreast of the door, where the strains of Mozart were unmistakable.

"Hold these," she said, then rapped twice upon the door. "He's moved on to Number 13 in B-flat major, and you know what that means. His budding romance has been nipped in the bud."

Viola thought that heartlessly glib, but she supposed her sister was right. Mr. Sparrow only played Mozart when he needed to forget. The complexity soothed him.

"No pestering him with questions, Viv," she whispered with quiet urgency as the young man opened the door, his handsome face somewhat splotchy about the eyes.

"Lala! Viv!" he said with a brightness made touching by his dejected state. "To what do I owe this pleasure?"

Vivian brushed past him, raising the plate of scones. "We thought we'd bring you a morning snack, Mr. Sparrow, and listen to a bit of—" She broke off at the sight of Mr. Sharma, seated cross-legged on the divan. He'd been rather cramping her style, of late, what with his stuttering inquiries that never seemed to get anywhere. But that was unkind of her. Really, why couldn't she be just a little more like Lala? "Oh, hello, Mr. Sharma," she said, giving it a try. "Great minds think alike."

The little man nodded sagely, looking up to guppy a moment or two before falling silent.

"You don't mind, do you, Mr. Sparrow?" Viola was saying, still standing by the door, dismayed by the tortured ruminations cavorting in the pianist's deep blue eyes. "Mozart," she said with a sympathetic shake of the head. This is the closest she would get to prying.

But good old Mr. Sparrow never had anything to hide.

"Her name is Alice," he said with a sigh, meeting her gaze with the trust of a small child who had lost his favorite stuffie. "And she's perfect."

"Not quite," Vivian said. He glanced over his shoulder as she settled into the Empire Revival chair and laid the plate on the coffee table. "If she were perfect, she'd hardly have put you into such a state, Mr. Sparrow, if you don't mind my saying so. I must conclude she's deficient either in taste or conduct, but either way, poor marks, all around."

Mr. Sparrow ushered Viola in and closed the door behind her, turning with a rueful grin. "I know what you're doing, Viv, but it won't work. Alice is perfect in every way. I'm afraid, this time, society's to blame." He crossed back to the piano, taking the ottoman in one lanky stride, then sliding onto the bench with a glissando across the keys. "How about 'The Hunt,'" he suggested, breaking into an experimental treatment of the opening bars of what was arguably Mozart's most complex sonata.

Vivian caught her twin's eye from across the room where Viola was perched on the edge of the rose stuffed chair—as if ready to rise at the first sign of imposition. And she was still fidgeting with that blasted rattle. Really, these dreams of hers were most concerning. Not that Vivian had enjoyed her own—well, she supposed *nightmares* was the only word that suited. Particularly the recurring one. She hadn't told Lala a thing about that. Her twin would be reading all sorts of destiny into the image of Vivian, tottering on the edge of a cliff while seven ravens circled seven blasted trees, when logically the dream was nothing more than a mash-up of all this rot Viola had been feeding into her ear. Vivian was becoming appallingly suggestible, and if she didn't watch out, she'd end up like Mistress Dubois.

What on earth does Sergeant Kowalski want to talk about? Or did he just call to lecture me?

"Do you suppose by 'society' he means those nosy parkers down at the club?"

Vivian started at her twin's appearance at her elbow, where she now sat in a cane chair she'd pulled up from the secretary. Suggestible *and* distracted. It was high time she took herself in hand.

"I'm certain of it, Lala," she said, relieved to turn her thoughts away from the mystical and maudlin. "They must have been found out, though I don't know who would have objected more, her friends or his. The world is positively set against them."

This phrase sat more comfortably on Lala's tongue, but Mr. Sparrow had that effect on Vivian, even now when she only thought of him as a sort of dashing uncle. The twins conversed quietly about the problem of Mr. Sparrow's star-crossed affair with the woman who could only be Alice Scott, the sensational night club singer with the honeyed voice and lovely, umber skin. Vivian nibbled at her scone but somehow it did little to quell her stomach's restlessness, and she finally set it aside as she and her sister drifted into their own thoughts.

Lark, indeed! Who is he to call my investigation a lark, even if he did use a fancier word! Well, I simply won't give him the satisfaction of returning his call.

Vivian was aware that she was doing a poor job of banishing the sergeant from heart and mind, but it was hard, what with him always lurking at the edge of thought, murmuring things like *Vivian, I—* and gazing at her with those brown eyes that were far less harmless than they appeared. But it simply would not do. He was probably much too old for her (though she didn't know precisely how old he was), and then they were of entirely different worlds (not that she was a snob, far from it), and . . . and . . . well, at the end of the day she'd probably make a beastly girlfriend.

"I say, Viv, are you listening? You're absolutely murdering that lower lip."

Vivian looked over to find her sister frowning, gray eyes contemplative beneath a lowered brow, though even that effect was charming. Looking at her twin was like living with a mirror.

"What was that, Lala? Something about the leader of all the baddies," she teased.

"I am impervious to your slings and arrows," Viola said archly, but with a wry undertone that had been rather more common of late. "I only said, I'm just sure this is one of those locket rattles, you know, like we saw in the window of Best & Co.?"

"Hand it over," Vivian said with a sigh as Mr. Sparrow launched into the next movement with such gusto, the canaries, Shiva and Devi, twittered in fright. Mr. Sharma was still sitting cross-legged on the divan, eyes now closed as the music washed over him. Vivian hoped he would stay perfectly lost in musical reverie. She squinted down at the rattle. "I see what you mean, Lala. There is a seam, isn't there." She remembered now—the rattle in the display case had opened along the handle to reveal a hidden inscription. "Oh, well done," she said, excitement mounting as she struggled with what appeared to be a tiny latch. "Does it go up or—oh, *there!*"

In her fervor, she had spoken rather louder than intended, and Mr. Sharma's eyes popped wide. But Vivian hardly noted him as she pried open the handle of the tiny rattle, squinting again to read three words, etched there in elegant script.

"Fire and brimstone?"

She had expected some profession of love that would put the *F* into *F & B forever.* But this?

"Of course," Viola was murmuring. *"That which binds us.* Oh, Viv, didn't I tell you?"

"Tell me what?"

"That the letters didn't necessarily stand for someone's initials, just like Hester's *A. F & B forever,* Viv. Don't you see?"

Vivian did see, but it all seemed utter nonsense. "Honestly, Lala, the *F & B* can't possibly stand for *fire and brimstone.* That's . . . that's . . ." But she couldn't say it was mere coincidence, for there were the ghastly words, plain as day, and whoever had given Babs the rattle had placed them there intentionally. But what did he mean by it? For the obvious candidate was Pastor Rathbone. Could he have meant the rattle as a gift? More likely a rebuke. Hadn't Mrs. Appleby said he was rather overbearing in his role as Babs's spiritual advisor?

"He *must* be the little tyke's father," Viola was saying when her twin tuned back in, "and not just because of Reverend Dimmesdale and Hester. *That which binds us*, Viv. The *baby*. It must be the baby that binds them, don't you think?"

Or the fire and brimstone, Vivian thought, just as she happened to look up and straight into Mr. Sharma's rapidly blinking eyes.

"I . . . er . . . rather fear, that is, there's s-s-something you should—"

But what Mr. Sharma thought they *should* was lost to the sound of a firm knock at the door. After a second round of knocking, Vivian rose and stepped smartly to the door.

"For goodness' sake," she muttered, thrusting the door open only to find Mrs. Lurch on the other side.

"Thought you'd be here," she said. "Telephone call for you, Missy," she said, raising one significant eyebrow. "Chop chop, now, or I can see I'll be fending calls all day."

CHAPTER THIRTY
Loose Ends

"Hello?"

Vivian cringed at the squeak in her voice. Cookie was right about these telephones. A wretched, unnatural invention.

"Viv—Miss Van der Beeck?"

Come to think of it, the sergeant sounded rather off too. Perhaps they should get the repairman in.

"Oh, yes, Sergeant, it's—it's you." Which was, of course, idiotic. "What can I do for you?"

The conversation continued in this preposterous vein for some moments, as if eternity had not once passed before them in the frozen instant of their eyes' embrace.

"I have some information for you," the sergeant said, finally. He hadn't even brought up the little incident at the train station, though Vivian was certain she'd been seen. "We got a break on our inquiries about Betty Boone. Had to dig a bit—seems Macavoy has an illegitimate sister that was kept on the hush hush because her mother is the daughter of a rival gang's boss."

Mobster relationships were so Shakespearean. "Do you mean to tell me that Betty is Macavoy's long-lost sister? Oh, Sergeant, then he is behind it all."

The stilted quality that had plagued their conversation vanished, as if it had never been. Sergeant Kowalski divulged what details he knew, that Betty was indeed Macavoy's half sister, and that her life-long dream was to take the Follies' stage by storm. The word on the street was that Macavoy had a sentimental streak known to show itself in extravagant gestures toward family, friends, associates, and even rival gangsters. He liked to be known as the big man around town, and to this end planted spies throughout the underworld to gather intelligence he could turn to his advantage. But his narcissism had a dark streak too. If he perceived that he'd been played, he'd put a mug in Sing Sing on the sly with a well-placed tip—or in the East River tied to a barrel full of concrete.

"We're trying to bring him in on another charge having to do with his club."

"I . . . appreciate that," Vivian said. The sergeant didn't need to explain that he was honoring his pledge to keep the blackmail threat well out of official inquiries, and of course Betty Boone's trail led straight to Ziegfeld's star-studded door.

"Miss Van der Beeck." Sergeant Kowalski paused, and it was almost as if he were in the room, as if the silence that had stretched between them in the police station was now connecting them through the telephone line. "Would you . . . do me a favor?"

"Oh, yes, certainly, Sergeant," she said, vastly relieved that no one was in the darkened hall to see her cheeks flame.

"Stay away from Macavoy," he said, simply. "As a . . . favor to me."

For a moment, Vivian did not speak. No rebukes for involving herself in police business, for surveilling a ransom drop that might well have put lives in jeopardy, including her own. No injunctions against future interference. Only a request that came so purely from the heart that she found she could not breathe. A favor. To him.

"Miss . . . Van der Beeck?"

"Oh, yes, Sergeant, of . . . of course. I will stay well clear of Mr. Macavoy; you can be assured of it." The strangled quality of her voice was appalling. She hoped the sergeant would take it for a glitch in the line.

"Okay, good. Then . . . I'll, I'll be in touch."

In touch. Language was beastly. Vivian snatched a magazine from the rack on the vestibule wall to fan her face.

"Yes, uh, do. We'll . . . talk then."

Vivian found her sister in the conservatory feeding chickens.

"It was the sergeant, after all," she said, nonchalantly, digging into Lala's bucket to throw some vegetable scraps to the marauding hordes. "As it turns out, Betty Boone and your Chief Weasel are half-siblings. Who would have thought?"

This offhand disclosure did the trick, and the two settled at once at a wicker table to dish the dirt.

"But what about the preacher, then?" Viola said, suddenly, as if struck by a sobering thought. "Oh, and I did so have him romantically paired with our heroine." Her delicate brow drew together. "Although, that required some artistic license, Viv, I don't mind telling you. He has a streak of Chillingworth that I haven't sorted."

"Well, at any rate, I think we've put *that* matter to rest," Vivian said, placatingly. "No doubt the pastor is just a busybody who can't help needling a poor waif for her ill judgment."

"Do you think?" Viola couldn't quite agree, though she couldn't quite say why, and in the end, she couldn't quite bring herself to do anything but go along.

But Viv was in a magnanimous mood. Indeed, she'd glided into the conservatory, oblivious to the pecking and fluffing and squawking all about her. She'd even grabbed a handful of scraps. As a rule, Viv did not hold with chickens.

"Fine, Lala It's against my better judgment, but I'll humor your whims. Even if it's only to prove that he's a harmless old coot, we'll make a visit to this preacher of yours. I can see there'll be no getting him out of your head otherwise."

Viola was fairly sure her sister was just itching for something to do on the heels of her conversation amoureuse. Come to think of it, perhaps a visit to the preacher would take her own mind off things too.

After a poorly attended breakfast that sent Cookie huffing off to the kitchen, glowering over her trolley, the twins headed up to their bedroom to change. Within the hour, they were ready to go, Vivian looking fashionable in a navy skirt, white blouse, and her favorite red neck scarf tied off to the side, and Viola looking whimsical in her polka-dotted dress. As luck would have it, Mistress Dubois's rheumatoid arthritis was still acting up, and lessons were canceled for the rest of the week. Not that anyone kept tabs on the twins' educational pursuits—nor their investigative ones. Vivian was sure they needn't bother with a chaperone for an expedition which would surely prove tame, not when a pretense would suffice. Mrs. Lurch was nowhere to be found, and Father was napping, so that left only Mother.

"Truly, mes chéries, must you? Les vêtements prêt-à-porter, they are so very gauche."

Giselle was in the second parlor which she had commandeered years ago as a studio for her artistic pursuits. She stood at her easel before the window, engrossed in her latest collage, a reimagining of the Eiffel Tower as a symbol of aberrant patriarchy in the Dada style.

"But, Mother, you know perfectly well that the couture houses are positively out of our price range at the moment. And

Lala and I haven't had a proper shopping spree in ages. I hear they've got a smashing sale on at Macy's."

The double whammy of "sale" and "Macy's" had the desired effect. Mother waved them off before placing the back of her hand to her forehead.

"How is it that the times, they come to this? D'accord, mes chéries, have your little spree, but do not show to me your acquisitions, oui?"

"Naturally, Mother," Vivian said with a conspiratorial glance at her sister. "Needs must, you know."

They were almost out the door when Mother called after them.

"And be careful, mes chéries. Remember: Il y a serpent caché sous des fleurs."

They turned to find her gazing at them fixedly, paste brush poised elegantly in one slender hand. With her long, blond hair plaited over her shoulder, she looked the very image of Diana at the hunt.

Outside, the twins paused in the hall to gaze at one another in the dim light. The single window at the end of the hall showed only a dreary, gray square.

"What on earth is she going on about?" Vivian said.

"Look before you leap, for snakes among sweet flowers do creep," Viola translated, though her sister's French was the equal of her own. "I say, Viv, do you suppose she knows?"

"Heavens, I hope not," Vivian breathed, aghast at the idea. "Can she have meant it as a bit of professional advice?"

Viola shrugged. "She did rather get up to things back in her rue de Fleurus days," she speculated, referring to the Parisian salons of the incomparable Gertrude Stein. All through the last decade, when whim struck, Mother would forsake New York (and the twins) for weeks on end, only to come home laden with sketch books, stories, and more than a few scandals to share. "Picasso is a communist, you know. Why, Viv, do you suppose she's a spy?"

This struck Vivian as one of Lala's less preposterous ideas. Still, on the whole, she rather thought not.

"Most likely, she's just guessing," she said, turning back to the stairwell. It felt strange, though, that Mother might know about their escapades, dangers and all, and implicitly approved. She was taking an interest, after a fashion, but by the same stroke rather leaving her children to the ravages of fate. Vivian felt a stab of loneliness so terrifying she quashed it at once.

"Come, Lala, it's high time we got out the door."

They headed down to the front hall to retrieve their wool coats, only to cross paths with Mr. Sharma, who was just tumbling in from the cold in a flurry of brown leaves. He looked surprised to see them, then hemmed and hawed most vexingly. Vivian had simply run out of patience.

"We're late for the bus, Mr. Sharma—so sorry, but let's do talk later, yes?"

They were out the door before the poor man could fumble a reply.

On the front steps, Viola turned a reproachful look on her sister. "Really, Viv. That was horrid, even for you."

But Vivian merely took her arm, ushering her into stride. "We'll miss the bus, Lala. Hurry along, won't you?"

The trip to Hell's Kitchen passed more uneventfully than the name would augur. Indeed, if hell had a kitchen, it might well have been this midtown neighborhood where even the roughest of New York's denizens could cozy up for a cup of joe. Irish, Italian, and German in character, with a mom-and-pop Jewish market on every third corner, Hell's Kitchen had earned its reputation from the gangs who fought for control of the docks, but the longshoremen were family men. Every household lost at least one child to diphtheria or pneumonia, but for every child that died there were ten hungry ones to take its place. Consequently, the prevailing rule was this: look out for each other because no one else will.

Religion was the opiate of the masses, and there was a dealer on every street.

Pastor Rathbone's Church of the Elect was located on the corner of 42nd Street and 9th Avenue, just down the block from the considerably more popular Holy Cross Church whose reverend, one Francis P. Duffy, had served as the highly decorated chaplain of the "Fighting Irish" 69th Regiment during World War I. Father Duffy was to Rathbone as Detective Johnny Broderick was to Flanagan, although Rathbone hardly noted the thorn in his side. While the intrepid Father was valiantly plying his faith in the trenches, Pastor Rathbone was holed up in a Hell's Kitchen garret, agonizing over the doctrine of predestination and the precise methodology of determining one's inclusion in the elect, saved from eternal damnation by God's whim. It was a difficult creed to sell, and his pews still sat empty. Folk from the neighborhood already lived in hell, or at least its kitchen, and did not care to be told that God had already made up his mind. And besides, the Catholic creed was just a bit cozier.

The twins noted the grand brick edifice of the Holy Cross Church on their second trip around the block.

"I say, Viv, didn't we already pass that one?" Viola was not strong on spatial reckoning.

"Quite so, Lala." She dug the small note out of her purse on which she'd jotted down the address. "This Church of the Elect is simply nowhere to be found."

Back to the corner they went, just up from Paddy's Market, once a warren of pushcarts, piled high with produce, which had dwindled now to a few carts with even fewer shoppers. Instead, a breadline stretched all the way down 42nd Street, men slouched into ragged overcoats with their hats pulled low.

"It's rather hard, isn't it, Viv?" Viola said despondently. "I say, perhaps we could get Cookie to put out our leftovers at the end of the week. We do rather eat like kings."

Vivian tended to agree. It was one thing to take in boarders, quite another to go hungry. "Right, Lala," she said, with a firm nod that startled her twin, who had expected to be chastised for distracting them from the case. "We'll talk to Cookie this very evening, just see if we don't."

"Oh, look Viv! There's the little fellow I met in Empire Park," Viola cried, pointing to a scrappy-looking boy of seven or eight who was loitering beside the line of men, hunched into his ragtag coat like a portrait in miniature. "I never forget a foot," she added, thinking of the poor urchin's bare toe, sticking out from his threadbare sock. "At least he has shoes, now."

But Vivian's charitable impulse had run its course. "Come, Lala, even you can't possibly save every lost soul. Is that a doorway over—"

Vivian had led her sister by the elbow into the slatted shadows cast by the Ninth Avenue El just as the train clattered by overhead, drowning out her next words. But Viola could see where she pointed, a brick stairwell beside an optician's storefront, advertising artificial human eyes. In the dimness above the stairwell, she could just make out a placard reading THE CHURCH OF THE ELECT: SINNERS WELCOME.

"Trusting no man as his friend . . ." she murmured.

"What's that, Lala?" Vivian had taken a step forward, craning her head to make out shapes in the darkness. "I'm afraid this preacher chap of yours is a dreadful stick. Who would worship here?"

Who indeed? Inexplicably, Viola had found herself transported to the scene in *The Scarlet Letter* when Dimmesdale first meets his nemesis, Roger Chillingworth, the man who will spell both his doom and his redemption. "Trusting no man as his friend," she quoted again, quietly, "he could not recognize his enemy when the latter actually appeared." Why that passage should jump to mind was beyond her, except that the placard's welcome bespoke a man whose world was so riddled with vice, he could no longer tell friend from foe.

"Really, Lala, we're hardly his *enemies*," Vivian chided, missing the point—or perhaps not, for Viola suddenly felt the thrill of premonition, all the way from the angled brim of her felt hat down to the toes of her heeled Oxford shoes. "Oh, do stop gawking, Lala," Vivian complained as she forged downward, into the darkness. "I'm sure your imagination is running away with you. Come along now, and I'll show you that this preacher chap is as harmless as a mouse."

CHAPTER THIRTY-ONE
A Sinner's Welcome

The main chapel of the Church of the Elect appeared to be deserted.

Vivian and Viola entered the small, low-ceilinged room, set with several rows of folding chairs all facing a narrow pulpit, raised above the floor on a dais built of rough boards. A single lightbulb dangled from a wire, leaving the room's perimeter in shadow.

"Good lord. This must be the most depressing place in the history of salvation," Vivian muttered, slapping her beadwork bag against her thigh in exasperation.

This offhand comment increased the frequency of Viola's premonitory thrill ten-fold. It was a peculiarity that beset her on occasion, the collision of numerous intuitions, inferences, and innuendos, forging a vibration that ran through her like waves through a tuning fork. *It ain't perdition that scares a mother half so much sometimes as salvation, no matter what the good book says.* That's what Mrs. Appleby had said that afternoon a seeming age ago, her gaze haunted by private—what, demons? But what on earth did demons have to do with salvation? Just what was it that Mrs. Appleby had feared?

"Lala, if you don't pay attention, how do you ever expect to solve this case? I *said*, it sounds rather like a someone's getting a right dressing-down."

Viola came to her senses to see her sister, now standing beside a closed door on the far side of the room, leaning in close to hear.

"Oh, quite," she breathed, hurrying between two aisles of chairs to join her twin, who had put a hand on the door handle. "It's just—Viv, who do you suppose the enemy is in *this* case? I do believe that's the key to the whole thing."

Vivian looked at her as if she'd sprouted a third eye. "Not *that* nonsense, again. I thought we'd agreed that we are nobody's enemies, Lala, quite the opposite. Perhaps you should book a session with Dr. Weber when we get home. I'm sure you're not yourself, these days."

The door stuck, then gave way onto a narrow corridor all but lost in gloom. The voice Vivian had heard immediately got louder, rising and falling in a certain cadence, but on the whole only rising, as though the speaker were building to a crescendo.

"They have become filled with every kind of wickedness, evil, greed, and depravity—"

"As I said, Lala, he's a bona fide oddball, this preacher chap," Vivian mused as she led the way down the hall.

"They are full of envy, murder, strife, deceit, and malice—"

"But I'm sure on the whole he's perfectly harmless. He certainly didn't *look* like much," she added, a tad shaken by the rising tirade that met their ears.

"They are gossips, slanderers, God-haters, insolent, arrogant, and boastful—"

"And now that we've confirmed the culprit is Macavoy— well, even if this chap is a bit of a raver, it's bound to be a simple case of religious fervor," she continued, with more assurance than she felt as the corridor turned, leading to a second closed door.

"They have no understanding, no fidelity, no love, no *mercy—*"

They came to a stop before the closed door, peering at each other in the gloom of the corridor for the breath of a second, one instant in which they might turn and venture back the way they had come. But that was ridiculous, of course. Vivian reached out and knocked firmly on the door, still holding her sister's eye.

At once, the voice stopped. After a long moment, the door creaked wide.

The twins had never been this close to the man. So firm in Viola's mind was the *startled, half-frightened aspect* of Hawthorne's Dimmesdale that for a moment, she could hardly register the reality of Rathbone's face until—in an instant—it breached the illusion, like the face of a drowning man, coming up for air. Viola stifled a gasp.

"Know the patience of God for his creations, though they be but vessels for destruction," he said, quietly, but with an odd light in his eye.

As for Vivian, she rather wondered if she'd made a mistake.

"Pastor Rathbone? I—well, but perhaps this is a bad time. You were working on your sermon—" She turned slightly to go but was halted by the firm grip of the preacher's deceptively slender hand.

"Nonsense, child. Come in, come in."

Decorum dictated that they follow the preacher when he turned to venture back into his study, furnished only with a desk, a few wooden chairs, and reams of scattered papers.

"I see you've been . . . busy," Vivian said, casting an eye over the mess. "This does appear to be a frightfully bad time. Perhaps we'll just—"

But Rathbone had already cleared two chairs of their rubble and pulled them before the desk, settling behind it to peer over the crest of books and papers littered there. He had a stilted, methodical way of moving, as if his body were a puppet on marionette strings that he manipulated from far above. The twins took their chairs as he made a temple with his fingers before his face, barely visible above the mound.

"What can I do for you, children?"

Vivian twitched uncomfortably in her chair. As usual, Lala had been right. The preacher might well be involved in Babs's disappearance, right up to his priest's collar. She cast a glance sideways to judge her twin's condition only to find her lost to the vagaries of her admittedly brilliant mind. Not that Vivian begrudged her sister's genius, far from it. It was only that—sometimes—she rather feared her twin would wander too far afield. Where Vivian could not reach her. Watch over her. Protect her.

She returned to the preacher, narrowing her gaze to take his measure. He simply could *not* be the kidnapper. They had seen the pastor deliver the ransom to Macavoy with their own eyes, just moments before *another* figure, quite different in stature and attire, had arrived on the scene to ferret Babs away. Unless Rathbone was in league with Macavoy, which seemed unlikely, he was what he purported to be—a man obsessed with Babs's spiritual welfare. And yet, neither was he *as harmless as a mouse.* Under normal circumstances, Vivian might disclose enough of the truth to gain his confidence. After all, he might be useful in illuminating the details of Babs life, her mental state, the circumstances surrounding her disappearance. But Vivian saw now that a disguise was called for, and instinct told her that the mantle of the acolyte was the correct one to assume.

"We seek your spiritual guidance, Father."

A change came over Pastor Rathbone's face, as if a breath of secret air lifted him from within, straightening his posture above the mountain of books and papers, raising even his eyebrows over the puzzled, angry gaze he habitually wore. A flicker sparked in his eye—of what? Hope? Humor? Yet his mouth remained fixed in that odd, humorless smile.

He tapped his fingertips together, still forming a temple before his face. "You have taken the first step. *He* has taken it for you, for of yourself you are nothing, can do nothing. The chasm between his righteousness and your depravity is absolute. Only when you have accepted into your heart the utter vileness of your nature can he guide your actions truly."

He was certainly an articulate fellow. Down came the temple of his fingers as he reached forward to clear a chasm through which he could see them better.

"Thank you . . . Father," Vivian managed, wondering how in heaven's name she could guide the conversation toward the subject of Babs. "Is there nothing, then, that we can do? We know *many* who are . . . fallen."

A shadow passed over Rathbone's gaze.

"One need only walk out one's door to be sullied by the world's filth," he acknowledged, that angry smile deepening at the corners of his mouth. "There is nothing you can do to earn God's grace, child. He has already elected those who are to live out eternity by his side, and those who will burn in the everlasting fires of hell. That you have come to me for counsel may indicate that you are among the elect, but none may know the mind of God. Do you have a burning for righteousness in your heart? Is it filled with love for your creator? With holy delight? With an irrepressible urge to enforce the lord's justice?"

Vivian felt her brow contract and immediately smoothed it. He hadn't taken the bait to talk about the *others* who had fallen—most particularly Babs. Indeed, his attention seemed to have wandered, his eyes fixed on the ceiling behind their heads, as if he were listening to something only he could hear. And with each question he asked, the torturous light in his eye grew, flecked with some inkling of dark humor that Vivian could not quite grasp.

"What is it that haunts and tempts me thus?" Viola murmured suddenly, startling her twin. The scene in which Reverend Dimmesdale returns from the wild wood, fresh from his liaison with Hester and their love child, only to find himself tempted by devilish imps at every turn—this scene had so utterly consumed her imagination that for one moment she forgot where she was. Her vision cleared by stages as Dimmesdale's face became Chillingworth's and finally Rathbone's, so that for the briefest of moments, all their faces were one. "What does it all mean?" she breathed.

The preacher seemed as surprised as Vivian by this small outburst. For the first time, suspicion entered his eye.

"I have not seen you in my parish before," he said as his gaze swept their neat, stylish outfits, their pinned felt hats, perhaps even registering their decidedly patrician air. "You have journeyed far for my counsel . . . children."

Not a question, or at least not the question he had asked.

Vivian was on the point of offering some excuse—perhaps a story they had read in the paper or a servant who had mentioned Rathbone's ministry—when she stopped short, a sudden rush of adrenaline coursing through her veins. Strangely enough, the thrill had the converse effect of calming her. What was life but risk? One either risked danger or the certitude of a life unlived, and for her part, she would take the former. Babs's life was at stake.

"Actually, we heard about your ministry from a friend, sir," she said evenly. "Babs Le Roy? I believe you are her spiritual advisor."

Synchronicity is a strange phenomenon, often mistaken for coincidence. Two strangers, destined to marry, bump into one another after missing their train. An eclipse darkens the sky at the precise moment that a woman stumbles, snatching her from the path of an oncoming automobile. As Vivian spoke, the preacher's reaction was both masked and augmented by what happened at precisely the instant the last word passed her lips, as if it were a summons. An invocation. A curse.

Thump.

Vivian and Viola looked over as one to see the closet door, hitherto unnoticed, pop open, a seemingly harmless event, quite ordinary if considered in isolation. The stockinged calf of a woman's leg protruded from the darkened crack, shod in a bright red pump.

"You were saying?" the preacher said, slowly taking a revolver from beneath the scattered heap of papers atop his desk.

CHAPTER THIRTY-TWO
Hands of an Angry God

When John Winthrop, governor of the Massachusetts Bay Company, warned his colonists that their fledgling settlement would be as a city upon a hill, before the sight of all the world, he thought not of wealth or stature but only of their covenant with God. It was New York, not Boston, which was destined to become the seat of enterprise, of *empire*, in the centuries that followed— a destiny marked by no monument so clearly as one glittering tower, rising above the avenues that flowed about its base like rivers of light. A beacon to the world—but of complex and contradictory import.

The Empire State Building.

The inaugural event had been held only last May, presided over by President Herbert Hoover as he lit the building for the very first time, setting flame to torch, so to speak, with the ceremonial press of a button from his oval office, miles away. Pastor Rathbone had watched the lights ascend to heaven from the streets below, like flames licking up a pyre, and in the months that followed, he'd mapped the building's secret architecture through diligent research—the freight elevators and steam rooms and maintenance entrances—information gleaned through books, pamphlets, and articles in *The Architectural Forum*. Like barnacles on that virgin ship so long departed from foreign shores, other evils had aggregated—the well-placed graft, the lies, large and small, the pistol in his hand—so that now, as he crouched with his quarry in a corner of the steam room, he had only to brandish his gun.

"Keep my commandments and live," he whispered in what Viola thought a vile corruption of Proverbs 7:2.

They'd entered the building shortly before closing time, pressed together in a tight knot, the tip of the preacher's gun wedged by turns into each of the twins' backs. Babs was slung over his shoulder in a burlap sack, poor woman, but Vivian found herself hoping the few guides who lingered before elevator doors in their burgundy jackets would *not* notice the odd group they made. She was quite sure that Rathbone would use that gun if the hue and cry were raised. Someone would be hurt.

Vivian cursed her stupidity as he herded them into a service elevator. How could she have missed the signs? Overconfidence, plain and simple. She could not puzzle out how the preacher was involved in the greater intrigue. Was he in league with Macavoy, then, or was Macavoy his dupe? Just how had Babs come to be in his custody after being released by the ransomer? Was the *third* man in fact Rathbone's accomplice? These thoughts hounded her all the way down to the steam room, where they huddled in a corner amid the hissing and knocking and clanging, the great hot pipes running overhead like the intestines of some leviathan that had swallowed them whole.

"Really, it's like something out of a dime-store novel," she complained under her breath as the moments dragged on. At long last, Rathbone waved his gun again, indicating it was time to go.

Up they went again in the freight elevator, returning to the lobby, now empty and dim with ambient light. The long ceiling stretched above, its gold-leaf mural almost lost in shadow, suns and moons and celestial orbs stripped of their constellations, transformed into the cogs and gears of the Machine Age. Gazing up, Viola was awash in impressions, surfacing from the depths of her mind. A meteor seemed to blaze the length of the room, firing the embossed gold to new configurations. "A light gleamed far and wide over all the muffled sky," she murmured as a glimpse of Dimmesdale's scaffold reared once again in her mind, surging skyward, even as she spied the grand door of the lobby elevator. Its etched surface depicted a great halo emanating from the spire of the building, as if in homage to Winthrop's premonition 400 years before. The doors opened at the press of a button, and up they sped, floor by floor, toward the building's summit where Pastor Rathbone would surely bare his own breast, his own stain—just as Dimmesdale had—his own scarlet letter before the sight of all the world.

"Lala, do remember to breathe," her sister hissed in her ear, steadying them both with a hand on the wood-paneled interior.

Several elevators, one steel ladder and a hatch door later, they stood upon a narrow walkway—the 103rd floor, to be exact—a small outdoor promenade that encircled the building's spire. The preacher had sent the twins up first, menacing them with threats of fire and brimstone from below, then followed, stuffing Babs up through the hatch door like some macabre Santa Claus. There'd been a moment there when Vivian had been sorely tempted to try her luck, just as the preacher heaved himself after, his gun hand planted on the promenade floor. But the moment was past almost before it arrived, and Vivian was left once more to curse her own stupidity, shivering into her wool coat against the rising wind. The first flakes of an unseasonable snow had settled on the low, limestone wall—all that separated them from the lights and bustle of Fifth Avenue far below.

"Pastor Rathbone," Viola said in a surprisingly sensible voice, the blast of cold having tempered her fevered mind. "You see, sir, we know all about your love child with Hest—Babs, that is, and, well, you mustn't let it bother you so. I'm sure God is not at all upset, *really*, sir, so you needn't bother with some grand gesture to placate his wrath. 'Lo, children are a heritage of the Lord,'" she quoted from Psalms, "'and the fruit of the womb is his reward.'"

Vivian shot a glance at her twin. What on earth was she on about? But the preacher only laughed—a low, garbled sound, rather like a sob. He waved his gun again, herding them until they were seated back-to-back, then binding them together with some rope that had appeared from thin air. But no—Vivian spotted the edge of some boxes, stacked just around the corner where Rathbone must have stowed them earlier. The balcony was little used, designed as a boarding deck for dirigibles, or so Vivian had once read. A violent gust of wind tore her felt hat from its pins, sending it whirling over the side and down to the streets below.

"My favorite hat," she fumed. Really, this preacher was too much, but what on earth was there to do about it? How was she to secure the freedom and safety of all three of them—unless . . .

Unless the preacher went the way of the hat.

But that was really too horrid to consider. There must be some other way, if only—

"As I was saying, sir, I don't suppose God cares a fig for your grand gesture," Viola continued, as if she were merely thinking aloud. "From what *I* know of predestination, which, mind you, isn't much—it's not the family creed, at least not anymore, although our forebears did worship in the Reformed Dutch Church for a time, come to think of it . . ." She paused, realizing she had strayed from her point. "But leaving that aside as neither here nor there, it's my understanding that *faith*, not *works* supply the evidence of one's exalted condition. I don't suppose God wants to see you and your beloved Hest—Babs, that is, go up in a spectacle of sacrificial flame just because the two of you had a secret child. Don't you rather think?"

What was Lala babbling on about? Vivian feared her twin had succumbed to the fright of their abduction, although she *sounded* rational, if one didn't take note of the words. It was horrid being strapped like this so that she couldn't even see her sister's face, only glimpse the preacher if she strained around just so . . .

"You think the child is *mine*?" he said, finally, leaving off his ghastly preparations, a few half-opened boxes, packages, and bottles strewn about him. His shadowed gaze was revealed briefly as the moon cleared a shred of cloud—a look so forlorn, so filled with longing, that even Vivian was taken aback. But then the moon passed behind the clouds again, and the dreadful chuckling returned as he bent to his work.

This glimpse of woe had not been lost on Viola.

"Oh, dear," she said. "Oh, it *is* tragic. That settles the matter—you *are* Roger Chillingworth, after all. 'It seemed not so wild a dream,'" she quoted, thinking of the twisted scholar's unrequited love for Hester, his estranged wife whose love—and child—were destined to belong to Reverend Dimmesdale, who had not even the courage to acknowledge them in public. Who then was the father of Babs's love child? And why had Pastor Rathbone not directed his wrath at *that* scoundrel, just as Chillingworth had pledged his life to destroy Hester's love? But perhaps the parallel ended there. Rathbone must have confused his own jealousy, his thirsting for revenge, with God's wrath. And now he meant to strike Babs down with his own bolt—of homemade fire! "But, sir," Viola pleaded, "don't you see? You needn't take your vengeance on Babs for, well, her sins if you must, for if you were truly among the elect, wouldn't your heart be filled with grace and forgiveness? With pity for her failings and, dare I say, for your own? Why—if you were *truly* among the elect, your heart would shine forth with love for all God's creatures, isn't that the case?"

It was as if the man had been struck a mortal blow. Vivian watched, astonished, as he fell backward, away from his mysterious sundries and the half-drawn circle already marked in powder upon the pavement, spanning the width of the narrow walkway. What was the infernal man up to? It really was the strangest enterprise. And what was *that*, almost around the corner, but a great—what—candlestick? Stowed beyond the boxes so that Vivian only now wondered at its purpose. *Like a giant firecracker*, she thought suddenly as a cold shaft of fear split her insides and she recalled the books Viola had spied the preacher reading that day in the library. And she had written fireworks off as a hobby! There was no one to blame but herself.

"Oh, dear," Viola said again, "It's much, *much* worse than I thought. 'He could not recognize his enemy when the latter actually appeared,'" she quoted once more, as she had earlier that day. "Didn't I tell you Viv? Why, it's just like the scene where Dimmesdale can't tell friend from foe. And I know now who Pastor Rathbone's enemy is, and it isn't himself, or the love child, or even Babs!"

Not that enemy nonsense again. But likely, Lala had cracked the code ages ago. Rathbone certainly appeared to be listening, steadying himself against the spire against a snowy gust, his head bowed as he recoiled from whatever psychic blow Lala had unwittingly dealt. It was hard to see him in the dark, but then suddenly the magic hour struck and lights came on below them and above, brilliant white light that bathed them like a shaft from the heavens. There was Babs's body, slumped against the spire, freed now from the burlap bag. She was still unconscious, head thrust back at an odd angle, hair tangled about her face. It was not her most glamorous hour, yet somehow she had never looked so beautiful. It was as though Vivian could finally see her, in a way she never had before. A woman, flesh and blood, not a figment of her own girlish imagination, nor an object of her prejudices, nor even the central character in her pet intrigue—for she saw now how very childish she had been. How sad, how pointless to only see Babs now, when their lives were all but lost.

"You have witnessed my secret shame," Rathbone cried now, gazing skyward. "It was for that I brought you here, that God might *know*, through the eyes of his innocents, the hatred for him that lives in my heart." He fell to his knees, hands grappling his shirt, his arms—as if to rend the flesh from his bones. He howled his grief. "How I loved thee!" he cried, head still thrust skyward. "How I searched every crevice of my black heart for signs that I might live for all eternity by your side!" His cries degraded to sobs, head collapsing into his hands as he knelt. "But I found only lust! Only envy and pride!" he sobbed, writhing from side to side. "And hatred! Hatred at the end! For she, after whom I lusted, she who revealed to me the baseness of my own nature! And for you, Lord, hatred for you above all! How could you leave me to the ravages of *hell!*"

This last word was ripped so violently from the preacher's soul that Viola burst into tears. Never had she beheld so tragic a spectacle as this broken man, whose unrequited love was not for Babs, after all, but for a god whom he could never touch. His greatest love, his greatest heartbreak, and now . . . his greatest enemy.

Pastor Rathbone lowered his gaze and wiped his eyes, turning back to his half-finished preparations with the ordered movements of the puppet he had seemed before.

"I serve a new master now," he said, quietly, as he got back to work, funneling chalk dust out of his cupped fist onto the pavement to close the circle he had made. Within it, he began to make a five-pointed star. "I serve the Beast, and to him I give my praise."

CHAPTER THIRTY-THREE
Absolute Power

What a disaster.

Tied back-to-back atop the Empire State Building, at the mercy of a madman, and not a soul knew where they were—though even Mother must be getting worried right about now, what with her children not yet returned home with their red-tag-sale items. At least Vivian dearly hoped so. If she'd gotten caught up in her collage, all bets were off.

The tenants? They'd simply think the twins were in their room. Father? Sleeping. Cookie and Mrs. Lurch? Well, at least they might notice the twins were gone, but no one, *no one* would know *where*.

It was exactly the sort of thing Sergeant Kowalski had warned her about.

Thinking of the sergeant brought a lump to her throat, which was utterly appalling. She mustn't be such a baby. There was work to be done.

Viola likewise thought on their predicament, though her mind was consumed with the preacher's tragic plight. The dingy chapel, lit by a single bulb, sermons delivered to empty rooms, pedestrians brushing by his soap box as if his strident words had no worth, no *reality*—all these images brought home his crushing failure. But surely the real defeat had come in solitude, sleepless nights spent searching his heart, his mind and soul for some crumb of *specialness*, placed there as a sign that he would not hunger in vain.

It was as if she had lived it herself.

"Oh dear," she said for the umpteenth time. "I'm not sure we can reach him, Viv."

"*I'll* reach him," Vivian said, thinking that tossing him over the side was not such a bad idea, after all. "Honestly, what a perfectly selfish man," she fumed. "As if the world revolved around him."

Viola supposed her sister was right, but then that's how people were, wandering the world alone, clutching secret woes, bereft, for even at the end, one died alone. It was the only thing that bound them all together on this lonely vigil through the thicket of existence, if only they could all grasp hands. For once, even the poetry of it all was no comfort.

"Pastor Rathbone," she tried again, "if you ever loved Babs—and I think, sir, that you must have done—don't you suppose that means *something*? She did so trust your judgment. Her mother said she positively lived by your word, which means . . . well, you must have touched her soul at least a little bit and, well, couldn't that be a sign that you *might* be among the elect?"

Vivian strained the fingers of her right hand to their limit, finally snatching the edge of her beaded bag to drag it close. At least Lala was keeping the confounded man distracted. A haze of snow whipped around the preacher as he rose from his chalkdust pentagram, now complete but already looking a bit bedraggled. With any luck, his dreadful little drawing would be ruined by the time he got around to . . . whatever came next.

Speaking of which, he began to lug the candlestick-like-thing toward his nefarious scribblings.

"But let him ask in faith, with *no* doubting," Rathbone said through his grunts. The thing was either blasted heavy or just awkward. "For the one who doubts is like a wave of the sea that is driven and tossed by the wind."

So *that's* what was bothering him. He thought his doubt itself was evidence of damnation. Viola had retained nearly all the Bible's verses. "And have *mercy* on those who doubt," she said, countering with a dose of Jude. "And doesn't Matthew 5:7 tell us 'blessed are the merciful, for they will be shown mercy?'"

The preacher shook his head so violently, it nearly sent him over the parapet. "Without faith, it is *impossible* to please Him." Somehow, Rathbone managed to wrangle the large firework into the center of the star without destroying its contours, though it took up much of the passageway. He paused to consider his handiwork, but when he spoke again, his voice was raw with contempt. He continued quoting verses: "He is a double-minded man, unstable in all his ways."

Hebrews *and* James. The poor dear. Always, the greatest wrath was reserved for oneself. She could feel Vivian squirming, tied together as they were. Hopefully, Viv had something up her sleeve.

"Don't be so hard on yourself, sir. 'For God gave us a spirit not of fear but of power and love and self-control,'" Viola tried, hoping the book of Timothy was not too obscure. "Maybe faith is about *forgiveness*, don't you think? 'For we walk by faith, not by sight,'" she added, throwing in Corinthians for good measure. Once again, this seemed to hit a nerve, and Rathbone took a step back from the pentagram, clutching his head.

"No . . . no! I am done with faith! With faith comes doubt, and you will not make me doubt again," he cried, abandoning his verses. "My *new* master knows no doubt, only anguish, no hope, only remorse!" He released his head and fixed her with his wild gaze, lit weirdly now in the brightness of electric lights. "He *too* languished on the lake of fire, cast down by God's own hand! Lo, the suffering! The burning despair! Cast down, and for what? Pride, ambition, deceit, all the sins I harbor in the blackness of my heart! His suffering is mine! It is in *his* likeness I am made!"

His voice rose, word by word, over the rising of the wind, as if God were weighing in on their little debate. *Good,* Vivian thought, *let them have at it.* She had managed to snag her ladies' pocketknife from her purse—beastly hard on the wrists. That was going to leave a mark.

As for Viola, she had to concede the preacher's point. Secretly, Satan had always been her favorite character in *Paradise Lost,* though she'd never felt comfortable saying so. She'd found herself downright rooting for him at times.

But she had to stay focused. "Isn't that just it, sir?" she persisted. "Your fallibility is what makes you human, what makes you *loveable,* why, it's exactly why you feel pity for poor Satan, lying there on that ghastly lake for all eternity with only his boorish henchmen for company. One can't help but feel sorry for him. And, well, perhaps, sir, if you don't mind me saying, perhaps . . . you could feel that way for yourself. Just a little . . . sorry." She could see she'd painted herself into a bit of a corner, seeing how it was God who had put Satan on the lake of fire to begin with. And if *God* didn't have pity on Satan, and Rathbone believed he was created in *Satan's* image, where did that leave Rathbone? Drat Mistress Dubois for teaching them syllogisms—dreadful, dry things. But then, theological conversations were always a muddle.

"Gotcha," Vivian whispered. Good old Mrs. Lurch had given her the slender, etched pocketknife when she was only ten and still rather a tomboy. Over the years, she'd spent long hours prying open locks, cupboards, and all manner of drawers so that it was almost like part of her hand. And now, she'd managed to cut through one of the thin cords that bound her wrists.

She kept it sharp.

Frightfully crampy on the hands, though. Vivian flipped the knife closed, easing it back into her purse, then worked her hands free. Now for the rope that bound her to Lala. She might be able to cut it, even at this odd angle, but not discretely. It was far too thick. Better to wriggle out, though it would take more of a distraction than Lala's drivel.

"There can be no forgiveness for the damned!" The preacher cried suddenly, turning from the twins toward Babs. "And if I am damned, why should I not worship at an altar of fire?" He pointed a finger at the unconscious woman. "And why should *she*, who was the agent of my revelation, not worship with me? It was she who first revealed to me the baseness of my nature, my jealousy, my lust! We will sacrifice ourselves to our new master that he may be pleased!"

We? Our? Fanatics were so self-centered. But perhaps this was the moment Vivian had been waiting for. Rathbone seemed utterly occupied with grappling Babs's body into his puny arms and hefting her toward his makeshift altar. Vivian supposed he planned to immolate her in some way, or the both of them—an entirely morbid affair, that. And he must indeed be fueled by some inner fire to manage these antics. He was rail-thin, while Babs, though petite in stature, was a bit plump around the curves.

Keeping one eye fixed firmly on the preacher, Vivian wriggled and squirmed while trying to push the rope tied around her torso upward, over her shoulders, but it was terribly tight. Best not to think about that—it only made her feel more trapped. Panic would take hold, and then where would they be? Blasted hard, though, not to think about something you had started to think about, which only made you think about it all the more until—she fought the wave of panic as she struggled to wedge the ropes up, inch by inch. *Goodness, Vivian,* she schooled herself, *don't faint, or you'll really be in for it.*

"Here, Viv," Viola whispered, "perhaps if I let out all my breath and relax . . ."

That was it. "Well done, Lala," Vivian murmured, working the ropes over both their heads, then kneeling to snatch her knife from her bag so she could cut the bonds around her sister's hands. But confound it, her own hands weren't working properly, between the cold and the lack of circulation. She was numbly fingering the pocketknife trigger when she cast another glance up to find Pastor Rathbone gone.

Or was he?

The arm came around her neck from behind. It might be rail-thin, but that grip was pure steel! Vivian only just managed to slip the knife into her coat pocket, then clawed at his arm as he dragged her backward. She skidded and scrambled, crab-like, across the cold, wet stone of the walkway. Before she could calculate a single maneuver, he had slung her onto the parapet, stomach down, as he reached down to grapple a hold on her kicking legs.

He was planning to toss *her* over the side!

Someone screamed. No, *she* screamed. The sound was all around her as she scratched and bit and tore, unleashing all her rage at this pathetic little man who had formed the preposterous intent to take her life. The nerve of it! How *dare* he? How dare they *all*?

"If you—*oof*—think you can just stuff—*ugh*—people in bags or toss—*humph*—them off buildings just because—*umph*—you've had a rotten time, you have another—*oof*—thing coming, you crazy old coot!" Like a wildcat, she fought, managing to get herself at least off the parapet and wedged against the inside of the wall. Her knife! If only she could get it in hand—but already, the madman was working his arm under her, scrabbling against the wet pavement in an attempt to heave her over once more.

Aha! The eyes. His chin was thrust upward as he struggled, all his efforts focused on wedging his arm under her. If Vivian spread her first two fingers just so . . .

"Take that!" she cried with a savage, well-placed poke.

It was an effective move, if a bit low-brow, and it might have worked had the preacher been of a milder disposition. But—

nearly blinded as he was—Vivian's attacks seemed only to goad him to new heights of diabolical fervor, as if the beast indeed lived within him.

"The chasm between his righteousness and my depravity is absolute!" Rathbone cried, now, cradling his wounded sight. "Therefore, do I embrace my fate!"

He heaved his weight against Vivian where she still struggled, wedged against the wall, and managed at last to encircle her with his arms. He stood, Vivian's slight frame gathered to his chest as he turned toward the parapet. One step, two—in a moment he would be at the edge, and then it would all be over.

Vivian screamed, and as she did, two things happened at once.

Viola lunged, and a gunshot rang out.

Hands still bound behind her, Viola caught the preacher on his side with her head, as if she were a human battering ram. Rathbone sprawled across the stones as Vivian fell from his arms and scrabbled away. The preacher slung one arm up and over the wall to pull himself upright, blinded, winded, but—like an animal cornered—fueled by rage.

A second gunshot split the air.

Vivian turned to see Sergeant Kowalski, down on one knee on the narrow promenade, his pistol pointed skyward but even now lowering to take deadly aim.

"Freeze!" he cried. "Freeze, or I'll shoot!"

CHAPTER THIRTY-FOUR
Fall From Grace

The gun!

Not the sergeant's gun, but the *preacher's*!

Vivian had almost forgotten it, and perhaps Rathbone had as well, caught up in his rituals and then the sudden grappling with his escaped captive. But now, it was as though Vivian had seen into the future, as if time had been inverted and she were living backward.

"Lala!" she cried as the preacher lunged toward his discarded pistol. "Not so fast, you creep!" Vivian seethed, charging forward. She reached Rathbone just before he reached the gun, his outstretched hand grasping only air as she laid into him with her shoulder, knocking him off balance. "Run, Lala!" she yelled as the preacher wrapped his arms around her own body from behind, the two of them falling backward onto the promenade floor.

Rathbone clutched Vivian to his chest, scrabbling crab-like back across the cold, wet stone, one arm around her neck as he reached with the other for the pistol that lay inches from his ruined altar. There was no way to stop him, Vivian realized, no way to free herself. She pawed again and again at that iron grip, struggling for breath. Having grasped his pistol, Rathbone now dragged them both to their feet and placed the barrel of his gun against her temple.

Drat that man! Sergeant Kowalski would never get a clear shot. It was up to her, now. Thankfully, Viola was safe, huddling behind the sergeant amid the handful of officers who had joined him.

"Put up your gun!" the preacher screamed with all his might.

No arguing with *that.* The sergeant raised his hands in surrender, slowly bending to place his pistol on the ground. "Pastor Rathbone, there's only one way out, here," he said in an even voice. "Let her go, and we'll take you in. We'll get you the help you need."

Vivian felt the preacher's laughter before she heard it, rippling up through his chest to erupt like some vile torrent. "*Help* me. *You?* And can you raise the dead as well?"

This little joke seemed to amuse the blasted man to no end, and for a split second, Vivian thought she might turn his distraction to advantage. But at the first movement, he redoubled his grip.

"You'd be surprised," Kowalski said, and it was such an unlikely answer that the preacher's laughter died, if only for an instant. But for all his skill, the sergeant was out of his league. If Lala could not get through to the blasted man, no one could.

Rathbone took a step toward the parapet, dragging Vivian with him. "But you *are* right. There's only one way out of here." Vivian felt him jerk a nod toward Babs's collapsed body. "I might have taken her with me, but I have decided this one will suffice as an offering of blood."

"Oh, sir, *sir,*" Viola cried suddenly, grasping the fullness of his intent before anyone else had even parsed his words. "Oh, *please* don't do it, or if you feel you must, don't take my sister with you. I do understand, honestly, I do—it's so poetic, retracing the path of your new, beloved master, down from the heavens to the lake of fire below, or in this case, Fifth Avenue. But, sir, if you don't mind me saying, Satan will be expecting *you,* waiting for *you* with open arms, and—why, when you think about it, my sister would only get in the way?"

Vivian frowned as the ridiculous meaning of her sister's words clunked into place with gut-wrenching finality. Rathbone was planning to jump. With her. To meet . . . not his maker, but his new master, in terrible mimicry of Satan's fall from grace an eternity ago. But the most preposterous thing was that her sister was urging him to *do* it, and merely arguing him out of taking Vivian with him in a brilliant and twisted psychological gambit.

Was Lala becoming a pragmatist?

Alas, the preacher did not take the bait. "I am bringing him a gift," he said in a tone far more chilling than his scream had been. "He will be well pleased." He placed one foot on the wall, which was only a few feet high. It would be nothing for him to spring off, into the ether, treating Vivian to a one-way trip to hell.

"Rathbone, *don't,*" the sergeant said at precisely the same moment that Lala cried, "Sir, please, *no!*"

Vivian felt the preacher's body tense. Was this truly it, then? Even if he'd not been armed, his strength was the greater, especially now, with him perched on the edge of destiny like some crazed prophet of yore. She gazed across the ten odd feet that separated her from her *twin,* so close that she could see her gray eyes, the mirror of her own, awash with tears. Her twin! Nature's best invention—to create the rarest love of all by splitting the soul in two! She felt her own eyes swell, not with tears of grief but laughter, with *love,* for it was exactly the silly kind of thing Lala would have said. Vivian put all her love into that gaze, her goodbye that said *we will never truly be apart,* then turned her eyes to the man who stood beside.

Adi.

The nickname was in her mind, but it must have passed between them, somehow, for she saw the sergeant's lips part. Such a fine mouth, it really was a dreadful pity. She supposed she might as well admit, here at the end, that he was absolutely perfect in every way. And if she could have said it to his face, she might have done—she'd been a coward and a fool. But perhaps some of it got through, because a fierceness entered his brown eyes that even from a distance, and with death hovering just over the parapet, brought that thrill of weakness to her knees.

Suddenly, she laughed. *The knife!*

Good lord, she truly was a nincompoop. Her hands had been quite warmed by their struggle, and with Rathbone distracted by impending doom, she managed to snatch it easily from her pocket, switching it open as she drew it forth. She raised it high. Rathbone gasped, and then she plunged it down with all her might, deep into his thigh behind her.

His grip spasmed, loosened, and Vivian struggled free. Four strides, and she was in her sister's arms.

Sergeant Kowalski grabbed his gun from where it lay at his feet and raised it, steadying his aim with both hands.

"It really is over now, Rathbone. Just come along quietly."

Vivian half-extracted herself from her twin's arms to turn and look. The preacher stared down at the knife protruding from his thigh, as if he could not fathom how it had gotten there. He looked over to Babs's slumped body, then up to the sergeant's gun. His own pistol was still clenched in his hand. He might have raised it against them or Babs, might have used it in yet another deadly stratagem, but he seemed suddenly to be much too tired for all of that. At the last, he turned to look at Lala, eyes sad but mouth still fixed in that dreadful smile, full of loathing for his god, for the world, but mostly for himself.

"Oh, sir," Viola murmured, as he leaned out, foot still planted on the parapet, and fell like deadweight over the side and out of sight.

They rushed to the wall. Down, down he went, his dark coat flapping out behind him like the ragged wings of a rook. The river of headlights coursed below. At the last instant, Viola flinched away.

"It's okay, Lala," Vivian said, gently, as they all drew back. She pulled her sister into the circle of her arm. "He really was a dreadful man."

But she wasn't looking at her twin. A few feet away, the sergeant was standing stationary amid the swirl around him as officers rushed forward to tend to Babs, to snap pictures of the preacher's handiwork and secure the crime scene. That *stillness* descended on them once again, so that even the bite of the cold could not reach her. Sergeant Kowalski seemed peculiarly moved, all the frustration and curiosity and puzzlement and humor of his regard now merged into something like longing—but so remote the word did not quite suit. She could never be like Jane with him, could she? Would he ever feel so easy as all that? Smile that smile that so unconsciously transformed him into a boy? Perhaps there was something wrong with her, some *thing* missing, that he would discover sooner or later, once he got past all her foolish airs.

At any rate, she was wretched tired.

"We'll need to take your statements," he said, stepping closer. "I don't think I've ever seen anyone fight like that, Miss Van der Beeck," he added with a sideways smile and a flash of admiration that, even through the strange foreboding that had gripped her, stirred her insides. "Let's get you both out of here. There'll be blankets and hot coffee for you down at the station."

CHAPTER THIRTY-FIVE
One Door Closes

It was nearly midnight when they trudged into the precinct office, the bright lights comforting after hours of gusting snow that had only gotten more unpleasant as it turned to rain. The office was still busy, proving the aphorism that crime never slept—nor *paid*, reputedly, though a group of well-heeled revelers was just being booked. As the errant party was led away, the clerk at the front desk pushed up the brim of his cap with a pencil, giving the twins a once-over, for they must have looked a frightful mess, all wet and bedraggled, dirt and chalk dust smudged on their coats and faces, and Vivian hatless having never recovered it from the street below.

Viola studied her sister as they followed the clerk through the maze of desks to an empty room on the far side where coffee and blankets would be supplied. In profile, Viv looked older than she had just hours before, damp flaxen hair slicked back from her high forehead and cheekbones, her gray eyes shadowed so that the smudged quality was even more pronounced—perhaps from lack of sleep—but undeniably becoming in an odd, exotic way. What strange creatures they were, the two of them, beautiful,

Viola supposed, as they'd always been told, though a tad waifish, as if they belonged in a world populated by gnomes and fairies, not murderers and thieves. Sergeant Kowalski watched Viv too as he walked on her far side, a frown in his sidelong gaze that revealed, not the speculative quality Viola had often noted when he looked at her sister, but another kind of question altogether. Reading books had taught her a great deal about human nature, and she was certain that the sergeant had *quite* made up his mind—if only he could gather his courage—and for a man so accustomed to sure footing, that must feel dreadfully strange.

"Mes petites," came a smooth, melodic voice, and sure enough, they turned to find Mother skirting desks effortlessly with Father in tow, still addled from his nap or more likely the nightcap that had followed. Mother had a way of clearing a path before her, officers stepping aside with unconscious deference to her beauty and—something else, that *je ne sais quoi* she had wielded for so many years, one could hardly fault her for it. *At least, she's come*, Viola thought with another watchful glance at her sister, for though she knew Viv considered *her* the impressionable one, she'd long ago mapped the limits of their parents' orbit. A *twosome* they would always be, like binary stars, like twins, Viola supposed. It was a trial for Viv, though, pretending that she didn't care. Ogres under beds were always there until you looked, but that had never been Viv's strong suit, and Viola feared her twin might be harboring more than one monster in the shadows.

"Mother," Vivian said, turning to clasp hands with her as she drew near. "You needn't worry, we're positively fine," she said with that perfect self-possession she had learned at Giselle's knee.

Father joined them as well, his sandy blond hair as disheveled as their own, but for no good reason, and Viola felt the pang she knew would come. He really was a dear, far too tender for the trenches, and she found herself thinking about Teddy and Titus, about the burden of history, of which she was custodian, and all the deaths registered in the family tome. *They so often died at twenty-one*, she marveled, the thought out of sync with the comings and goings of the moment—but then, Father crushed her into a hug and she gave herself over to a few indulgent tears. He reached out an arm to pull Viv into their huddle too, and it was all so lovely Viola rather wished it wouldn't end.

Father really was such a dear.

But in the end, Mother intervened. "Come, mon cher," she said, gently drawing him off, "We will wait with the others," and the twins followed the incline of her head across the station to where not only Mrs. Lynch and Cookie but the entire brood of tenants stood, some still in their pajamas, all crammed into the waiting area and craning necks like watchful hens.

It was enough to swell one's throat.

"They shouldn't be long, ma'am," Sergeant Kowalski said, holding open the nearest door. "We're just going to debrief. I'm sure you'll want to see them home as soon as possible."

Giselle inclined her head in appreciation, then led Father off to join the others, leaving Vivian and Viola to follow the sergeant into the debrief room.

"Can I get either of you some coffee?" he said, though his eyes never strayed from Vivian's face.

"I rather think not," she said, sounding peaked, and Viola wondered if the strain of nearly dying had finally caught up with her. Viola demurred as well, and so the sergeant brought them both blankets, draping Viv's about her from behind, then resting his hands on her shoulders for a moment so that Viola looked away, thinking it bad taste to pry.

He came around to sit behind the desk. "You might be wondering how we found you," he began. "We nearly didn't—it was just a stroke of luck that the hit-and-run witness finally came clean right at the end there."

The woman from the flower shop on Broadway! Viola recalled her at once as the sergeant went on to explain that the witness to the Appleby hit-and-run, the accident that had killed Babs's brother, Eddie, had revealed that it was no accident at all. The day they'd seen the mousy, little woman at the station, handbag clutched to her chest, she'd had every intention of naming the culprit, but then the sight of him—of Pastor Rathbone—where she'd least expected to see him had robbed her of nerve.

"Do you mean to say it was *Rathbone* that ran Eddie down?" Vivian said, perking up a bit as she leaned closer, the blanket falling from one shoulder. "But why would he—*unless,*" her gaze sharpened. "He must have been trying to stop Eddie from bringing Babs back to the family farm . . . which means—"

"He was plotting this all along!" Viola cried.

"Or something very like it," Vivian agreed. "Only his plot got waylaid by Macavoy's—goodness, the *both* of them after that poor woman. What is the world coming to?"

"It took a fair amount of coaxing to get the witness to make the ID," Kowalski said, running a hand through his hair as he leaned back in his chair. "She was terrified of the man, and for good reason, it turns out."

Exactly what had scared her wasn't clear unless it was merely the fact of having witnessed murder, and perhaps the preacher's strangely menacing airs. But finally, conscience had gotten the better of her, and she'd explained how she'd seen Rathbone through the windshield of that dark sedan, had seen the car swerve to *hit* Appleby, rather than avoid him. And even though she was the sort to mind her own store, thank you very much—in the end, a chance encounter with the preacher had made her think twice.

"She saw him, preaching on a soap box outside her flower shop," the sergeant explained, and although some might call that serendipity and some might call it luck, Viola knew that all of time and space was but a tapestry of inscrutable design.

"But how did that lead you to the Empire State Building, of all places?" Vivian asked. "I don't mind telling you, Sergeant, I could have *thrashed* myself for taking Lala to that infernal man's parish, and all on our own, never once thinking of danger."

It was an olive branch, Viola suspected, the admission of the reformed meddler, though both she and the sergeant surely knew better than to take her at her word. But he accepted it for the apology that it was, with more than professional courtesy, Viola thought, the determination in his eye suggesting that he felt he finally might be getting somewhere.

But Viv will never let him, will she?

For all the possessiveness of twinship, Viola found herself suddenly and fervently hoping that she would.

"I found this at the chapel," the sergeant said, opening a desk drawer and reaching inside to remove a red silk scarf. He rose, moving around the desk to where Vivian sat, then made a gesture, as if to brush the strands of drying hair from her shoulder.

"May I?"

Vivian nodded mutely, then inclined her head forward as he knelt down to lace the scarf gently round her neck and tie it off to the side, exactly in the style that Viv so often wore it.

"How did you . . . know it was mine?" she managed.

"I . . . well, I . . . just noticed."

He cleared his throat and stood, leaning back against the desk, arms folded across his white shirt. "We saw all the schematics of the building on his desk, plus a bunch of books on pyrotechnics, and figured out the rest."

"Yes, well, that *is* lucky." Vivian's eyes were cast down as she fingered the scarf. "I guess in this instance it's a good thing you . . ." she looked up, "you followed us."

The sergeant reached up one hand to ruffle the back of his head, then let it drop with a grin. "I always seem to be a step behind you, Miss Van der Beeck."

The high color in Viv's cheeks made her look all the more bewitching, but Viola thought it high time she came to her sister's rescue.

"So, who was the third man at the train station?" she blurted, quite out of context, but it was the first thing that had come into her head, and after all, the sergeant clearly knew about their little lark.

He perched on the edge of the desk and swiveled a bit toward her, forearms draped over his thigh. "Frankie Morgan. Can you believe it? We figured he'd go straight back to Macavoy after we rattled him, but our tails came up empty-handed. Macavoy had gotten greedy after Ziegfeld put Betty into his show, guess he felt he deserved a little more for his efforts and a big payout would do the trick. Your instincts were right about him," the sergeant cast Viola a grateful look. "He's a weasel, through and through. Sure enough, it was Morgan who gave him the scoop on Ziegfeld's little secret, but Morgan insists he didn't know about the kidnapping idea up until the day of the show, and by then it was too late. Says that with the ransom drop, he saw his chance to set things right, so he swooped in to grab Babs after her release, thinking he could make good with her if he had one more shot. Strange way to do it, but I guess he figured he could pretend to be her savior. He didn't get far—someone jumped him on the train and picked up with Babs where he left off—Rathbone, no doubt. We've got both Morgan and Macavoy in custody now.

"She has a strange effect on men," Vivian mused, looking reasonably recovered from her attaque d'amour. But what the sergeant said next made her cheeks flame all over again.

"Some women do."

Oh dear. Time for another diversion. "But what about the love child, then," Viola said. "Oh, I mean Babs's child. You know. The secret one."

"The father?" Kowalski said, then gave a laugh, shaking his head. "Never saw *this* one coming. Our best guess is that Luigi Luciana is the baby's father—or at least that's the word on the street. After your visit to his nightclub," his rueful gaze returned to Vivian, "it appears he did some sleuthing on his own. He didn't know she was pregnant—they'd been carrying on again, quietly, you see—and when she disappeared from the stage, he assumed she was making a clean break from him. Got to hand it to him, for a wise guy he's a decent man. He appears to have resolved to leave her alone—until he found out about the child. I'll bet you he'll be back in Babs's life before the night is out, picking up the pieces."

"That *is* romantic," Viola couldn't help but comment. Of all the men who had darkened Babs's door, he seemed the least detestable.

"Yes, romantic," the sergeant said in a considering tone, quietly, flicking another look at Vivian before standing up from the desk. "Well, uh, ladies, it's late. You must want to be getting home. I'll see you out."

Vivian looked up, as if startled out of her thoughts, then shrugged off the blanket, draping it over the side of her chair as she rose. Viola stood as well, wishing suddenly she had some pretext for leaving them alone. After all, when on earth would Viv and the sergeant see each other now? Suddenly, the silence seemed full of unspoken words.

"Oh, um, might I use the ladies' room first?" Viola said, hardly knowing what words tumbled out of her mouth.

The sergeant leaned forward to point. "It'll be just out the door and down the hall, third door on the right."

"Thank you, yes, well, I'll . . . I'll be right back."

Vivian watched her sister scurry out the door, then turned back to see the sergeant, for once, not holding her with his steady, inquisitive gaze. He was looking at the floor, in fact, until—with what seemed a force of effort—he raised his eyes. So serious. It pained her that she seemed to bring that out in him. If only she could make him feel at ease, like Jane, that boyish grin flashing across his face that made her knees weak merely thinking of it. But then—suddenly—it was as though a scene glimpsed through the reflection of a window came into focus, *flipped,* and she saw the boy inside the man, not in his smile, but in his eyes that showed a note of such touching uncertainty, she reached out to place a hand on his arm.

"Sergeant, I really must apologize for—"

"Adam, please call me Adam." He put his hand over hers where it rested on his arm.

"Adam, I—" She barely got the name out. What was this wretched panic that closed her throat? "I . . . know you must think I've been rather a nuisance during this entire—"

"Vivian, don't," he said, and she looked back up into his eyes, not realizing she had looked away. "You don't owe me any apologies. If it wasn't for you and your sister, we wouldn't have broken this case. I'm the one that should be apologizing, only, I can't seem to do it."

"Apologizing? But what on earth should you have to—"

"For . . ." he set his jaw, then sighed, "for a breach of protocol. I'm afraid I've let my . . . feelings interfere with my professional judgment."

"Serg . . . Adam, I—what are saying?"

But she knew what he was saying. His feelings for her. For someone who was involved in the case. And for a person like . . . *Adam,* acting on such feelings, even just a little, must feel like an awful breach of his integrity.

"I'm saying, it isn't fair to you, to put you in an awkward position," he said, carefully, looking down again, "and I know that, believe me, I've told myself this a thousand times, because—who knows, you might be confused about *your* feelings. These are the kinds of situations that can really mix people up, and I would never want to . . . to . . ." finally, he looked up again, into her eyes, "take advantage of you."

Vivian's heart hammered in her throat. The warm weight of his hand on her own, the tan of his neck against the whiteness of his collar, the way her body drifted toward his of its own accord—it all made words impossible. Were her feelings just the result of being thrown together into strange and perilous circumstances?

He cleared his throat again. "But now, well, the case is over." He let his words settle for a moment, along with their various meanings. They would not have cause to see each other again, but there would also be no case to come between them. "Under ordinary circumstances, I . . . well, I guess I would . . . call on you."

It was an experimental statement, and he watched her closely.

"I . . . you . . . you want to . . . call on me?" For once, Vivian's mind could not outpace the intensity of her feelings, the wave of longing that touched and opened, not only her body, but her heart in places she had not known existed. She was like a universe expanding, a study in equal and opposite forces, the overwhelming desire to submit countered only by the terror of extinction. Because—what then? Would she be blown apart? "I . . . I'd make a beastly girlfriend," she said, too overcome to feel mortified by her idiocy.

But these words seemed, finally, to put the sergeant at his ease. He looked so relieved, so *energized*, that Vivian was flooded suddenly with dread. She had made him *happy*. Good lord, how on earth could she bear it when she one day let him down? For it was inevitable, what with her being so cold and stiff and, well, awkward in all the ways that mattered for a . . . girlfriend. He was sure to notice at some point, and then where would they be?

"Vivian, I—" he began as Viola barged in, a repetition of what struck Vivian as destiny. He bent to her ear as she quickly slid her hand from his arm and turned to go, adding softly, "Tomorrow, then?"

Tomorrow? She could picture him standing on the doorstep, a bouquet of flowers in his hands. What on earth would she say?

She looked back at him, over her shoulder. Did she nod yes? She hardly knew as she turned back to her twin. "It's about time, Lala," she said, breathlessly, then headed out the door.

CHAPTER THIRTY-SIX
Hat in Hand

The next morning found the twins deep in conversation with the tenants in Mr. Sparrows' chambers. They were all there, for once—or at least the six of them. Babs was still recuperating at Bellevue, where Ziegfeld had made sure she would receive only the finest care with his newly returned ransom funds. Madame Koslova was camped out on the low divan in her high-collared nightgown of stiff linen that resembled the kind of tents Victorian adventurers pitched on the savanna, while Miss Sphinx sat criss-cross in the Empire Revival chair, resplendent in wide-trousered pajamas of Moroccan silk. Dr. Weber sat nearest the piano, away from the door for once, his velvet smoking jacket with the tasseled belt as neat as a button, while Al and Mr. Sparrow made an odd pair in identical pin-striped pajamas—Mr. Sparrow having gifted his spare set to Al when it was discovered the man slept only in boxers. Only Mr. Sharma was fully dressed, his dark gray suits of combed wool always strictly 1910, complete with detachable collar, cufflinks, and thin, woven tie.

"How is it that the culprit can be both the gangster and the preacher and the boyfriend?" remarked Miss Sphinx, whose grasp of English grammar was still in its adolescence. "And then yet the baby—he is of someone else entirely! It makes the head does spin."

Everyone agreed that this was strange, with various interjections suited to the purpose. Madame Koslova maintained she had always known it was so, while Al expressed astonishment, as a lapsed Catholic, that a man of the cloth would turn out to be a goon. The good doctor thought the three culprits to be apt representatives of the id, ego, and superego—though Rathbone rather stumped him—and Mr. Sparrow played them through with a sprinkling of Debussy, adding a thought here or there, mostly to the effect that he hoped Babs was okay. Mr. Sharma did not speak, which was typical, though Viola thought him more agitated than usual. Viv was silent as well, curled up in the pillows of the overstuffed chair while she chewed on her bottom lip.

"I suppose we're rather out of mysteries," Viola said with a concerned glance at her sister, whom the others clearly thought to be recovering from last night's trauma. But Viola knew her sister far too well for that. No gun-toting, gospel-spouting maniac could rattle her sister, whose nerves were made of stern stuff. It was Viv's heart that quailed, walled up behind that flawless demeanor of hers, like a prisoner exposed to light after too many years of solitude. Naturally, *Viola* was allowed entrance to that chamber—goodness, where would Viv be without *that*—but it wasn't the same, was it? And for the first time since the sergeant had entered their lives, Viola's fear that her sister would leave her was overtaken by the fear that she would *not*. "Speaking of mysteries . . ." Viola said, hitting on another diversion. She removed the family diary from her day bag, which she'd taken to keeping with her most hours of the day.

"Allah! Such a beautiful book!" Miss Sphinx exclaimed.

"I suppose you've never seen it," Viola realized, for until last year, the book had lain dusty and all but forgotten in the family library, shelved between *The Railway Children* and *The Enchanted Castle,* though how it had made it into the E. Nesbit section was beyond her. "It's a sort of domestic chronicle, you know—births and deaths, marriages and annulments, bankruptcies and felony convictions—the usual sort of things." She opened it to a random page where, sure enough, fraternal twins Willem and Wilhelmina Van der Beeck were noted as dead at the age of twenty-one when—while visiting the van Rensselaers at their manor house on the banks of the Hudson River—they'd tripped during a three-legged race and died of lockjaw after being impaled upon the tines of a garden rake. "I suppose every family has its version," she added, thoughtfully, thumbing the pages.

"'M-m-may I see it?'" Mr. Sharma said, out of the blue.

Poor dear, she thought again as she rose to hand over the book. His stutter did so seem to come and go. "I've been noticing some frightfully strange patterns," Viola mused, relieved to be talking about the subject which had occupied her thoughts. "As you can see, it goes all the way back to the mother country. Does it interest you as a history buff, Mr. Sharma?"

But the little man did not appear to hear her as he bent to the well-worn pages, leafing forward until he paused to peer closer. Then, he rose from the cane chair he'd pulled over from the secretary and proffered the open book back to Viola.

"There is a sm-smudge," he said, pointing.

Viola glanced down at the book in her hands. "Oh, yes, I noticed that. Wretched strange, that. I'm quite sure neither Viv nor I would have desecrated the diary in such a way, though it's such a recent entry, I can't think who might have done."

The spot was halfway down the last page of entries, a wide smear that obscured whatever had been written there, right after *Married: James Van der Beeck and Giselle Adilene de Bourbon in the Trinity Episcopal Church, May 29, 1912, service attended by the Duke of Chartres.* Viola recognized the crabbed script as that of Aunt Lavinia, from whom Viola had inherited her duties due to Auntie's negligence and a tendency to embellish certain details to salacious effect.

"I suppose Auntie might have smudged it," she continued, frowning. "Though it does seem rather careless, even for her. I always thought it must have been a first attempt at the recording of our *own* births," for, there they were, listed just below: *Born: Vivian and Viola Van der Beeck without complications at 63 Central Park West, 2 a.m. and 2:05 a.m., respectively.*

"I-I-I'm afraid that's not c-c-correct," Mr. Sharma managed, growing visibly more distraught by the moment—and syllable. "I-I've been tr-trying to find a way to t-t-t—" he broke off with a grimace, then tried again, "t-tell you what I discovered in my r-r-research."

"Research?"

So, Vivian was listening. Viola turned to find her sister straightening up from her slouch.

"Yes, Miss Viv-Vivian," he persevered. "A-As you know, my services have been enlisted by the Society to p-p-place certain manuscripts in historical c-c-context, including the papers of certain p-prominent families, and I've . . . dis-dis-discovered certain p-papers which seem to indicate a . . . a . . . that is, it's not my p-p-place to say, b-b-but . . ."

"For goodness' sake, Mr. Sharma, are you quite well?" Vivian said, a tad sharply.

"The existence of an older brother," he said, seeming to spit the words across the room. "Who died," he continued, drawing in a long, gasping breath, "shortly after birth."

"An older . . . brother?" Viola said, wonderingly. "You mean *our* older brother?" She flicked a finger between her and her twin.

"Qu-Quite."

It was at precisely that moment that the door opened wide to reveal Mrs. Lurch, already wearing her dusting apron and looking as though she'd discovered a nest of mice in the attic.

"Breakfast will be served in five minutes. Best look lively," she said, instilling fear in all their hearts. Cookie was a tyrant when it came to stragglers.

They all hurried off to their chambers to dress, and none more vigorously than Vivian, who would not say a word as she exchanged robe for day dress and combed her hair. She looked a fright, but Viola supposed the news had hit her awfully hard, what with her lonely heart already flinching from the light. As for Viola, she thought the revelation a tad delightful—*a secret brother! Positively like something out of Dickens!*—but that was only because she'd never known the tyke enough to love him and therefore grieve him. He wasn't Teddy or Titus, after all, though that's likely just what Viv had pictured in her mind's eye, a mischievous scamp, a secret brother they'd never gotten the chance to know—or even know *about.* Yes, a secret. That was the rub. Viola had never really minded having the rug pulled out from under her, not having a firm footing in this world to begin with. But she could see it all through Viv's eyes, felt betrayal on her twin's behalf. For they all must have known—not just Mother, Father, and Auntie, of course, but Cookie and most distressingly Mrs. Lurch. How could they have kept this from them? A brother! What other secrets were they keeping? And if that was the case, who on earth could they trust but each other?

And so it continued all through breakfast, with Vivian fuming or perhaps trying not to cry. Viola thought the latter more likely and made their excuses halfway through the meal, saying that last night's trials had rather wearied them. The tenants exchanged worried glances—the meal had been a painfully silent one—and even Madame Koslova abetted their escape, noting something about the imbalance of the humors whose alchemical effect on the human spirit had been lost to the ravages of modern science.

They were passing out the door when they almost bumped into Mrs. Lurch, who was just coming in.

"The very person I wanted to see," she said, folding her hands in front of her without even a hint of contrition, though she must have known something was amiss. Vivian had refused to meet her eye all through breakfast, even when directly addressed. "That young sergeant is at the door asking for you, Vivian. I've shown him in."

Good lord, not now.

Vivian cast a panicked look up into her sister's eye. Already, she had been dreading the sergent's arrival, not because she did not want to see his face, to feel his presence, which had come increasingly to feel like her own, but because she was so dreadfully sure she would have nothing to say. But now—*now*, well, she didn't even have it in her to exchange passable banter, let alone sparkling wit.

"Come, Viv, I'll walk you down," Viola said, comfortingly, taking her by the hand as she allowed herself to be led out of the morning room and down the stairs. Lala's sympathetic gestures were nothing like normal people's, which always smacked of judgment, and by the time they were on the landing, parting ways, Vivian felt almost herself again, except for that gaping pit where her stomach should be.

With a squeeze of her hand, Viola let go, and Vivian continued down into the front hall with measured steps, the front hall canaries chirping their welcome.

He was sitting on the boot bench beside the door, overcoat folded over one arm, elbows on knees as he twirled his fedora. But when he saw her, he got at once to his feet, laying coat and hat on the bench and thrusting both hands into his pockets. His shirt was still white, though of casual cut and worn without a tie, and he looked every bit as handsome in his khaki sportscoat as his usual navy suit—only youthful, somehow. Away from the police station, he seemed nearer her own age, eyebrows drawn together over the slight jag in his nose in a way that suggested he too might be feeling awkward.

"Vivian," he said, taking a step closer. "How . . . are you?"

"Oh, Serg—Adam, I—I'm well, thank you—I—it was a dreadful night, if you must know, but I suppose that's to be expected." Her cheeks were warming already, and they'd hardly gotten through two sentences. Her mind flashed on Jane, swiveling from the filing cabinets to parry anecdotes with her laughing coworker, as effortlessly as Clara Bow playing the carefree shopgirl. *Blast her.* What a stick Vivian must seem by comparison. Why, the serg—*Adam* must already be plotting his escape. "And you, are you . . . well?"

He extracted one hand from his pocket to reach up behind his neck, inclining his head forward in that way he had of doing, like a boy caught at mischief at the penny store. Vivian's heart gave a *pang*, but that only made up her mind all the more that this would never do, and the only solution was to get as far away as possible, as fast as she possibly—

"You know, I think I've never been better." He looked up from under those dark lashes with a grin that fairly destroyed her, then dropped his arm. "I was thinking you could help me celebrate my birthday."

"Your . . . birthday?"

"I'm turning twenty-one today. I know it's cold out, but I thought maybe a walk in the park? I should speak to your parents, of course, but then I thought we might take in a matinee." His grin turned mischievous. "I might even let you buy me a soda at Gor—*oh*, hey, Vivian, I . . . I'm sorry—" he broke off, brown eyes deepening with worry as both hands came out of his pockets and he took a solicitous step forward. "You must still be getting over everything that happened yesterday, how stupid of—"

Vivian waved him to silence with a small gesture before clamping the hand to her mouth, mortified as tears streamed down her cheeks. She had seen their expedition in her mind's eye as he spoke, seen them drifting through Central Park, side by side, leaning in toward each other to exchange words meant only for each other's ears, and Adam, *Adi*, placing an arm around her shoulder as a few early snowflakes wafted to the ground. And it was all so otherworldly, so peculiar and lovely—a scene glimpsed in one of those snow globes, just before it crashed to the ground— that she could not bear it. A moment frozen in time, and if she could not bear to have it snatched away now, how much worse would it be later, when she had lived it? Because things never lasted, and even those you trusted eventually betrayed you—all except Lala, and wasn't having one person to love quite enough for any person, really?

"Vivian," Adam said, his voice soft yet rough with worry as he took another step toward her. In another moment, he'd be close enough to touch. "I was an idiot not to realize how this all might have affected you," he fumed at himself, "after all my fine words at the station about not taking advantage. This isn't the time for . . . for *this*, I just, I just—" She could hear what was behind his words, how much he'd hoped, how *happy* he'd been, which wrenched another gasping sob from her lips. "But we can *wait*," he said, "of course we *should* wait, and when you've had some time with your family to really get over—"

His hand touched her arm, and she flinched away.

"No . . . Adam, *no*." She had taken her hand from her mouth, and it hovered, under her chin, but her words were still garbled. She strengthened her resolve. "Please, you . . . you must understand, this . . . this just wouldn't work, surely you can see—" She broke off again, unable to speak through the closed shaft of her throat, but it didn't matter. Already her words had done their awful work. Adam stepped back—one, two, three steps. Frame by frame, as if a projector had guttered in the darkness of a theater, his face progressed through an unbearable sequence—from confusion to shock to mortification to despair—until finally, Vivian looked away. "Adam, I—I'm *sorry*," she managed, unable to take anything back, unable to even think. Surely, *this* was who she really was, a dreadful mannequin in the place of human flesh, and it was better that he saw it now than that he should be disappointed by degrees. *Better to see him crushed now than to be crushed myself,* she thought, flinching again. And wasn't that the truth, the horrid, beastly truth?

Adam Kowalski, newly twenty-one and the youngest cadet ever to be appointed to the Detective Bureau placed both hands on the top of his head, then let them fall with a sigh. If Vivian had been able to meet his eye, she might have seen that—beyond the despair—something else lingered, that *determination,* for the sergeant was too young to have ever failed at what he set his mind to. His confidence, though capable of being shaken, had never yet been broken. Yet. And his mind was of that rare type that, once made up, was rarely unmade.

But she could not meet his eye.

He turned on his heel and headed toward the door, grabbing his coat and hat from the bench, wrenching the door open, then pausing for the briefest of moments. Vivian looked up to see the silhouette of his back against the gauzy backdrop of a November day, dead leaves playing at the threshold.

And then, he was gone.

CHAPTER THIRTY-SEVEN
Turn the Page

In the months that followed, Vivian learned to forget her brush with true love, or nearly so, except for certain nights when she would end up on the widow's walk, watching the sunrise with Lala by her side, the two of them shivering into their robes. This had the desired sobering effect—or perhaps it was penance—and by throwing herself into every pursuit of which she could conceive, Vivian managed to make it through even the spring, when flowers bloomed and leaves budded from their winter cocoons and, worst of all, the park was rife with lovers, strolling arm in arm.

Spring brought another tenant into their lives, and into Canary House, the turret room having lain empty all winter long. Archibald Abercrombie, Scottish archaeologist and old family friend, took up lodgings for an expected term of eight months. He'd been enlisted by Columbia University as a visiting professor where he would be organizing an exhibition on ancient treasures. But his true passion, and his secret pursuit, was the search for artifacts on the isle of Manahatta, as the Lenape had called it, or *hilly island*, now transformed into a landscape of glittering towers and spires, like some impossible crop, sown by the gods. The professor had not sought official recognition for his pet project, the field of Native American Studies being still in its infancy due to disagreements within the citadel, and then too, Archie was something of a black sheep, visiting professorship notwithstanding. Perhaps this is not surprising given his association with the Van der Beecks. The clandestine nature of the project quite charmed the twins, adding romance and offering ample opportunity for volunteer assignments, be it as scribes or scouts or glorified research assistants who snuck biscuits for the professor from Cookie's larder. Viola was even inspired to pick up a new book, *The Last of the Mohicans,* which chronicled the travails of a doomed wilderness and people—though she found the prose rather stiff for her tastes.

Had Professor Abercrombie possessed a magic ball instead of just a PhD, he might have known the precise spot in which Johann Van der Beeck sat with a Lenape shaman shortly before the onset of the Wappinger War—also named Kieft's War for the first governor of New Amsterdam who had ushered in two years of bloodshed with the ambush and massacre of 120 men, women, and children. Certain remnants of this fated meeting would not have survived the intervening centuries—the beaver pelt, gifted by Johann to tribal elders in friendship and gratitude, the meal of rabbit, corn, and a flatbread made from acorn paste—but other items would surely remain, buried under concrete and four hundred years of sedimentary strata. Who knows what treasures the professor might have found? But possessing no such divinatory sphere and claiming only the assistance of two unpaid teenaged research assistants, it is hardly surprising that when a letter arrived at their door two weeks into his tenure at Canary House, he could make neither heads nor tails of it.

It was addressed to Vivian and Viola Van der Beeck.

Postmarked January 26, 1932, from the city of Cajamarca, high in the Andean peaks of Peru.

No sender was noted on the envelope, but inside, at the bottom of two pages of ruined script, was the barely legible signature of Cornelius Ambrose Van der Beeck.

Grampy Cornelius was *alive?*

In the nearly three months it took Grampy's letter to reach Canary House, it must have undergone a terrible ordeal. It was a miracle it arrived at all, the address being so besmirched with mud and clay and the excrement of unknown quadrupeds that it could hardly be read. It had clearly been delivered to other residences, the address being crossed out and over-written several times. The letter itself was unmarked by gross contaminants but moisture had wrought its own destruction, every second or third word corrupted until the whole of it seemed nonsense.

"It reads like a cipher," Vivian complained, giving up after countless attempts to create meaning from mayhem, but Viola persevered, thinking it a lark.

"It's just like something out of Sherlock Holmes," she said, perusing the archives in her mind for words, phrases, and grammatical formulations that might breach the divide. "And how does he even know our names?" To their knowledge, no one had had contact with Grampy since he absconded with the mystic.

But in the end, Grampy's letter seemed little more than a curiosity. Someday, if he were to show up on their doorstep, they might understand what had possessed their prodigal grandfather to reach out across half the globe to pique their interest and Vivian's ire. But that seemed hardly likely, and so the twins contented themselves with archaeological expeditions and the occasional trip up to the attic to continue their own excavation of the family treasures. Even *the curse of the turret room,* as Viola had termed it, seemed unlikely to bear fruit, what with Archie being so staid and bookish, unless he had a trowel in his hand.

And what of tapestries woven by fate? Who can say? Sergeant Kowalski in his bachelor's apartment, burning a casserole intended for a friend; Vivian and Viola, knee deep in family papers as they labored below the rafters, seeking clues; Professor Abercrombie, welcoming the research fellow just appointed to assist him at the college—a choleric man with small eyes and a politician's smile. What had these lives to do with one another?

What indeed?

ACKNOWLEDGEMENTS

This book, and the series it inaugurates, hold a special place in my heart. The idea was planted in an instant, as the seeds of books so often are, in a Spanish village overlooking the Mediterranean in 2018. We were sitting in an outdoor café when I saw a girl whose strange, waifish, tow-headed beauty struck and intrigued me. Or were there two girls? I can't remember, because immediately she became twins in my mind, and Vivan and Viola were born – though it would be a while yet before I named them.

I've always been a fan of the *Thin Man* movies, and originally, my fledgling idea centered around a witty, urbane couple with oddly beautiful twin daughters who solved crimes. *The Thin Man* came out in 1934, and I knew this was my setting; I love this era with its style and wit, the Jazz Age prodigal of the 20's having sobered and matured into the clear-eyed, wise-cracking realist of the Depression era. I can't recall exactly how or when Nora and Nick evolved into the Van der Beecks with their quirky, patrician, disreputable charm, reminiscent of a Wes Anderson film (though I only made that connection later). But the book and its voice proceeded apace without any real help from me, and I knew I would have to see this odd little experiment through.

In came other strands to flesh out the book's DNA, remnants of my love for classic literature, for theme, and for the question of what constitutes the American character. Max Weber was in there, and *Paradise Lost,* and of course Nathanial Hawthorne, one of my favorite authors of all time. And, lastly, glorious New York was at the center of it all with its contradictions and vitality, its ethnicities and neighborhoods, and its privileged classes (distinguished from their Bostonian and Philadelphian cousins by very distinct norms and ideals).

The cast of supporting characters in my life has not changed in the three years since I started Starr Creek Press. I would like to thank my writing group, which is the best specimen of its kind, anywhere. In addition to those who simply listened and cheered me on during our monthly zoom sessions or the occasional backyard gathering, I'd like to thank those who read and offered suggestions and edits that helped me make this book its best self. Here's the list, in no particular order: Linda Marie Zaerr, Carolyn McAleer, Nancy Matsumoto, Gabi Snyder, Margaret Anderson, Angie Voss and Kimberly Olford Wear. My parents, Dan and Mary, are my biggest fans and have been so from the time I can remember. I have no words sufficient to do homage to what they have contributed to my development and happiness. Let's just say they are the Alpha and Omega of both my creative life and my personal one. My husband of twenty years, Johnny, provides me with the unconditional love and support that makes all of this possible. I live in Johnny's world and wouldn't have it any other way. My children, Jacob and Phia, now teens on the edge of adulthood, are not only stalwart supporters of my journey, they are the light of my life. All parents should feel so proud. Deep thanks to all the friends I get to share my ups and downs with, over a glass of wine and often with a dose of laughter. You are my urban (or, in my case, semi-rural) tribe. You know who you are, and I hope you know how much it means to me, sharing my life's work with you.

As for the "contractors" I work with in producing my books, that seems far too cold a term. My copy editor, Nevin Mays, once more provided the kind of detailed, smart, and nuanced edit that I have come to rely upon. She's also become a friend – even if we only correspond a few times a year. My cover designer, Robin Vuchnich, never fails to amaze me with what seems to be effortless talent. I have only to sketch the contours of my vision and she gives me back something that far exceeds it.

And that leads me to the final acknowledgement, that of my reader. If you have picked up this book, if you have been swept away for even a moment, if you have fallen in love at least a smidgeon with my imaginary family, then you have fulfilled my life's purpose. Thank you for giving me the gift of your readership and all it entails.

Julie Mathison is the multiple award-winning author of books for the child in everyone. Her novels, whether coming-of-age, fantasy or mystery, all contain elements of history and emphasize complex themes and a love of language. Her author imprint, Starr Creek Press, is founded on the principle of "books not boxes," the belief that a good book should transcend genre and category, and should be enjoyable to readers of any age. She also writes and speaks about the interface of traditional and independent publishing, and the role of quality self-publishing in maintaining a robust and healthy literary ecosystem.

The Canary House series will feature five volumes. Sign up for updates and to hear about new releases at www.juliemathison.com.